Michéal mac Liammóir was an actor, director, designer and playwright in both Gaelic and English. Born in 1899, he was on the London stage as a child, and then studied art, travelled widely in Europe, and finally returned to Dublin. In 1928 he co-founded the Dublin Gate Theatre, and from 1928 to 1931 directed the Galway Theatre, where he was responsible for the production of a number of new Irish plays and foreign classics in Irish, making translations of Chekhov, Shaw and other dramatists himself. Among his own plays, the best known are *Diarmuid an Grainne, Ill Met by Moonlight, Where Stars Walk* and *Home for Christmas.*

Michéal mac Liammóir died in 1978.

Michéal mac Liammóir

Enter a Goldfish

Memoirs of an Irish Actor, Young and Old

A PANTHER BOOK

GRANADA
London Toronto Sydney New York

Published by Granada Publishing Limited in 1981

ISBN 0 586 05388 3

First published in Great Britain by
Thames and Hudson Ltd 1977
Copyright © Thames and Hudson 1977

Granada Publishing Limited
Frogmore, St Albans, Herts AL2 2NF
and
36 Golden Square, London W1R 4AH
866 United Nations Plaza, New York, NY 10017, USA
117 York Street, Sydney, NSW 2000, Australia
100 Skyway Avenue, Rexdale, Ontario, M9W 3A6, Canada
61 Beach Road, Auckland, New Zealand

Printed and bound in Great Britain by
Cox and Wyman Ltd, Reading
Set in Plantin

Granada ®
Granada Publishing ®

Contents

Acknowledgment

I would like to express my profound and cordial gratitude to Mrs Tom Corbett, our secretary – for which purpose she has, like an actress, kept the name by which she is known to my partner and me: Miss Mary Cannon – for the unwavering patience and helpfulness of her work during the creation of this book. Much of it had to be dictated to her because of bad eyesight and inability to hand her any sort of legible script, and I cannot conceive how the task could have been achieved by anyone else on earth.

Michéal mac Liammóir

For Máire and Hilton,
who will recognize
many of these characters

CHAPTER ONE
A Dream of Childhood

And the powerful baritone whisper grew louder and softer, the smooth palm stroking the little boy's body under the sheet grew deeper and lighter, and slowly it faded and the child was asleep again . . .

And back in that room again.

Not the one he knew in the daytime with the window looking out on the front garden and the Blackrock Road, but that other room he only knew when he was asleep (if he really was asleep) and he was a grown man waiting for the end to come.

For he always knew it would come. He would come.

Or was it they?

And there they were, out of sight still. Tramp tramp tramp outside on the stone floor in the passage. Nothing in the world could stop it happening now.

And then the two thunderous blows on the door and the door springing open, and he appeared. His men were behind him, their spurred boots clanking to a halt, and they were still out of sight.

But not he. Into that room he came, but of course he had not foreseen the step that led down to the room, and as he tripped forward the black stiff hat he wore slipped down over his eyes.

It was Daddy with the Hard Hat. And Oh God, the child who was now a grown man knew, yes he knew, that the other would push the hat up over his forehead and then his eyes would come into sight.

The eyes were small, hostile, black as night, and set too close together in the pale face.

Ah no! Ah no! No!

And the child woke again, screaming.

Scratches and matches and the squeak of the lamp glass, and then it was brighter and Mother had him in her arms.

'What is it my pet, my darling? You're all right so you are, you're all right.'

These were Martin Weldon's first memories. And being walked up and down, up and down he heard her say, 'Daddy with the Hard Hat? Ah sure that's only an old dream. Don't worry darling, Sing a song of sixpence, come on pet.'

And then in a whisper she said to Father, 'Dr Harrington's right, you know he is: didn't he say the other day the child's mind is too active. And he's right. Too active. That's all it is.'

And Father's deep voice as he murmured through a yawn like a cloud: 'Wouldn't he drive you out of your mind? Here, give him to me, I'll sing him to sleep . . .'

A sort of policeman: that's what Daddy with the Hard Hat was, and he'd come to bring Martin away with him, he and those others with their swords and their helmets and their spurred boots. And Martin and his friends were in great danger from the police because of the sort of army they belonged to that was making trouble so the beloved country might be free, and the damned enemies and tyrants be banished forever. There was a woman among the friends and she was so beautiful, with eyes like violets. Yet she was the most violent of the lot of them in her opinions and her passionate speeches. But Martin could never remember her name. And there was a man who was his greatest friend of them all. He was called Giovanni. What was Martin's name in that double alien life when he was a grown man? He could never recall it, but the memories of hurried conspiratorial meetings that teemed with fanatical excitement and with the looming danger of arrest and imprisonment, perhaps of a firing squad at the end of all, were vivid with the

10

reality of terror, and sometimes they would descend on the child Martin in the middle of waking life, like the pleasant image of walking arm in arm with Giovanni when the meetings were over, strolling together through moonlit streets of amber-coloured stone on nights that smelt of fresh lemons and roasting coffee, over the long bridge that spanned the river, and sometimes they would linger there to throw crumbs to the seagulls and the pigeons. Then the goodnight embrace at the house on the corner and then that room, into that same room, down the step that had caused Daddy with the Hard Hat to stumble later on, oh much later on, but when? But where?

Yet apart from these moments of what seemed a painful memory of aeons ago, Martin's waking life was happy enough.

Its beginning had been in Cork at the very end of the last decade of the old century, and perhaps that was why, when he first began to look about him, it was quite clear that men and boys had two legs each. And so did little girls, but grown-up ladies all had their feet sewn onto the bottom of their skirts. He believed this for many years and could never remember when or how he discovered that it was not a fact. Nor had he ever been puzzled by the question of at what period during puberty the girls' legs vanished or how they had been replaced by the neat tripping shoes: by magic, he supposed. Look at Mother: look at Aunt Kate: look at any of them.

Mother was home to him. As much as the cot he slept in and most of the rooms in the house, especially the kitchen where they had most of their meals, except on grand occasions when friends came to visit them, and then they ate in a room called the dining room. All these things were home, and so was the River Lee and the hills on the far side that were like tea cosies embroidered with green trees and little houses, and his father, dark-eyed and almost invariably kind and always full of stories and songs accompanied by clapping hands.

Besides, Martin had four sisters, all of them older than himself and maddeningly exciting. There was Debby, the eldest, quite a young lady she seemed to Martin from the beginning. Pretty Deborah with the rippling bronze of her hair, and her flower-like complexion and brilliant hazel eyes, she was the beauty of the family. So wise and laughing, and so tranquil too. What a contrast to Tina, the second. A terror she was with her dense sombre hair, her deep olive skin, her enormous eyes that seemed to be a brownish green when she was looking at somebody else, and black as Egypt's night when she looked straight at you, and Mother was in despair about her.

Maimie was smaller even than Tina, and as fair as a cowslip, though there was a hint of red in her hair and her eyes were not blue like her mother's but green, and her mouth was too wide for her thin little face. She was delicate too, and Dr Harrington advised raw meat sandwiches which she artfully smuggled into the lavatory when nobody was looking, and stealthily pulled the plug. Nobody knew of this wasteful undermining of her own health but Peg, the youngest of the sisters, and Peg would have preferred death to betrayal. She was as high-principled as Brünnhilde, and was destined as she grew older to look rather like her, being as fair as the changeling Maimie and taller than any of her sisters.

Peg was six years older than Martin, and although on the day of his birth she, with the other young ladies of the family, being firmly convinced that, owing to the scarcity of riches among the Weldons, the arrival of a baby brother in their midst meant there would never again be enough money for a pretty frock between them, let alone one or two apiece, had rushed up to the bedroom she shared with Maimie, where, falling on their knees, they opened the heavens with their prayers that God the Father and Our Blessed Lady who had so unfeelingly sent him to Mother would take him back to themselves where he would have a halo and a gorgeous pair of wings and be blessed and blissful forever.

Two days later, when Martin had engagingly blinked and gurgled at them from the cradle of his mother's arms, they had a wild reaction, and there was another panic-stricken scamper across the passage, another meeting in the bedroom and another opening of the heavens to implore forgiveness for their vanity and a definite change of mind on the part of the Holy Will.

Not that the Weldons were a religious family. Father, as he said himself, was violently vague on the subject of dogma and always terminated a theological argument with, 'Ah, but none of us know for certain: I'd say they have their differences even in the Vatican.' And Mother, who had endured a childhood shadowed by an over-zealous father who insisted on the nightly Rosary, and loved to describe the terrors of Hell: Mother was positively lax. They went to Mass now and then and their irregularity shocked their neighbours, but they prayed frequently in privacy whenever they wanted any special favour for themselves or their friends.

'From Limerick too, can you believe it?' was whispered here and there. 'Of course, 'tis all that time they spent in London before they decided to grace Cork with their presence. Is it the Weldons? Wisha, they're nothing but a lot of old fly-by-nights.'

Still the Weldons did have their fits of piety now and then, and sometimes their prayers were answered. As indeed they had been about Baby Martin's life on earth being spared to them. They adored him and spoiled him and bullied him in turn. Peg was at once the most enthusiastic and the most severe. A scatterbrain, Peg was, known to her family as Scatty Peg, but her brain teemed with ideas about the upbringing of others. Especially of Martin.

'What that child needs is training,' she'd say. 'Look at this lovely dolly now, Martin. Do you want her?'

'Yeth, pleathe.'

'Well, you can't have her,' she'd say, firmly setting the doll down on the very middle of the table where he couldn't possibly reach it. 'And that's the way to bring him up,' she'd go on. 'Education. That's what he wants . . . No, darling, don't try to climb onto the table, you'll only hurt yourself. And you are *not* to have Dolly till you recite for me. Now then, *Sleeping Beauty*, Act One. Come on now! "It is our baby's Christening day" . . .'

13

'"What thall we call her? . . ."'
'No darling, begin at the beginning.'

> 'It ith our baby'th Chrithening day,
> What thall we call her? Born in May
> A thweet May flower, she came to bring
> Into our heartth the joy of thpring.'

'That child's lisp is not only not improving, 'tis getting worse,' Tina said, gazing sombrely at him. 'He's nearly five now. Thilly baby Marty,' she gibed at him. 'Thay "Puth, Puth, Puth", and my black cat will fly down from the sky and spit fire at you.'

'Have you a black cat?' the child asked.

'Of course I have. She's flown down and she's sitting on my shoulder now, but you can't see her because she's invisible to everyone but me.'

'What'th invithible?'

'Phantasmagorical,' she whispered, waving her pale hands in front of his face.

Naturally it was Tina who was cast for the part of Fairy Nettlesting in the 'Book for the Bairns' version of the *Sleeping Beauty* to be performed by the Weldons and their friends the Moores and the McCarthys at Christmas in the sitting room, with a select audience in the dining room and the folding doors as a proscenium.

The cast was select too, and all the best parts were to be taken by the family.

The King (essential but not striking) – Master Tom Moore.

The Queen – Miss Deborah Weldon.

The Nurse (negligible) – Miss Annie McCarthy.

The Baby (non-speaking and in a cradle) – Master Martin Weldon.

Mayflower (the Baby, now grown to the lovely sixteen-year-old Princess) – Miss Peggy Ruth Weldon.

Fairy Nettlesting – Miss Tina Weldon.

The Prince (appearing in Act Three only) – Master Denis McCarthy. (Later to be doubled with Nettlesting, by Tina, who had her eye on it from the start.)

Fairy Lily – Miss Maimie Weldon.

Fairy Rose – Miss Maggie Moore.

Fairy Crocus – Miss Eileen Moore.

Martin, by the time Christmas was come, would be five years old, and he felt for the first but not the last time the disadvantages of age and sex. What? He, a boy, five years old, to be presented as a female infant not yet even christened? But he was determined to make the most of this, his first bow to the public – could it be called a bow when he would be cabined, cribbed and confined in a cradle to be lovingly constructed and gilded by Father? Could it be called a public, this handful of neighbours sitting condescendingly in the drawing-room? Anyway, he would make the most of it.

And so, when his birthday party was over and he had wallowed in enough kisses and presents to last him a lifetime, the great night had come and with it a sudden, a brilliant, a diabolical inspiration flared in his mind and he acted on it.

When the Queen (Miss Deborah Weldon) came to her lines:

> 'We'll call her Mayflower!
> Nurse, just peep and see if she is still asleep:
> She sleeps so long.'

And the Nurse (Miss Annie McCarthy) had replied:

> 'They all do so!
> They sleep and sleep and grow and grow!'

Martin Mayflower threw both arms above his head and gave a resounding yawn, followed by an impressive series of panting breaths that sounded like an excited fox-terrier. So that in poor Nurse McCarthy's following speech:

> 'I know what babies are, you see,
> I nursed his Royal Majesty,
> His brothers and his sisters too,'

15

the lines were completely drowned by unleashed giggles from the audience and ill-concealed fury from the rest of the cast, and even the King's jovial reply:

> 'Yes, I remember, Nurse, don't you?
> The naughty pranks we used to play!
> Mayflower will hear them all some day,
> For the children always love to know
> What Father did long, long ago,'

was only just heard, and not much helped by Nettlesting who, having had a tiff with Father two days earlier, audibly commented from the wings: 'I question that.'

Martin slept in a cot in the corner of his parents' bedroom, and one morning he woke earlier than usual, and when he looked over as he usually did to the bed where as a rule his mother lay drinking tea, behold the bed was empty, and there was Mother coming in through the door and she was wearing a dressing-gown. So, she'd been in the bathroom, had she? and Martin hadn't heard her going out. But now he watched her as, not noticing him, she went over to the looking-glass and threw off the dressing-gown. And there she was, her back to Martin, but he could see her plainly in the glass and she'd nothing on her but a white petticoat with three frills on it, and the top part of her was all bare, and Martin for the first time he could remember saw her two breasts and oh God! How strange! How wonderful! Like two pale inverted flowers. Would he one day have two beautiful breasts like that? Would he? And what was more, if Mother was formed with a chest so luxurious, and she was nearly as small as Tina, what must Father's be like and he so much bigger and taller than she? Everyone said what a well-built man he was: what must he be carrying in front of him? So it was that Martin took to following his father about, waiting for him to take off his shirt, opening the door of the bedroom or the bathroom softly and peeping inside, but no, the bathroom door would be locked as a rule and, even when it wasn't, there was never a sign of Father or anything else in the least interesting, and one day his father, emerging fully clothed from the bedroom, said: 'What are you looking for, boy? What do you want, creeping about like a cat? Be off with you now. Be off!'

But one morning Father left the door of the bathroom unlocked and Martin stealthily peeped through, and there was Father, with a towel knotted around his waist, shaving at the wash-basin.

Ah no, it wasn't fair!

Nothing in the least like that vision of Mother: just nothing to compare to her, and instead of that dazzling whiteness and the two round inverted roses there was a sallow, muscular chest, hardly anything you'd notice, but a cross of dark hair that stretched up and down and across and across.

'Ah what do you want now, child? What is it you want to be following me round for? Be off with you now: be off with you like a good boy.'

So that was the end of that search for the fulfilment of his own future, and Martin felt bitter about it for a few days. But then he didn't think about it any more until the night when they all went to the pantomime, when it returned with a puzzle attached to it like the tail on a kite.

It was the first time Martin had been in a real theatre, and its name, he felt, described it perfectly. It was indeed a Palace with its glittering lights, its rows and rows of luxurious chairs whose seats folded under you when you sat down on them and sprang to attention as you rose, its golden enormous frame at the far end with gorgeously coloured curtains, rich with tassels and fringes, and what in Heaven's name was hidden behind them? Then there were the two mysterious gilt cabinets: one on each side of the frame, they had curved lids on them, or were they roofs? *Domes* they might be called, Mother explained, though even she seemed vague, as well she might, about the purpose they served. And there were a few pretty ladies standing about with elegant dresses and white caps on their heads. They were offering programmes and some of them offered sweets, and

Father bought one programme and two big boxes of the sweets, so everyone was contented as they shared them and listened to Father impressively reading out the list of characters.

There was Dick Whittington himself, there was somebody called Idle Jack, there was King Rat, there was a lady called Alice Fitzwarren, and – ah! but now the musicians were coming in from a door at the side of the golden frame. They were carrying their fiddles and their trumpets and their flutes: cool as cucumbers they were, and they sat down and began to play softly and loudly the strangest music of tinkling and squeaking with no tune to it at all but tinkle and squeak and big heavy blasts blaring through like fiery snorts out of a giant's throat. Martin said in a loud voice, 'What are they playing? Ha?' And Mother whispered, 'Hush now darling: tuning up, that's all they're doing.'

Diddledy fiddledy la la la la prang footle ootle ting tang oom oom boom diddle de flutter o day come all a play ta ra ta ree ta rohoho bluhulu hulla.

And all of them with white sheets of printed music on their easels in front of the gorgeous curtains that were framed in gold with the little honeycombs of cabinets at each side of the frame, and a man with a red face and silver curls like a frill round the back of a bald head appeared, and he had a little stick in his hand and when everybody started to clap their hands at the sight of him, he bowed and smiled three times, centre and right and left and then – now why? – he turned his back on the audience and gave two loud raps with his stick on the top of his tall easel and ah! and oh! the loudest loveliest music began, a real tune this time, and the theatre grew slowly dark and the gorgeous curtains grew suddenly brighter and they trembled a little, and then ah! and oh!, they rose up in the air all shaking with joy and they flew away, and there was all Fairyland stretched out in sunshine, with little coloured houses and crowds of boys and girls in the most wonderful clothes you ever saw moving with tripping steps in circles here and there, and they were singing in high laughing voices. Like angels they were, made out of coloured sugar, all the colours of the rainbow they were and how happy they must be all of them, glancing from right to left and always with upward glancing as they swung round and round, and Martin began to shout with joy, and Scatty Peg said, 'Isn't it gorgeous?' and Mother whispered, 'Don't shout or talk aloud, my pets. Just watch it and enjoy it Martin, there's my good boy.'

'Would you wonder at him?' Scatty Peg whispered, 'Isn't it heavenly? And all the lovely colours! Wouldn't they dazzle you?'

'I think there are too many colours,' Maimie said in a tiny voice. She was, as her mother had once remarked, a 'martyr to good taste'.

But none of the others thought there were too many colours. Not even Deborah, who as the eldest was often listened to with respect. Not even Tina who was usually given to caustic criticism, and who, when Dick Whittington himself appeared to a fanfare of trumpets and merry laughter from the villagers, murmured, 'My God, if I'd legs like that, I'd hush them up.'

Dick's legs, Martin thought, were the most rapturously superb he'd ever seen. Such mighty curves, such heroic strength and grace! No wonder Dick slapped them every now and again, it was to congratulate them on their manly beauty. And ah! Would he have legs like that one day? Not a bit like Father's legs when he went for a swim in the river, and Martin, remembering how often he'd seen him in a bathing suit that was skin tight and only exposed his legs and arms, realized suddenly what a fool he had been to expect Father to have two beautiful chests like Mother's. Yet surely, oh surely Dick had! Ah, what a magnificent creature! What masses of golden curls, what flashing azure eyes – even the lids of them were blue – what snowy teeth, what a laugh, what a daring devil-may-care walk, what legs, what a waist, what a chest! And the glorious talk of him, and the soaring voice of him when he sang of his love of adventure and his determination to leave 'this dull village' (what could he mean by that?), and make his way to London town.

And the big enormous black and white cat danced round with him, and off they went together arm in paw as the gorgeous curtain came down and the lights in the theatre went up, and Martin was faint with emotion and dread as he asked: 'Is it all over?'

'Not at all: that's only the beginning,' Father reassured him, and the rest of the evening was a whirlpool of enchantment.

At home in his own cot in the corner Martin couldn't close his eyes for a long, long while: the dark air of the bedroom was thronged with dazzling pictures and loud crashing harmonies and the crowning glory of Whittington, that last glimpse of him glittering in a jewelled tunic and a vast feathered hat, hand in hand with his beloved Alice: Dick Whittington, the shining triumphant star of the Palace, King Street, Cork: thrice Lord Mayor of London! And it was many months after that night that Martin learned that Dick's real name – off stage of course – was Miss Daisy Bates.

And then, a couple of weeks after that, Anthony Weldon presented his son Martin with a new toy. He had made it himself out of odd bits of wood and canvas stuck together with glue, and he had painted it carefully, with helpful advice from his wife as well as Deborah and Maimie, who were anxious about his uncertain colour sense, in crimson and black, with loops of festively knotted cords, fringes and tassels of yellow-gold, and all of them so dazzling in their beauty that Martin gasped and stammered with pleasure as he gave his father thanks. Besides, it was practical too with a raised-up stage just like the one at the Palace in King Street, and a red and gold curtain you pulled up or down as you chose, and the scenery was a forest glade with miles of dark and light green trees with the pinnacles of a grand castle rising up out of them and above them all a clear blue sky.

'But you must make other sets as well,' his father told him. 'And Maimie and Peg will help you to cut out the little actors and actresses in cardboard, and push them on and off on wires, or dandle them maybe, from the top like this, look.' And he gave a demonstration with his fingers.

20

And so Martin's toy became an institution, and he never seemed to tire of it.

'How ominous it is to watch that child,' Tina remarked one rainy day, when neither she nor anyone else could lure him from his toy stage and his dandy dolls. 'Obsessed. The poor little creature is obsessed. He'll fly away from you all one day and go on the stage.'

Anthony Weldon was a singular type. Handsome and good-humoured, with the features and colouring he had inherited from his mother, who had come from Seville, he was also talented as a teller of tales and a designer of funny pictures as well as of toy theatres, though his drawings were always in pencil or in black and white, for he was colour-blind and could barely distinguish between red and green. He was not by nature or training a businessman. He dealt in corn and flour, as his people had done before him – the family on both sides were millers – but Anthony Weldon had no mill and had come to Cork from London seven years ago with the hope of establishing a corn chandler's shop, as his father had, first at Limerick and later in London. But the shop had never materialized, and he was working now as a commercial traveller selling oats and barley, and lately he had been cursing the inventors of the motor car who, he swore, were discouraging Nature more and more from the breeding of horses.

'The curse of Cromwell on the lot of them,' he regularly cried. 'We'll be in the workhouse, the whole lot of us, if business gets any worse.' And his wife worried, which was unlike her, and began to wonder would it be possible to take in a lodger.

'If Tina would ever consent to sharing her room with Debby,' she said, 'we'd have a grand spare room, and wouldn't that bring in a pound or two to help things along? And you know, Tony, Martin is getting a big boy: too old he is for sleeping forever in a cot in our room. If we'd a nice lodger – a business man or something like that – maybe Martin could share the room and have a little bed in the corner there.'

'And maybe the lodger wouldn't care for that,' her husband said, gazing out of the window. 'Still, 'tis a possibility. Thank you Mary: you're a great comfort to me. My God will you look at the composition of those clouds over the river . . . would the colours be yellow now, with the setting sun, or green?'

'Rose red, me poor blind man.' Mrs Weldon laughed at him. 'Isn't the human eye a very curious contraption?'

The four Weldon girls all went to Miss Cotter's for piano lessons, Deborah on Monday, Tina on Wednesday, Maimie and Peggy Ruth on Saturday morning. Miss Cotter was strict but patient, and seemed mildly pleased with them all; but Tina, though she was pronounced difficult and moody, was by far the most talented. In fact Miss Cotter asssured her that if she worked very hard she might be able to appear in public one day.

'Like a performing seal,' Tina said, purposely playing a handful of chords in the wrong key. 'And *they* have no knuckles for spiteful spinsters to rap,' she added, closing the piano with a bang, and was later reported as 'ungrateful and ill-mannered'.

That was true, but all the same she had verve and brilliance, and all her relations listened to her with envious pleasure. Martin was the most enthusiastic of them all, and one day Tina lifted him onto her shoulders and brought him pick-a-back on a magical journey 'all round Europe', which in bare fact was the house. The kitchen was Ireland, because one was almost always there; the hallway England, 'because it was so strenuous and draughty'; her own room Russia, because it was 'all upside down'; Mother's and Father's room Spain, because of the white walls and sunshine; the stairs Switzerland ('Ah the mountains . . . up and up we go. Do you feel how cold it's getting? And look at the snow on the peaks!'). The dining room France, because the best meals were there, so down they went and back through France, through the folding doors into the sitting room.

'Italy, the land of music,' Tina, in one of her best moods, cried, and letting Martin slip from her shoulders onto an armchair, she sat down at the piano and began to play.

So beautifully she played, Martin thought, closing his eyes in rapture, and as she went from one luscious, facile melody to another, she murmured, 'Now this one isn't Italian music like the others, 'tis a French thing from an opera by a man called Gounod,' and she started to play, and Martin's eyelids grew luminous and he heard through the light notes the rich depth and volume of an orchestra with a woman's sweet voice floating over it, and then he saw . . . where he was in a box at the right side of a big theatre, much bigger than the Palace in King Street, but where was it, where? And he was a grown up man again and he stood on the left side of the box, half hidden by a curtain, and he was glad of that: it wouldn't be safe for him to be recognized with all these friends that were in the box too, and many of them known to the secret police . . . the secret police, ah dear God what could happen at the end of all? Tomorrow everything would happen and they would dare or die, but they would all be together, and then he noticed the birds – or were they bats? He couldn't make out – pigeons maybe or swallows and they were flying round and round over the heads of the audience and the woman's voice floating out from the stage singing, still singing, and then it all died away into what seemed the notes of a piano, that was all, and then he was walking back home through the cool amber streets, arm in arm with, yes with Giovanni. And across the long bridge again and over the street to the house on the corner and after the goodnight embrace Giovanni whispered, 'Courage, courage, tomorrow we prove ourselves.' Then they parted and he went into the house alone, along the stone passage opening another door with a second key and down the step into that room.

It was that room again, yes, and terror swept over him like a bitter wind and took him into its arms, and then it was not the wind that embraced him or cried aloud, no: these were Tina's arms and Tina's voice that was saying:

'Were you asleep my pet? What were you calling out for? Why? And you missed the end of Siebel's Flower Song, you bold boy! Never mind, I'll play it for you again – another time – don't cry now, don't cry! Why you're shaking, my poor boy, you're all upset . . . now what's this all about? Tell Tina, tell it all now to your own Tina.'

'Ah!' he sobbed, 'it was that room again where Daddy with the Hard Hat is always coming in through the door. A-a-ah!'

'Now Martin – Martin you know that's only an old dream, darling. You know it. Daddy with the Hard Hat? Sure there's no such person.'

'There was once. There was once. Oh Tina! It was that tune you were playing. That brought the room back and everything.'

'Now my own sweet love, how could the Flower Song in *Faust* bring anything that was bad back to you? How?'

Deborah, usually so calm and indifferent, was in a condition of hilarious enthusiasm when she came home from a tea-party at Turners Cross to which she and Tina had been invited. It was a party for young, but not for little, girls, and Maimie and Peg, to their fury, were left at home.

'Maisie Hunter, that English girl whose father is a coast guard at Crosshaven, was there,' Deborah said. 'Met her for the first time. Me dears! You never saw anyone so beautiful! She's sixteen, but she still has her hair down – as fair as Maimie's but all curls, and such style – and quite a long dress. Nile green, she said it was, with short sleeves and pink ribbons and a bouquet of pink roses, and she was so gay and grand, and she told the funniest stories you ever heard, and she said that one day she's going to go on the stage in London. What do you think of that?'

'That's if her father and mother will allow her and any stage will want her,' Tina said. 'Silly affected doll, all frills and flutter and can't sound her R's. At least she pretends she can't: "My bwotha's name is Jack you know. Daddy calls him Jack Tah sometimes 'cos he looks so like a sailah." What you can see in her, Debby, honest to God, I fail to imagine. Yes, she's pretty I suppose, if you like that sort of thing. She has a face just like a marshmallow. She's not any prettier than you. You are more

24

than pretty: you have a certain beauty. She has none. None at all. Unless of course you can find beauty in a chocolate box. I can't. She's more like a chocolate box than a marshmallow, a blue-eyed chocolate box. What's more she's too tall. Much too tall.'

'But that's so fashionable just now. I think she's fascinating.'

'Fashionable! Deborah, I'm ashamed of you. What is fashion? Some blithering fancy that changes every month. And every fashion sillier than the last. You might as well be fascinated by a monthly magazine. You probably are. Ah well, if chocolate boxes and monthly magazine covers are what fascinate you, have it your own way: grovel at the feet of your painted maypole. Don't ask me to admire her.'

'I'm not asking you to anything. But I'm going to ask her to tea if Mother will let me. I suggested to her this evening would she like to come and she said she'd love to, and could she bring her brother too, as it's such a long way from Crosshaven to here. So now, Madame Tina Tempest. May she and her brother Jack come here to tea Mother?'

'They may of course, why not?'

So Maisie Hunter came to tea, and with her she brought her brother Jack, a pleasant Londoner of twenty years, and even Tina smiled on him. He was tall like his sister, and well built, and although his face was plain it had a reassuring strength and character. He had, too, a shy, friendly charm of manner, and paid a great deal of attention to them all, especially to Tina. The family were astonished: they had been prepared for her to be either absent or belligerent, or silently hostile; at the least they had expected some caustic witticisms about poor Maisie, probably of a somewhat sinister nature.

But no. After a rather frosty 'How do you do?' she melted and was at her most charming to everyone, and although, normally, mention of the works or even the names of Gilbert and Sullivan in her presence was enough to bring a curve to her lips and an outburst of her most malevolent mockery, today she cried, 'What fun!' on hearing that Jack Hunter was enthusiastic about them, and was fond of 'trying to sing some of the numbers' himself, and she electrified everyone by asking for a performance and offering to accompany him. Father, who shared Jack's simple musical tastes, eagerly produced a copy of *The Mikado*, and soon Jack Hunter, brilliantly accompanied by Tina, was singing 'A Wandering Minstrel, I' in a light, rather husky baritone.

'Tremendous,' said Tina when she had finished, and firmly closed the piano. 'You should have your voice trained. And take care of that cold in your head.'

'Cold?' Jack Hunter enquired, looking startled, 'I haven't got a cold in my head.'

'Your poor throat then, perhaps,' she murmured. 'And that's terribly dangerous for a singer. Corns on the vocal chords.'

But in spite of Tina's comments, Jack was a great success with the family, especially with Martin, and the tea party went along very nicely. While Maisie kept the conversation at full and frantic swing, with occasional admiring interpolations from Deborah, Jack was having a sober talk with his host about his own plans for the future, with Martin stretched out on the floor at their feet, gazing from one to the other in rapt and totally uncomprehending interest. Grown up people always thrilled him, and the less he followed what they were discussing the more intrigued he became. The rise and fall of their voices had all the fascination of the incomprehensible. There must be something of mysterious importance afoot, or why did they go on so long? Who knew what jungles of mystery Jack Hunter and Father were not exploring in their rapid gabble?

'You see Mr Weldon, I've not got any really unobtainable ambitions in my head for the moment, but there is the possibility – the likelihood in fact – of a reasonably remunerative temporary job,' was what Jack was in fact saying. 'A job in a bank. Oh, nothing particularly inspiring, nothing adventurous, nothing that you might call epoch-making. But it would be a stepping-stone, if you see what I mean: a stepping-stone to what I really want to do in the future. And that is – I hope you won't think this too high-falutin', I mean too sort of far-fetched – that is a sheep-farm in Australia.'

Martin understood 'farm' though what sheep had to do with it he could not make out: but what in God's holy name was Australia?

'Down Under, as they call it,' Jack went on, getting more and more wrapped in mystery. 'Now this bank – it's the Cork branch of Barclay's, you know – is in Pembroke Street, in the heart of the city, as you know—'

'Going to plant trees in Pembroke Street, is he?' thought Martin, 'A branch of Barclay trees? My God!'

'And Crosshaven's really a long way away to come in and out of on a bike four times a day, and what I'm hoping to discover is a room somewhere nearer to town – well not *Town* I mean, in the literal sense, but near Cork – just a room and a bit of breakfast and possibly a bite of something in the evenings.'

'He'd better not try biting Tina,' Martin thought.

'Well now, did you make any enquiries?' Father was saying now. 'For it just occurred to me. Mary!' he said to his wife, who, after a polite excuse to Maisie, dragged herself with a faint expression of relief from a bubbling description of a pantomime at Drury Lane, and joined Father and Jack Hunter, with Martin still lying at their feet, all eyes and enchanted ears.

'Do forgive me for a minute, dear,' she said, 'I think me husband wants me. You'll go on with it all later, won't you? 'Tis fascinating. And you're looking lovely, dear. Debby was right about you. You're beautiful, God bless you.'

'Mary,' Father said in an impressively homely voice, 'this charming young fellow . . .'

Jack Hunter paid Mrs Weldon twenty-two and sixpence a week and, as Mrs Weldon remarked, 'twas a great help to the housekeeping, 'even though he has the appetite of a bull, God help him, and he likes more to eat than the green grass, well why wouldn't he, hasn't he the big frame and what would you expect? A very nice quiet decent fellow, and I wish to God

27

you'd stop your teasing him, Tina, not that he takes any notice of it, only you'll never get a good husband if you go on that way with your mocking talk and your scornful glance.'

'Have I ever in my life expressed a wish for a good husband?' her daughter enquired smoothly. 'A bad one would amuse me a thousand times more. I think I've something of the lion-tamer in my make-up.'

'So that's what it is on your cheeks!' Deborah unexpectedly cried. 'Rose-pink on a yellow skin! Maisie was saying the other day you were far more interesting with your own natural pallor. And she said, if you insisted on using rouge, a brownish tint would suit you far better, and she could give you a hint where to get some.'

'Hints on tints from the painted maypole? I see. Thank her a hundred times from me, will you?'

'Such notions you all have,' Mother laughed, in a way which both comforted and annoyed them. 'Listen, there's the door. That'll be Jack. Run and let him in, Martin. He gets on wonderfully with Martin,' she added as the child scampered out of the room. 'He says he's no bother at all.'

Martin's cot was getting too small for him now, and a larger one had been procured and put in a corner of the room Deborah had occupied in solitary peace. Now she shared with Tina who, she declared, spent half the night telling her that the room was haunted by three women with green hair who danced in a circle of fire and disturbed her own slumbers with their singing, and that if she, Deborah, had any sensibility she would see and hear them as plainly as herself. 'But of course, to help the housekeeping bills one sacrifices everything,' she muttered. 'Deborah! Do you seriously mean you can't see them?' she would intone. 'Look! Listen! and now the tallest one – the one in black with the tears streaming down from her eyes – has plucked a huge blue flower out the air and is laying it on your bed at your feet. That means she is sorry for you and will do you no harm if you do nothing to offend them. Lucky for you, that's all I have to say.'

'Then let it be! I hope it is all you have to say, and I wish to God you'd shut up and let me get to sleep,' Deborah told her. 'With your blue flowers and your blather.'

'Poor blind Deborah: deaf and blind, like all the rest of them,' Tina muttered. 'Foolish of you too: you've offended her now and she has turned the blue flower into a crimson thorn. Oh well, I suppose you can't help it, and luckily for you your hide's so thick you'll never feel the evil winds she is at this moment blowing over your future life. So goodnight and sleep in happy ignorance. I'll make a spell to protect you from the curse of the thorn . . .'

The unintelligible muttering grew fainter, and at last the sisters were both asleep.

In the room that Jack Hunter had consented to share with Martin things were far more peaceful. They got on together splendidly during the day. Jack failed to stimulate the child to the faintest interest in football or cricket or any other form of sport, but he told him stories of adventures by sea and land, of strange, faraway countries where there were deserts, and mountains much higher than any that Martin could imagine, and jungles where tigers and lions and snakes and humming-birds lived, and all the terrifying marvels of tropical creation. He told him of the north too, of Lapland and Greenland, and of reindeer and icebergs, and boys and girls who lived in clothes made of fur and leather and ate little but dried fish.

'And in the winter it's dark nearly all through the day, and in summer it hardly ever gets dark. The sun goes on shining all through the night, you see – the Midnight Sun they call it.'

Martin recounted all that he heard, with many embroideries, as was his family's way, to his mother, for he felt he could ask her questions he would have been too shy to put to the all-knowing, experienced Jack.

'Are there any deserts here in Ireland, Mother?'

'Ah not really, darling. 'Tis bare and stony enough in Connemara and in bits of Kerry too. But not the sort of deserts you mean. Ah no.'

29

'No jungles with tigers and snakes?'

'For Heaven's sake, no!'

'What about reindeers? And icebergs?'

'No dear, it isn't cold enough. Not quite cold enough anyway, thank God.'

'And why isn't there deserts and jungles?'

''Tisn't hot enough, thank God.'

One thanked God for the strangest things, Martin thought. Nothing exciting was to be found at all in Ireland it seemed. It was not hot enough for them. Or even cold enough. Ah well.

But peace and friendliness reigned between himself and Jack all day long, and at night in the room they shared the child would try to stay awake till the young man came up to bed. Because then perhaps he would tell him more. Why, for example, Jack was so enthusiastic about going to Australia. He must ask him about that. Why Australia? Where there were no jungles, and no icebergs and no reindeer or anything more, apparently, than one could find in Cork? Nothing but sheep.

Why Australia in God's holy name? The question was never asked because the child forgot about it during the day and was always asleep before his room-mate – that was how his English hero described himself – appeared.

One night Martin was sleeping peacefully, and in dreams that changed their colours and their moods from one moment to another he found, suddenly and strangely, that he himself was a grown man and walking arm in arm with another who was – Giovanni. Through the coolness of moonlit and moon-shadowed streets they walked in silence together, and presently Giovanni spoke and said:

'Why are you joining with us at all – you who are so afraid?'

He had no answer to this but muttered something about believing in the cause and feeling ashamed of his fear if he did not join with his friends and go through with things to the end, as he had sworn to do.

'But you know what the end may be? Our chances are small, our enemies strong. You know that as well as I do. And if the thought and the fear are poisoning your life?'

Yes, that was it: his whole life was poisoned by fear. He could say nothing that would make all clearer, but he did manage to murmur something about being true to what one believed to be the truth and continuing one's labours.

'Even if you disapprove of physical force?' Giovanni said, 'And you do, you know. It is against everything in your nature. Everything in yourself. I am anxious about you, my friend.'

They were over the bridge that spanned the great river now, and across the road to the house on the corner, and Martin found himself weeping as they said goodnight and Giovanni whispered: 'I know, I know. Well, it is inevitable now: the day after tomorrow will tell all. And tomorrow night: the opera. Don't forget! Dine with me beforehand. At Magali's at seven. Courage. Courage, dear friend.'

Then it was the dark stone passage again – and down the single step into the room again – and as he lit his lamp the old terror swept over him so that his hand shook and he began to cry out in his loneliness.

'Ah!' he cried. And 'Ah – ah – ah!'

And Martin woke screaming and the moon was shining brightly into the room in Cork, and he was chattering in broken words about Daddy – Daddy with the Hard Hat. 'He'll be coming tomorrow: he'll be coming in the morning.' And there across the oblong of moonlight, in a long white shirt down to the middle of his calves, came Jack. Straight over to the cot he came, and lifted the child in his arms.

'What is it? What's wrong with you, poor old chap? Had a nasty dream, did you?' The crisp English voice with its peculiar vowels was muffled by sleep and sounded kind and reassuring.

'Ah, Jack! Ah, Jack! Ah, Jack!' was all he could answer. Then he murmured something about the 'same old black dream, and on a morning later on Daddy with the Hard Hat would come in and look at him and then he'd be dead.'

Again. He would be dead.

Jack repeated something under his breath about 'Daddy with

31

the Hard Hat – what on earth? Poor kid. Poor kid. Gosh! You're in a pretty state. Come along to bed with me, you'll be all right with me.'

And now they were in the bed and Jack's arms were round him and he was safe. For a long while then Martin did not sleep. He had no wish to sleep, for he was too happy. Nearly all his waking life went by in happiness, it was only sleep that brought terror that descended in dumb empty darkness, and drowned him under clouds of black windswept gauze, clawing at his throat and blinding his eyes with daggers of flame. All the rest was happy and funny sometimes too, and there were his four sisters to tease and bully and spoil him, and Mother laughing and humming old country songs to herself about Shannon's green banks and the grandeur of Sarsfield's men, and Father telling his stories of Beppo the Brigand, and drawing rapid pictures in crayon, whistling to himself as he drew. But happiness like this the child had never dreamed of, lying there warm and safe in the bed with Jack's arms about him and Jack's steady breathing in his ears.

'This is lovely,' he thought to himself, and he pillowed his head on Jack's chest and thought for a moment of what Aunt Kate had once soulfully referred to in his hearing as 'heavenly bliss', but Jack gave a snort and tapped his cheek and murmured, 'Now don't you start fidgetin' or you'll keep me awake. Just you stay quiet, there's a good little chap,' and Martin removed his head but stayed close to him, and thought what a funny accent he had, and how beautiful and simple life was after all . . . and a long while after that he went to sleep.

Martin was as artful as a cat, though it was a very innocent sort of a cat. For, a few nights after the warmth and comfort of those hours in bed beside Jack Hunter, he decided that he would like to repeat the experience. So, waking for a moment in a moonless darkness when the rain was falling with the sound of faint feathers brushing the leaves of the lilac trees in the warm night air, he gave a most admirable performance of nightmare horrors, and of course succeeded in waking up the lodger. Almost at once Jack was pounding across the room, and his cheerful 'Hullo, hullo, hullo, what's up with you *this* time, sonny?' was music in his ears.

'Ah, Jack! Ah, Jack! That bad old dream again. There he was coming in through the door dark as night, yes he was! Honest to God! Daddy with the—'

'Well don't you bother about him. What is he, I should like to know? Nothing but a silly soppy dream. You ought to laugh at him, Marty! Pluck up your courage and laugh at him, that's what you've got to do!'

'Jack, don't leave me alone. He'll come back if you go away, he'll come back and eat me up.'

'Well, you'll be a nice mouthful for him. Give him indigestion, that's what you'll do to *him*. Oh all right then, all right, come along with me or you'll drive yourself potty, and me too if you don't look out. Come on then, upsy-daisy! here we go, I suppose I'll have to put up with you, only keep still now won't you and don't fidget, there's the good chap!' And for the next half hour Martin lay in warm bliss until sleep took his body and mind in her embrace and poured her music into his soul.

It became a habit, this purely histrionic nightmare that enabled him to share Jack's bed, and Jack himself was not unaware of the fact that, after the first occasion, there was no foundation at all to the heart-rending summons to rescue a human soul from terror by sharing the night with what was clearly a play-actor in embryo. But he humoured the child, and three or four times a week the two of them would sleep together in blissful comfort and innocence. Neither of them had even heard of psychoanalysis, nor would the study of it have aroused the faintest reaction in either of their conscious or unconscious thoughts.

And if his nights were peacefully spent, but for the occasional return of what became gradually revealed to him as the Italian nightmare, Martin, now that he had arrived (as the century had arrived) at the age of seven, discovered that his days were filling

33

with two new and novel interests. These were both inspired by his sisters, as every event of these early years seemed to be, and one of the sisters was Tina and the other – unexpectedly as it seemed at the beginning of things – was little Maimie.

Maimie had developed at her convent school not merely a passion for learning, but an even stronger urge to impart the fruits of her studies to others, and she fixed her attention on Martin who was the soul of willing cooperation about anything in the world as long as he was himself interested in the proposition. And in this he was deeply interested, especially as the alternative would mean that he would have to go next term to a boys' school, probably to the Christian Brothers, the thought of which filled him with dismay. But he was considered too large, not to say too old, any longer to continue among the young ladies' classes at the convent, and without hesitation he chose to spend two hours every evening with Maimie whose plan was to teach him reading, writing, and the elements of drawing.

So it happened that, quite soon, Martin was reading Lamb's *Tales from Shakespeare* aloud, and doing little sums of addition and subtraction – arithmetic was not Maimie's forte, and the sums were nothing more than embryonic – and drawing cups and saucers and chairs that he peopled with imaginary figures of gnomes and fairy women; and reciting 'J'ai, tu as, il a, elle a,' which he was told was how French people spoke to each other, and enjoying his nightly lessons with his diminutive teacher.

It was the reading of Lamb's *Tales* that intrigued him most, and one day he discussed them with Tina. 'Shylock was a devil,' he informed her. 'A pound of flesh he wanted to cut off from poor Antonio, just imagine.'

And Tina, unconsciously perhaps, started the child off on a new and significant path.

'Of course you would get that notion from Maimie and Charles Lamb,' she scornfully cried. 'No word of Shylock's suffering or his point of view at all. Now listen to the real thing: wait now till I get the book for you,' and she pulled the collected

34

works of William Shakespeare from the shelf in the sitting room, and flicked through the pages.

'I am a Jew. Hath not a Jew eyes? hath not a Jew hands, organs, dimensions, senses, affections, passions? . . . If you prick us, do we not bleed? if you tickle us, do we not laugh? if you poison us, do we not die? and if you wrong us, shall we not revenge? . . .'

The actress's small brother, moved to tears by the passion and pathos in his sister's voice during the first few lines of the speech, was numb with terror at what seemed like the approach of some hideous torture ending inevitably with death, for Tina's voice as she read the part was filled with such violence and fury, such venomous hatred, such unendurable pain that she seemed for a moment to have become some stranger he had never seen before. Her eyes while she was speaking were like two lakes of dark flame, and yet, when she had finished, Martin saw that tears were running down her cheeks.

'Oh Tina!,' the boy cried, for he could say no more, 'Oh Tina, oh Tina!'

'Now I'll read you a funny scene,' she told him, brushing the tears away and speaking, to Martin's amazement, in a perfectly normal voice. 'At least, 'tis supposed to be funny: I can't see anything funny at all about two people, a brute of a man and a bad-tempered demon of a woman, being hateful to each other, and the two of them going to be married if you ever heard of such a thing. Listen to this now.'

And flicking the pages over she commenced:
'The he-devil's name is Petruchio, and the she-devil is called Katherine. Now . . .

"Good morrow Kate, for that's your name I hear."

"Well have you heard but something hard of hearing.

"They call me Katherine that do speak of me."

"You lie i'faith for you are called plain Kate . . ."'

Tina finished the scene which she had played with precisely the same tragic fury as that she had used for Shylock, and when she ended with the line, 'I must and will have Katherine for my wife,' she gave a snort of contempt. 'And that,' she continued, 'is what is known as the Wooing Scene. I, if I had my way, which of course I haven't nor ever expect to have, would call it the "Come with me into Hell till I torture the life and the spirit out of you" scene.'

Martin had never realized that humour had no place in Tina's conception of the drama. Her considerable talent was lurid and tempestuous, her strength was sheer passion, her weakness sheer melodrama, and both of these qualities she carried with her all through her life. They made her at once a vivid yet limited personality, for although her imaginative insight was sensitive and powerful, her interpretation, whether she read aloud or acted some short scene in poetry or prose, was marred by over-emphasis, and her scorn for any form of what was merely pretty, or fanciful, or humorous, would have been fatal for her development in the theatre if she had chosen it for her profession.

But she showed no signs of doing so. In this – for the Weldon family – eventful year of 1907 Tina, at the age of seventeen, was as uncertain of what she wanted to do with her life as were Peg and Martin, and they were both so young that nobody bothered their heads about them. Deborah and Maimie were far more decided: Maimie, she hoped, was going to be a teacher somehow or other, and Deborah – somehow or other – had her luminous, lazy, good-natured eyes firmly and avowedly fixed on matrimony.

'You see, my dears,' she would smilingly explain, 'marriage may not be much of an institution, but 'tis the only career if you're a woman and you don't happen to be a genius like Emily Brontë or someone. And so, I've set me heart on a nice husband. I'll find some charming young man I really feel I could pass my life with some day, not one of your Jack MacCarthys or Jack Hunters, and none of your Tim Murphys or Paddy Mulhares either, and I'll have a beautiful house somewhere and I'm going in for the study of cookery because all men enjoy good food, though of course if I'm lucky we may be able to afford a cook. A

French one, who knows? Wouldn't that be grand? And you can all come and stay with us now and then.'

'And be given bacon and cabbage à la française I suppose?' Tina said, 'Thank you, Debby, it sounds irresistible. But if you get as grand as that won't you be ashamed of common-or-garden people like us?'

'Oh we're *not* common-or-garden,' Deborah assured her. 'We're not, you know. I think we're a very original family, even though we haven't a penny to bless ourselves with. Look at you, Tina. You'll probably be a great actress one day.'

'Oh no I won't. I can only do it really in my imagination. One should never twist a dream about and try to push it into everyday action. For me it would be a catastrophe: I think it would kill me if I tried and failed.'

'In any case you'd not have much of a chance in Cork,' Peg observed sadly. 'I often think 'twould be a marvellous thing for all of us if we could get back to London. After all I was born there. Though I can't remember anything much about it.'

'Mother and Father were talking about it the other day, I heard them,' Tina said. 'And I think if we do go it'll be horrible. I can't imagine listening to English voices all day long . . . half of them talking like Jack Hunter and the other half like that appalling sister of his. And 'tis no good glaring at me like that Debby, because your precious Maisie Maypole is a silly, affected, fluttering fool, and she puts on that fwightful sopwano to hide the fact that her natural voice is like a steam engine, and her natural accent is more Cockney even than Jack's.'

'You're jealous of her, oh yes you are,' the loyal Deborah cried. 'But what's all this about London? I never heard a thing about it at all, and I should have been told first. After all I'm the oldest, *and* I'm the only level-headed one among the lot of you.'

'There's some big shop called Whiteley's, and part of it is devoted to corn and flour . . . chandlery or something, I think Father was saying . . . and he's hoping to get a job there. And so, my poor delusioned Peggy, your dream may come true and we'll all be living in that great whirling English metropolis,

37

with theatres and concert halls and restaurants as thick as grass about us, and a fat lot of all that will *we* ever see. I know Father: he makes a mess of everything he touches. He has no more talent for making money than a tinker's ass, and we'll all be living in some poky little God-forsaken hovel in the depths of some desolate God-forsaken little suburb, and Father, who ought to have been a painter or an actor instead of a failure of a businessman—'

Maimie was profoundly shocked.

'You oughtn't to talk about our father the way you do, Tina,' she cried indignantly. 'And he so good and kind to us all.'

The rumour about a move to London turned out to be quite true, and astonished them all, and the four girls added delight to their astonishment. London, they were convinced, would be a wonderful adventure, but Martin was tearful at the thought of parting with the river and the Marino, and with his friends the McCarthys and Maggie Moore, and most of all with Jack Hunter. How could he get on without Jack? Whom would he be able to impress now with his nightmare terrors so beautifully acted for three, if not four, nights of the week? Who now would reward these performances with the half of his bed and the reassurance of those warm, powerful, poetical arms?

'There'll be lots of people like Jack in London, Martin,' Maimie informed him. 'There'll be a thousand of them in London, won't there, Mother?'

Mrs Weldon looked over the pastry she was rolling on the kitchen table. 'There will, of course. Sure, nearly everybody over there is the spitting image of Jack. So don't worry your head, child. Jack Hunter's not the only pebble on the beach.'

'Well, I don't want to leave him, and if I'm not here to mind him he'll go off to Australia and I'll never see him aga-a-in!'

'Ah, don't cry, God help you,' his mother implored him, and she put down the rolling-pin and, sitting down near the fire, took him into her arms and stroked his hair. 'Only babies cry,' she told him. 'Big boys like you, they never cry. They'd be ashamed to cry.'

38

'Well, I'm *not*, then. Ah hah hah!'

'Shameless, of course,' said Tina, passing through the room and regarding her reflection in the glass on the wall with critical eyes. 'Curiously shameless. I think that's rather interesting. I wonder why he's so shameless. Look at him! Listen to him! Sheer abandon!'

CHAPTER TWO
London Reality

The Weldon family felt that London was terribly close to becoming a reality when it was known that a small house had been settled upon by Father as being suitably cheap as far as rent was concerned, and situated in a northwestern suburb in a quiet street with fields in the vicinity, and something called Queen's Park close by. The prospect of imminent adventure in unknown surroundings took the edge off any dread of exile that they might have felt, and there was more curiosity than sadness in the air. But when the house had been stripped of nearly all its furniture, and almost everything had gone away with Mother and Deborah as forerunners to the new home, nostalgia swept over those who had been left behind for two more days. In spite of Maimie's lively interest in the future, and her heroic assurances that it was all so exciting, Peg who had to share her bed with her (for Maimie's own had gone ahead with the rest of the things), poor scatty Peg cried herself to the threshold of sleep and continued to repeat her conviction that she would 'never see her Irish home again'.

'And I don't imagine for a moment that you'll feel at home in London, even though you were born in it,' Tina had said in what was for her a sympathetic tone. 'Don't imagine I will either,' she continued, 'But there'll be nothing new about that for me. I don't feel at home anywhere. I feel utterly out of place on this earth. I wonder would Mars be a more sympathetic place?'

'Will you listen to her?' Peg demanded through her tears. 'Isn't London far away enough for you without blathering about Mars?'

Martin's last night in Cork was a melancholy one, for Jack Hunter had left the Weldon household already, and after saying goodbye to them all had settled himself for the nights and days to come not a stone's throw away, at Ballintemple. His parting with Martin was an embarrassment to him and everyone else except the child, who with the lack of shame, that abandonment, already remarked upon by sister Tina, cried and kissed and cried again while loudly repeating his wish that he had never been born, and demanding of the world why a cruel fate should choose to make him suffer so much.

'Pull yourself together, Martin,' Peggy Ruth begged him.

'How can I help it if I'm falling to pieces?' the child wailed. 'Oh Jack, oh Jack, why do you have to go away?'

'Come on, cheer up darling,' Maimie coaxed him, 'You're making poor Jack quite sad too. And he'll send you a nice postcard now and then, you will now, won't you, Jack?'

'I should say so,' Jack said heartily, 'Come on now, old chap. Never say die, you know.'

'But I do say die, and I wish I could die. I do so, and what's the use of a postcard? You'll forget all about me Jack, yes you will, you will!'

And that night he slept all through the dreary hours in his lonely cot, and his father, swathed in blankets, slept on the floor where Jack's bed had been.

The first contact with England – arrival at Bristol – was probably exciting for the girls. Even perhaps for Father, though heaven knew he had seen it often enough. But for Martin everything was obscured by his own sleepiness, and by the time they reached London, after what seemed a lifetime in the train, they were all exhausted but intrigued. Yet Martin felt it was all a dream, as dreamlike and unreal when he was awake as were the vivid ever-changing images that crowded about him through the hours when he slept.

Paddington Station was all in turmoil: there was no sign of Mother or Deborah or of any familiar face, but a cloudy confusion of strangers hurrying to and fro, of a rattle of milk cans and piles of luggage being wheeled or carried in a myriad directions by porters frantically followed by anxious passengers. Father was wildly gesticulating at the open doors of the luggage van to two uniformed men who also, it seemed, were porters, and Martin followed them to what appeared to be a huge shuttered chasm in the wall, where he heard talk about something called Carter Paterson.

'What's Carter Paterson?' Martin demanded of Tina, who was the nearest person, but Tina only clasped his head in her hands and did not answer.

Presently they were bundled into a thing that Father called a four-wheeler and rattled away, but it was nearly an hour later before Mother was clasping them all in her arms, and Deborah was saying, 'You creatures. You poor creatures! You must be famished! Come along now: we've rashers and tea and everything ready.'

It was a different sort of a kitchen: there was a bay window, and one of the doors, Mother proudly announced, led to the coal cellar. A different shape and, through the bay window, a different-looking garden. But it was home again because there they all were, and Mother was saying that there was gas all over the house. All the lights were gas, and there was a gas oven in the kitchen as well as the range.

'Oh, very up to date altogether,' Mother said proudly. 'And won't it be grand not to have to light the fire every time you'd want a cup of tea? All you have to do is to turn one of these little taps and crack a match – come over here till I show you – here we go now: houp la!'

'Wouldn't that terrify you?' Martin, full of awe, whispered to his family.

'Ah, you'll get used to it,' Deborah soothed him. 'Give me a match, Mother, till I show him. I'm used to it already,' and she lit another ring of bluish flame.

'Why does it go *pop* like that?'

'Because it's so delighted to get free from prison,' Tina explained. 'Now listen to it complaining with another sort of pop when it has to go back again. Sheer fury and despair, you see,' and she turned both rings off. 'Aha! Now they're back in

42

the dark. But don't you play with them or you may be blown up in the air and never come back.'

'Now why do you want to frighten the child?' Father demanded, and his family agreed with him.

'Maybe 'tis nothing to any of you if he sets himself on fire like Harriet and the Matches in *Shock-headed Peter*,' Tina responded. 'I happen to be fond of him. I hate the thought of him wrapped in sheets of flame, and—'

'Well, think now,' her mother hastily interrupted her, 'think of all the lovely things I'll be baking in that! Chickens and cakes for your birthdays – only Martin's birthday comes just a couple of weeks before Maimie's, and Peggy's comes two days after that.'

'Ah, yes,' Tina replied thoughtfully, 'Martin's a Scorpio and Peg and Maimie are Sagittarians. And poor Deborah is a Gemini. That's why they can't understand me. Not their fault, I suppose. I belong to the Air.'

'What's she talking about at all?' her mother asked. 'Where on earth you get all that old stuff from Heaven knows.' And she turned off the oven and closed the door. 'And there's a lovely little room for you, Martin, and a door opening out of it into Father's and mine so you'll not mind being on your own.'

But he did mind. For a while at any rate. He was lonely for Jack Hunter, and lonely for Blackrock and the river, and for Maggie Moore and Kelleher's shop and the nuns at the girls' school. For a long while he felt that London and loneliness went hand in cold hand together, and it was very meet that the two words began with the same letter: London and loneliness. Lonely in London.

One day as he stood at the bay window in the sitting room, looking out at the rain falling over the row of neat houses and prim front gardens all exactly alike with their iron railings and ornamental iron gates, he said to his father, 'Are we going to live here always?'

His father was filling a pipe, and now he took from his pocket a long box of matches. Swan Vestas, he called them. The boy

43

had never seen such a box before, and the size and shape and bright colours of it intrigued him, yet somehow increased the sense of isolation and strangeness. Then his father took out a match, put the pipe in his mouth, and lit it carefully before he spoke, regarding his son with eyes nearly as darkly brooding as Tina's. He blew a puff of smoke into the air then and he took the pipe out of his mouth with his left hand and, holding the box of Swan Vestas in his right hand, he pointed it at Martin.

'Yes we are,' he said. 'And I feel that you don't like it very much yet. But you will you know, boy. You'll grow to love it. 'Tis one of the world's great cities. The very greatest of all, I'd say. And slowly – very slowly maybe – you'll get to understand that. 'Twas here in London I met your dear mother, you know. And 'twas here that my father met my mother. And she didn't like it here at all. Why? Because she didn't stay long enough. London is a place you have to know and understand before you love it. She – my mother I mean – she was from Spain as you know, from Seville, and she used always to be saying, "Quien no ha visto a Sevilla no ha visto a ninguna maravilla" – Who has not seen Seville has never seen any marvel. That's absurd of course, I mean, Seville is a lovely place. Beautiful, beautiful, there's no denying it. But compared to London it seems lackadaisical, self-important, trivial somehow. For all its liveliness, all its courteous manners, all that thing that's called vivacity, 'tis less truly throbbing with life than London. Ach, I know of course that on the surface of things London seems a grey, chilly sort of a place. Like the manner of the people. They don't wear their hearts on their sleeves. They don't smile at you much or seem to notice you're there at all half the time. But they're good people as a rule. They're very true. At least I've found them so. You make a friend of an Englishman and he's your friend for life. Not like an Irishman – ah, not every one of them of course, but a great many of them, and I'm one of them myself, no matter about my mother and I ought to know – an Irishman will take you to his heart in five minutes if he likes you, but he may forget about you altogether the next day, or he'll tell stories and

44

scandals about you that'd take the skin and hair off you: anything at all to get a good laugh. You may not like it here so much for a while, but the day will come, mark my words now, when you'll agree with me. London is the greatest city in the world.' And he waved the long box of Swan Vestas in front of him with the air of a prophet.

'Yes,' said Martin from some remote place from which he was gazing through a window at the grey monotony of the street under the falling rain. And it seemed to him that he would always be looking out of a window at a grey monotonous street, looking out and dreaming of somewhere else, of somebody else. But of where? Of whom?

And to the end of his days Martin never saw a box of Swan Vestas without recapturing the desolation of that moment.

Anthony Weldon's wholehearted admiration of London did not meet with the exchange of compliments he had half anticipated, at any rate as far as financial success was concerned. Whether or not it was, as he and the big store he worked for averred, because the steady advance in the streets of the motor car, and the steady retreat of the horse as a means of transport, was responsible for the increasing slackness of the corn trade, the slackness was certainly there. And the Weldon family grew poorer and poorer: when they looked back over their shoulders, as they often did, the old days in Cork seemed positively luxurious by comparison. There had been Katty O'Driscoll for one thing, a buxom young lady from Youghal, who came in four times a week to do what Mrs Weldon called 'the rough work, God bless her: heaven knows what I'd do without her!' But now the most that could be afforded was a half-a-day, once-a-week visit from Mrs Vokins, a dim, middle-aged, exhausted-looking creature with a grey face and crimson hands knotted and wrinkled with toil. Mrs Weldon was sorry for her and easily persuaded her to stay for the midday dinner, which she ate in the kitchen with the rest of the family. This annoyed Tina, who was going through a stage of what her mother called 'grand notions', and who frequently vowed that it 'really was going rather far in democracy to be forced to endure eating one's lunch in the presence of raw hands, sword-swallowing, and the deafening music of the Voskins's mastication. Why can't she eat in the scullery?' she would demand. 'She'd be far happier, and so would I.'

But Mrs Weldon only laughed and said, 'Ah but the poor creature, God help her: what harm is she doing you?' and on the following Saturday – the charring was always done on Saturday – she would pile Mrs Vokins's plate higher than ever, until Mrs Vokins would say at last, 'Oh it *is* good of you I'm sure, Mrs W., dear, but really I couldn't take no more. Fact is you see, I like bacon and cabbage, but bacon and cabbage doesn't like me. Not if I take too much of it. Wot? A cup of tea too? And a bit of plum duff? Well this is a bit of alright, no mistake. Thanks ever so.'

'And then she bangs with her fist on her chest and burps,' Tina would say in her deepest tones. 'The woman is impossible. 'Tis so bad for the soul to have to put up with her repulsive manners.'

All the same, Tina had to earn some money like the rest of them after a year or so had passed and there was no sign of improvement in their father's business. Maimie, brandishing the scholarship she had earned from the nuns in Cork, was sent off to a boarding school in the Midlands, where she meant to win a teaching certificate. Deborah found a job at a telephone exchange, and a month later Tina followed in her wake, declaring that her nerves would swiftly be destroyed by the incessant ringing and buzzing of the mechanism but 'Of course, for one's family one sacrifices everything, though I have never understood why.'

And then one day Peggy Ruth came dancing into the kitchen with a determined gleam in the blue eyes she had inherited from her mother.

'I've the offer of a job at Hillman's Handy Shop: one pound a week to begin with – only to begin with you know, 'twill go up

46

and up maybe after a month or so – and what do you think of that?'

To her own distress and the embarrassment of everyone, her mother suddenly began to cry.

'Ah Mother, what's wrong? Isn't it enough? Do you think it won't help at all? It'll save me school fees anyway and bring in a few shillings, won't it?'

It wasn't like Mrs Weldon to cry, and she put her arm around her youngest daughter and wiped her tears with her other hand.

'Sure of course, of course it would, Pegeen,' she said. 'And 'tis wonderful of you. You're a great little girl. But you mustn't do it, child: no you must not. You're too little, you're too young. You're only fourteen.'

'Fourteen and a half, and I'm as tall as yourself already,' Peg said proudly, pulling herself up to her full height. 'Ah, let me take the job, Mother, please. Do, ah do, ah do! You'll save the half a crown every week that goes to the nuns, and I know quite enough – as much as I'll ever learn from those old fussy ones anyway – and I'd hate not to be helping like the others.'

Peg, in spite of her mother's pleading, got her way, as she so often did throughout her life, not only by persistence but by her frank and simple and very direct methods of attack: a rare quality among the other Weldons.

The only member of the family who appeared untouched by the scarcity of money was Anthony Weldon himself. He set out in the mornings, apparently delighted with life, and when he came home somewhere between five and seven in the evenings he was always full of stories.

'Met a most interesting fellow in the City today,' he would say. 'Ah yes: in the City all day I was, on a new deal Whiteley's are trying out: don't suppose it'll come to anything, but that's what kept me so late. These jaunts to and fro on the buses you know, they take a hell of a time. But now the Vanguard is coming in, you know what I mean: buses driven by motor engines. Much faster of course, but they'll not do anything to brisk up the trade, I can tell you that. But this fellow: in a pub where I was having a bit of lunch, and there he was, sitting up at the counter the same as myself, and what do you think he was reading? Homer's *Iliad* if you please, and in Greek too. Well, of course we got chatting, and I had to confess that I hadn't a word of Greek, but he was all amiability about that and not in the least condescending: said he envied my knowing Spanish, and how he wished he could read *Don Quixote* in the original and begod, do you know, by the time we'd finished our talk and I'd made a very rough drawing of him – a fine head he had and a beard that made him somewhat old-fashioned looking, but I don't mind that at all, a beard gives great dignity to a tall man and this fellow was six foot if he was an inch – what's this I was saying? Ah yes, by the time we were through, do you know, six o'clock, and too late of course for my appointment at Duffle and Dawson's, but what harm, a person can't have everything. Homer's *Iliad*, well God knows the world is full of surprises.'

'So you missed your appointment with the cornflour people,' Mrs Weldon murmured patiently. 'Ah Tony, that was a pity: Whiteley's won't be too pleased about that, you may be sure.'

'Well, haven't women a very sordid practical point of view?' her husband countered. 'There are more interesting things in the world than business, my blessing. And how's the young fellow this evening?' he went on, grasping Martin by the shoulder. 'Look now what your father has brought home for you!' And he fished from his pocket a battered book. '*Don Quijote de la Mancha*, por Miguel Saavedra Cervantes, Primero Tomo.'

'And what do you imagine the poor child is going to do with that?' the poor child's mother demanded. 'He won't be able to understand a word of it.'

'Oh, later on he will then,' Weldon remarked hazily. 'A great bargain too – just sixpence. A secondhand shop in Mark Lane. They're going to try for the second and third volumes, and then he'll have the whole work. Tell me, are you pleased with it now, Martin?'

'Oh it's lovely and thank you very much Father. And if you

see a copy of *A World of Girls* by L. T. Meade, would you ever get it for me?'

'*A World of Girls* by L. T. Meade, my God,' his father said, breathing through his nose. 'What sort of a son have we brought into the world? The triviality! The – the – my God, you'll be asking for *Little Women* next.'

'I've read that,' Martin confessed. 'And 'tis gorgeous. Like our four girls. Only Tina's not much like Jo. Jo was a tomboy, not mysterious a bit. Oh, but I love this too Father,' and he looked fondly at the battered copy of *Don Quijote*. 'Will you write in it for me? An intro – introduction.'

'You mean a dedication,' his father told him. 'Don't play about with words you're not sure of, son. I will of course, why not?'

And on the flyleaf he wrote 'Para Martín de su afmo. padre, Enero 1908.'

'What does it mean?' Martin asked.

One day, an inspector from something called an Educational Board decided that the boy must be sent to school. And now it was Maimie's turn to cry as she was preparing to leave for her own boarding school, and Mother cried too for there was less money coming in than ever, and even Father looked gloomy and remarked that God alone knew where his son would go to what he called 'a decent school. The curse of Cromwell on these bloody motor cars,' he concluded, and finally, on the softly spoken but hearty advice of Mrs Hathaway next door, it was decided to send the boy to a Council school.

'A Board school is it?' Mother demanded with a shake in her voice.

'Make a man of him, dear,' Mrs Hathaway cooed. 'It's a good sound education. Our Sydney went to one, the one at the top of those steps close by the station, and Sydney got on very nicely there. Ever so happy he was, and passed three exams and got home every day to his dinner and tea, and not a penny to be spent on his schooling. You take my advice and send your boy along.'

49

So Martin went to the Board school at the top of the steps near the station, and for the rest of his life that first day there was to haunt him with as great a horror as the recurring dream that ended with the appearance of Daddy-with-the-Hard-Hat, though in a very different fashion. Because there was no waking out of it, no lamp being lighted, no walking up and down the bedroom in Mother's arms, no warm and dim delight of lying safely in the arms of Jack Hunter.

There were four hundred boys in the school at the top of the steps close by the station, and in some of the subjects included in the preliminary examination by Mr Brace, the headmaster, Martin was so advanced that he was put in a classroom that was occupied by boys much older than himself. But this did not last for long, because the first subject was Arithmetic, at which he was so bad that when the lesson was over he was firmly removed to what was known as the Babies' Class, where everyone was younger than himself. He would have felt far more humiliated than he did by this if his feelings had not already been so numbed by his surroundings, by what he had already endured, that he was in a condition of abject indifference to all things around him.

Empire day was approaching, and the first event after his brief interview with Mr Brace was a rally of all the boys in the school. All four hundred of them were there, most of them dressed in dark knickerbockers and stockings, hobnailed boots and dark polo-necked jerseys surmounted by an Eton collar. Their heads were cropped, and they all seemed to have big mouths and small eyes and voices that sounded like raucous machines as they marched round and round bawling patriotic songs:

They may build their ships, me lads, and think they know the
  game
But they can't beat the Boys of the Bulldog Breed 'oo made
  old England's fame.

They shouted it out impassively as they pounded around the hall, and Martin, tramping with them, realized slowly and painfully that something he had read in a story about somebody having 'a lump in his throat' was no mere literary fancy, but a grim and depressing reality.

Mother came to the gate of the school to meet him, but he could not say much to her. His tongue was deadened by a sort of grey emptiness of spirit that choked any utterance of speech. Besides, he was half an hour later than either he or his mother had expected. Some boy in the middle of the classroom had let out a resounding fart, and the smell of it had not only filled the room but had reached the nostrils of Mr Woodley, who was the teacher of that particular group.

'Who made that horrible noise and that disgusting smell?' Mr Woodley demanded in deathly tones. 'Whoever it was had better own up to it. Was it you, Sykes? Was it you, young Buckley? Was it . . .?' and a dozen names were mentioned from the suspected quarter of the room. 'I'm patiently waiting.' A few more minutes passed in silence. 'Oh very well,' Mr Woodley said at last. 'If there's not one among you who's manly enough to own up I'll be obliged to punish you all. *All* of you,' he thundered, bringing his fist down on the top of his desk. 'You're all kept in for half an hour. And I hope the culprit (he pronounced it colpritt) whoever he may be is per-oud of himself.'

So they were all late, and for once Martin was speechless on the way home, and for tea there was Mother's soda bread and celery, and a pot of last year's homemade blackberry jam and a seed cake, and to the end of his days these things reminded Martin of his first day at an English school.

The boys were quarrelsome and punches and kicks were the rule of the play hour. But no one punched or kicked Martin. They called him 'Irish' and 'Paddywack' and 'Curly' and some of them were quite friendly. One day a boy called Cyril Hopkins said, 'You're Irish aren't you?'

'I am, yes.'

51

'Ah See, I suppose?'

'What's that?'

'You don't know wot Ah See is? Ah See of course. You know: Roman Catholics.'

'That's right.'

'Oh but it's not, you see. It's wrong. It's Idolatry. I suppose you know that? They worship idols and they worship the Pope's Toe. You know that don't you?'

'I didn't know it. No.'

'Well it's true. My Dad says so. And he says the Irish are alright but they're not ready for self-government. So it wouldn't be right to give 'em 'Ome Rule *which* my Dad says is just another word for Rome Rule. That's what he says and it's true.'

'Ah well.'

'Wot do you mean by Ah well? You're a rum one, you are really, Curly. But you're all right. Of course I guessed you was an R.C. when I spotted you at Scripture day before yesterday, sitting next to that other Irish bloke – wot's his name? O'Neill or something – and you was both reading *Ivanhoe* instead of listening to the Scripture. I suppose you're not allowed to listen to the Good Book, bein' R.C.s.'

'Maybe not, I don't know.'

'There you are you see. You just don't know. Yet you go on 'ollering out for Home Rule. Enough to make a cat laugh the Irish are, my Dad says.'

Cyril Hopkins, with his brief and salty summing up of the Irish and their absurdities, diverted Martin for a while rather than annoying him, but did little towards making him feel at home. The monotonous dullness of his scholastic hours grew gradually into an acceptance of a dully monotonous life, which at least grew easier as the term went on, but he made no friends among the other boys. Terry O'Neill, his desk companion during the Scripture lessons, was a dreary little fellow in ragged clothes with a waspish and often obscene tongue. When they were both supposed to be absorbed in the reading of *Ivanhoe*

52

together, he used to make muttered observances about Mr Woodley out of the corner of his mouth, and call down curses on the school, Sir Walter Scott, and the English race in general, describing them as bloody old bloodsucking tyrants and lousy old bashtards that wouldn't even fight you decent, sure all they could do was to half pull off their jackets and say, 'Want a fight do you, you mad effing son of a Hirish bitch,' then carefully replace their jackets, turn their back and say, 'Gahn, you! I wouldn't dirty me 'ands fighting with the likes of you, you lousy Hirish worm,' at which he, the bold courageous Terry O'Neill, would chase his victim round the playground until he got him into a corner and pummelled Hell out of him.

All this sort of thing would happen, of course, in the hour ironically described as 'Recreation'. Filled with terror at the almost universal punching and kicking and shouting, the yells and threats from the momentarily victorious bullies, the altercations and opposing shrieks of laughter, the piercing screams, nose-bleedings and whimpered imprecations of the victims, Martin would turn away to the long pebble-strewn passage, flanked on one side by the school walls and, on the other by tall iron railings forming a barrier to the street. Here he would stand, at the right-angle of similar iron railings that separated the boys' playground from the girls', and peer through.

Ah, the girls' playground! How sane, how sensible, how restful, how infinitely desirable it was! There they stood in groups or trotted about, some of them holding dolls in their arms as though they were real live babies, some of them whispering and giggling together, some of them quarrelling, but none of them yelling or kicking each other. The worst fighting that went on would be the pulling of a curled or plaited lock, and a resentful high-pitched squeal:

'Oh you spiteful thing, young Elsie Wood: I've a good mind to go round to your Mummer and tell her all about you.'

That was the worst and it was all, in Martin's opinion, absolute heaven! 'How lucky they are,' he would murmur to himself as the big iron bells rang on both sides of the frontier railing, summoning boys and girls alike back to their lessons in the big bare rooms that smelt of sunlight and ink and varnished wood and humanity.

But he was getting used to it all, and with Cyril Hopkins as his champion and Mr Woodley as a slowly increasing defender of his better qualities as a scholar, he was more and more at his ease. A year and three months went by, and Mr Woodley decided to revive the subject, long since abandoned, of Composition. Twice each week, each boy was given a half hour to write a 'composition' on any material that occurred to him, and if, as in numberless cases, nothing occurred at all, Mr Woodley, with many sarcastic interpolations, kindly provided one.

'Wot about "A Day at the Seaside and how I Like to Spend it"?' he would inquire in his swift, clipped baritone. 'Or how about "My favourite subject in school": history, jography, or wotever it may be? Or "Wot I'd like to do with my life when I grow to manhood"? Now another thing,' he went on, warming to his subject. 'If any of you have got an idear in your heads for an Original Story, there now, w'ich of you could have a go at that?' and he looked around the room with eyes that seemed full of doubt behind his thick spectacles. 'I don't imagine,' he confessed, 'that many of you have got many ideas for such an undertaking. However, it'll be interesting to see the results, and there'll be a small prize at the end of term for the boy, whoever he may be, who can cough up the best composition. Right-oh! Now for our next. History. Let me see: w'ere were we? Yes. The Roman Occupation of Britain,' and lessons proceeded in the normal fashion.

Martin, his head blazing with a new ambition, began to dream of a story of two Indian sisters, princesses, who were mysteriously cast out by their mother, the Ranee, a beautiful but merciless creature, and were sent to live in a hut in the jungle where they were guarded by an ancient peasant who had nursed them from their cradle days, and by a purple serpent that had magical powers. The sisters' names were Chandra and Gulga – Martin had pinched these from a story in 'Books for the Bairns,' but his story was really and truly from his own inventive though addled brain – and the serpent was known as Baharuda, also a creation of his own.

And so he wrote the story at spare moments at home, and Tina was most helpful in giving advice and suggesting the most lurid incantations and spells, and the day came at last when the results of the competition were to be read out, as well as four of the most promising essays. Mr Woodley called Martin out to stand in front of him by his large and alarming desk. He put his hands on his shoulders and, twisting him from side to side as though he were an exhibit at an auction, he spoke:

'This boy, this boy Martin Weldon, has won the first prize. A fine edition – here it is as you can see – of Sir Walter Scott's *Ivanhoe*. And now, before presenting it to him, and the other three prizes to three other pupils who shall be named by me in a moment or two, I should like to say something about him.

'It is this.

'When he first came here to our school we didn't think much of him, did we? He wasn't any good at Arithmetic, and although he has worked hard he still isn't what you might call striking. As well as that he seemed to many of us a bit of a softy, didn't he? You know, a girly kind of chap with his curly hair and his namby-pamby ways. We thought he was a bit of a milksop, didn't we? Well, we were wrong. See what I mean? We were mistaken. And when we are wrong about something the best thing, the most manly thing, the most English thing, is to admit it. Right? We thought because he wasn't the same as ourselves, because he wasn't an English boy, that there was nothing to him. We thought because he'd pipe his eye when things went wrong, that he was a crybaby, didn't we? Well, I mean to say, look at him now! . . . Oh my good Lord, he's doing it again!'

For Martin, overwhelmed by the compliments and the sympathy of Mr Woodley, for whom he had always nurtured a secret sentimental admiration, was shaking with emotion and showering his own face and the front of his home-knitted jersey with tears.

'Oh all right, all right, all right.' Mr Woodley said hurriedly. 'Cheer up, young Weldon, and congratulations.'

And he hurried the shameless Martin from his presence and announced:

'Next pupil please. Young William Perkins!'

Martin, ever since Tina's reading of Shylock and the wooing scene from *The Taming of the Shrew*, had long since acquired the habit of acting, for his own delight, in front of the long mirror which had stood in Mother's and Father's room in Cork, and which now occupied the same sort of corner in the London home. It was a very secret delight, for the glass which held his reflection was his only audience. Yet, in spite of Tina's performance, and the interest which Maimie's lessons from Lamb's *Tales* had awakened in him, Shakespeare was not his only material. Often he would improvise, after the manner of the *Commedia dell' Arte* (of which he had of course never heard), and the most lurid and impassioned speeches and scenes would flow from him, and inspire him to bodily contortions and frenzied gesticulations as he mouthed scene after scene of treachery, of thwarted love, of deaths from poisoned cups, or daggers, or lightning bolts. Such imaginings were frequent features of his repertoire.

For in those early days Martin had no trace of humour in his nature. No funny incidents, no light and laughing jokes, made any impression on him. All he wanted, as far as acting was concerned, was murder, murder most foul, strange and unnatural. Murder, despair, and death in dungeons deep, and blood, blood, blood! And though he was unaware of the fact, his tastes and preferences were all perfectly known to his family. It did not bother them.

'Ah, the poor child,' his mother would say. 'You'd think almost that he was two people, wouldn't you? I mean, there's the Marty who plays bat and ball and Thrift Clubs with Peggy,

56

and who nurses the cat, and does those little drawings of leprechauns and the like, and runs messages for me and runs races with the Hopkins boy at the school, and reads all the girls' story books and Grimm's *Fairy Tales*, and writes letters to Jack Hunter, and goes mad with delight when he gets the odd postcard from him, and then there's this other Martin acting away in front of my looking glass till you'd think he was half demented or something . . . Sometimes I wouldn't know what to make of him at all, but sure there's no harm in him. Not a bit of it. He'll be all right.'

Martin's father was even more interested in his son's histrionic tastes, which he felt, quite correctly, were inherited from certain traits in his own temperament, and one evening when a certain Mr Lambert came for tea at the Weldons', Father suggested to him that it might be amusing to watch 'the Boy' at his antics in front of the mirror in the bedroom upstairs.

'I think 'twould amuse you, Joe,' he said. 'I think the boy has something remarkable about him. You've seen a couple of his drawings, and I told you about the prize he won for his writing in that terrible old school we had to send him to, God forgive me, so what do you say now? He's at it this minute, I happen to know, for I saw him a couple of minutes ago sneaking up the stairs with a big bath towel he'll be using for a cloak; so what do you say? Shall we sneak up and watch him? I don't think he'll have the door locked; in fact he often leaves it half open.'

Joseph Lambert was an old London friend of Anthony Weldon, someone he had known in the days before the family had returned to Ireland on account of the 'great prospects' in Cork. A more successful businessman than his friend, Lambert had wisely removed himself from the corn trade and was now treasurer to the famous Beerbohm Tree at His Majesty's Theatre. A chance meeting with his old Irish associate had led to this invitation to take tea and meet the family, and it was the beginning of a change in the life of its youngest member which seemed of importance to them all.

The two spies found the bedroom door ajar and, peeping

through, they saw the back view of Martin as he crept across the floor until he reached the long mirror, the mirror that had revealed his mother's breasts to him so long ago. Now as he reached the chosen spot where he could gaze at his own reflection, he rose slowly and with apparently agonizing difficulty and, still bending low as if under some nameless torture, he twisted his face upwards and hissed in a broken voice, 'You imagine, because you represent a power in my unhappy land, that you have power over me. But you have not! You have not, foul tyrant of the mountain gorge. I laugh at your threats. I laugh at them. Ha ha ha ha ha!'

Then, turning to face the spot where he had crouched and standing erect and menacing, he shouted in a completely different voice.

'Yes, you can laugh! Laugh then! Laugh away! But when my demons come to bear you through the air, far, far from this place, you will laugh no more. No more, you hear me well? When you are face to face with the Witch of the Seven Moons you will laugh no more! No more!'

'Ah, do not attempt to frighten me. For I have that within my soul . . .'

'Your soul? Poor feeble victim of delusion . . .'

And so the improvisation wound its lurid way to a most impressive climax, with shouts of joy from the once cowering victim as he flung his arms high above his head and cried, 'Victory! Victory! Victory!'

To the actor's astonishment there came from the doorway the sound of applause and, to his disgust, some loud shouts of laughter.

Laughter? What was funny about it, pray?

The two men came into the room, and Father's friend Mr Lambert shook him warmly by the hand.

'Congratulations, old chap!' he said heartily.

Really, the English, thought the ungrateful Martin, with their bellowing laughter and their eternal 'old chaps'.

Aloud, he said, 'I didn't know you saw me.'

'Well we only saw a bit of you, but we heard you all right,' Mr Lambert went on. Father for once was saying nothing. But he was looking at his son with a gleam of self-congratulation in his eyes. Then he looked at Mr Lambert.

'What do you think of him, Joe? Will he be any good?'

'Any good? I should say he ought to be. And who was the play by, sonny?'

'Ach, I was just making it up myself.'

'Well aren't you a clever chap? Making up your own plays? Do you always act your own plays? Make them up as you go along, eh?'

'Oh no. I do Shakespeare sometimes.'

'Shakespeare, eh? Yes, I'd say he'd be the man for you.'

Later that evening after Mr Lambert had thanked Mrs Weldon and said goodbye to the family, Martin heard him say to Father, 'There's money in that boy of yours, Tony. No, I mean it. I wish you'd let me talk to the Chief about him. He might arrange for an audition for him. Well worth while, you know.'

The rest of their conversation was unheard by the family for the two men were walking to the gate together. But Martin's brain was buzzing with questions.

Who was the Chief? Could he be a Red Indian? Feathers and a tomahawk?

And what in God's name was an Audition?

He soon found out. His father smiled with a sort of tender affection at the question about 'the Chief', and began to explain the true identity of the man in tones of lofty yet sombre reverence.

'The Chief,' he said, laying his hand on his son's shoulder, 'is the name that the men who work for him – the actors, the technicians, the secretaries, the stage-managers, the electricians, the scene-painters, even the scene-shifters and the call-boys . . . the pet name that all these men, it may be the ladies too, call that great actor-manager, the owner of His Majesty's Theatre, Sir Herbert Beerbohm Tree, the grandest, the most impressive figure in the English theatre since the death of the great Henry Irving, the Lord be good to him. Aha. And you, me son, you – thanks to my good friend Joseph Lambert – are going to meet this wonderful man. You are going to meet him face to face, to act a scene or two for him the way he'll be able to tell us have you any talent for the art of acting or no: my own opinion is that you may have but we must wait for the Chief's judgement about that mustn't we? So now: within a week or so we'll hear what Mr Lambert can do to arrange this meeting, and I'll bring you to His Majesty's Theatre in the heart of the West End, and I sincerely hope your mother will see to it that you are dressed in your best clothes and that you'll behave yourself in a manner that'll do credit to the lot of us, and act as if you were setting yourself and everyone else on fire. Now what do you say?'

Martin said nothing for a while, for he scented danger here. He had an inborn resentment against anything in the world that seemed to push a secret dream into the realm of facts which could prove and reveal, or disprove and destroy. He loved acting but shrank from action. He dreaded anticipation: he dreaded planning and contriving. It cast an indescribable gloom over his spirit to feel he was to be put on trial. If he lost his case it would be as though he would be sent to hell: if he won it, would the heaven that awaited him be as monotonous as that heaven he had heard the nuns describe with such complacency at the convent in Cork?

'Well?' his father asked him, with an impressive upward inflection.

'Oh yes,' he replied at last. 'I'll get Mother to finish me new blue jersey.'

'And what piece – I don't want to hurry you, mind you, but you must be prepared – what piece will you act for Sir Herbert Tree?'

No, this was going to be awful. What piece indeed?

'Ah I don't know yet. I'll think about it.'

'I hope now that doesn't mean you'll just put it out of your head?'

'Ah no. No . . . maybe I'll do something out of my own mind.'

'I wouldn't, son. Honest to God now. Your own material is not as good as your acting.'

'What material?'

'The scene you enact,' his parent exhaled the verb impressively. 'There are better writers, finer dramatists than yourself you could choose from. Shakespeare, for example.'

'Well, what about Katherine and Petruchio?'

'But that scene surely is for two players? And one of them is a woman. You're only a boy.'

'Well didn't boys play the women's parts as well in Shakespeare's time?'

'My God, aren't you the holy terror,' his father told him. 'You've an answer for everything.'

They had lived on the outskirts of London more than three years, yet Martin had never seen anything of the city, and knew with any intimacy only the suburb where their house was, and where the sprawling school stood at the top of the steps close to the station. The world referred to by everyone as the West End was as unknown to him as the City, where Father's business brought him for many visits during the week. However, today Anthony Weldon and his son were not bound for the grim mysteries of the City, but the light and carefree haunts of the West End where, for some reason, Martin imagined everything would be in a constant flutter of movement both languorous and gay, and there would music in the air and pretty ladies laughing back at you over one shoulder as they rustled their skirts or shifted their luxurious furs from one white shoulder to another, or smiled with a sort of gay mystery from behind spotted veils.

They took the train from their local station: 'Two singles to Trafalgar Square please.' It ought to have been Piccadilly Circus, but Anthony Weldon was not nearly as familiar with the geography of what his wife alluded to with a sort of nostalgic admiration as Theatre Land. They had to change at

Baker Street and crowd into an enormous cage called a lift, which brought them down to a Tube, which produced out of a circular cavern at one end of the platform a long glittering train. Away they rattled – Regent's Park, Oxford Circus, Piccadilly Circus, Trafalgar Square – and out they fled and into another lift and then out through a maze of stone passages, and up a short flight of steps and ah! there was the West End in pale dappled sunshine, and the first thing Martin saw was a flight of pigeons soaring away to the sky, and behind them and under them a big and beautiful building in ivory and pearl-grey stone, and that, Father explained, was the National Gallery, and there was an enormous pillar with a man on the top – Nelson, Father said, and who was *he*, for Heaven's sake? – and a bewildering panorama of houses and streets scattering away in all directions, and they went, Martin clutching Father's hand in his own, right on and up towards that wonderful National Gallery and round the corner and across the street, and past a hotel that Father said was the Carlton, and there, next door to that, was an impressive pearly-coloured palace.

'That's His Majesty's Theatre,' Father said, 'and now we must find the stage door.'

This was situated round the corner from the Haymarket in Charles Street, and was not nearly as enchanting as the other part: the last door of a long row, quite small and ordinary it looked with a little bench for two people to sit on as you went in, but you didn't stop there but turned to the left up three little steps, through another door and into another little hall with a sort of office in the corner where a large man in a uniform looked out of a window and said:

'Name please.'

'Martin Weldon.'

'Oh yes. Got an appointment, haven't you? Chief's expecting you, I think. This way please. I'll take you to his office.'

He looked at Martin in the new blue jersey Mother had knitted for him for the occasion, and the dark blue shorts she had bought him in the Kilburn High Road, as if he didn't think much of him or them and, leading the way through another door, he was about to ascend another flight of stairs when he stopped suddenly.

'Oh good morning Sir 'Erbert, good morning, sir,' he muttered in reverent tones. 'I think this is the young gentleman and his – his father? – you were expect—'

'Yes, yes, of course,' the murmur came in what seemed to Martin the strangest and most impressive voice he had ever heard. A soft, powerful, effortless humming it was, almost like that of bees on a golden summer day: a low heavy sweetness was in it that suggested the colour and scent of honey. Yet with all this sweetness there was behind it somewhere a deep, purring strength.

'Oh how interesting,' he exhaled, and gave the child his hand to shake, and the hand too was soft as velvet and inexorable as iron. 'And Mr Weldon?' he asked them, and shook hands with Father.

'Mr Weldon . . .' was there a faint, a very faint suggestion of a lisp in the 's' of the Mister?

'So pleased.'

Yes: there was a faint sibilance as of a lisp, and yet, instead of weakening his utterance it gave it an added power. Then, suddenly:

'So, Boy Blue, you are going to perform for me. What can you do? Can you stand on your head?'

'I can't, Sir Herbert.'

'Oh, what a pity! Can you juggle?'

'I don't think so.'

'No? Perhaps you can dance a hornpipe?'

'No, I can't, Sir Herbert.'

'It's a pity. But there are other qualifications. Now tell me, if you can't stand on your head, and you can't juggle or dance a hornpipe, . . . what in Heaven's name can you do?'

'Oh, I can act.'

'But how interesting! Because only a few people can. Well, will you act for me?'

'I will of course.'

'I shall disappear in the stalls with Mr Weldon, Mr King and Mr Dana and you will go with Mr Pickens here to the stage . . .'

It may have been Martin's inflammable imagination that gave to the Chief's pronunciation and drawling emphasis on that last word such mystery, such finality, such a sense of destiny, such vistas of doom and delight. In any case, the moment was soon lost in a series of small facts: doors that were opened and shut, little passages through which he followed the trim trotting figure of young Mr Pickens, who seemed hardly more than a boy himself, until at last a pair of double doors was reached with a big notice 'Silence' on the wall above. Martin passed through somehow, and found himself in what appeared to be a vast, dark, empty space will no walls near enough to touch, and no visible ceiling or windows. No, there was nothing here but a faint smell of glue, perhaps even Pickens had gone away and left him in this spectral place: no, no he hadn't, for there was his voice. 'Give us your hand now for a moment, will you? That's the style: now follow me.' They proceeded a few steps. 'That's about it now.' Picken's voice went on: 'Bang upstage centre, that's where he'll want you. Hey, I say, Syd Buckridge, what about a bit of a working light eh? And the Chief wants the Safety up, see?'

Two shocks came then: a long narrow bough of what seemed innumerable luminous globes of amber, white and red sprang out of the darkness overhead and then: ah, nameless mystery, the great wall facing him rose up into the air. In leisurely calm it rose: there was no hurry and no surprise anywhere, it seemed, but in his own soul: the solid dun-coloured wall just went up and vanished, and in its place was the dim eternity of nothing. Nothing at all but space and mysteries and – who knew? – maybe this was death, and angels and demons would appear to welcome or destroy him.

Yes, for there perhaps they were, by the little light that blinked its way into being, shining on what seemed a white scroll and the faces of two men: was it St Peter and some attendant judge? And then the voice he knew: warm, powerful and consciously soothing, that said most unexpectedly:

'Give him a spot. A white – no, not a white, a pale amber spot. That's better.'

He was bathed in light. So it wasn't the worst of all.

'Now then, Boy Blue, show me how you act.'

Suddenly he found his voice.

'This is the Wooing Scene,' he began. 'The Wooing Scene from *The Taming of the Shrew*: I am Petruchio first and then Katherine.'

'A little louder,' came the voice. ' "The Taming of the Shrew" was good and so was Petruchio: Poor Katherine was almost lost. Go on, go on!'

'Petruchio says, "Good morrow Kate, for that's your name I hear."

(*Turn furiously to face right.*) "Well have you heard but somewhat hard of hearing: they call me Katherine that do speak of me."

(*Turn toweringly to face left.*) "You lie i'faith, for you are called Plain Kate".'

And he went through the scene with the roll of the Cantos of the *Inferno* translated into Cork via Mr Woodley at the Board school, and at the end sailed out of his spot into the shadows of upstage Right, walking backwards with pointed hand and a volley of Mephistophelian chuckles.

Then he didn't know what to do so he just waited – no applause. And Martin stood in the shadow for a moment, motionless, wondering what was going to happen next.

'Don't go away, Boy Blue,' the voice boomed softly out. 'I'm coming up to the stage.'

And presently he appeared with Father and two satellites in his wake. He came straight over to Martin and laid two enormous hands on his shoulders.

'You will be an actor,' he half whispered. 'Oh yes. And what you did was full of acting. . . . I don't suppose,' he went on at once, 'that you realize that the scene you played was written for comedy. For comedy,' he repeated, his voice growing softer and softer, and more like a gentle wind among young reeds, 'To make people laugh, you know. Oh yes. You will understand that very soon. And never mind, what you did was, in its own way, very funny. Really and truly funny in its own extraordinary way.'

Martin felt absolutely furious, but assumed a rather awful smile and said nothing at all.

'And you will hear from me again, Mr Weldon,' Tree added, looking round at Father. 'I should like your boy to play at my beautiful theatre. Remind me, Mr Dana.'

And he flashed away with the satellite he had addressed as Mr Dana and left the other one, Mr King, to take notes and addresses from Father.

But no word came for a long time, and one day Tina, returning from her office in time for tea, said: 'I thought Martin was going to be an actor. When does he begin? Begin to rehearse, I mean? Surely actors rehearse? I mean they don't just appear by magic: or do they?'

Father, who had unexpectedly returned to his family earlier than his habit, unhesitatingly took up the cudgels.

'The Chief', he proclaimed, 'was most impressed by what he saw the boy doing, and I've no doubt at all that we'll hear soon. But you see, *Henry VIII* is still running, and looks like going on until Christmas, 'Twouldn't surprise me. So patience all of you, patience. The boy will surprise you yet.'

'Tree might have a part for him in a Christmas pantomime, wouldn't you say so?' Peg asked.

'But sure Tree never does pantomime, I'm sure of that,' Deborah cried. 'You'd have to get in with Drury Lane for that.'

'The Chief,' observed Mr Weldon, 'does not specialize in pantomime. That is true. But there are other plays in the world with roles for a young boy.'

'There wouldn't be much in Shakespeare, though,' Peg observed sadly. 'Would there now?'

'I don't know. Actually there's Robin in *The Merry Wives of Windsor*,' said the learned Maimie in the accent she had acquired on her quest for a teaching certificate. 'And plenty of fairy children in *A Midsummer Night's Dream*. Martin would make a lovely Mustardseed.'

'How curious it will be to be the sister of a stage child,' Tina murmured. 'Clutching a Teddy Bear, I suppose, and with wet-whited knees. Ugh!'

'Well isn't that a sort of a badge for them?' Mrs Weldon demanded with shameless anticipated delight. 'And I wish you wouldn't smoke cigarettes, Tina. You know your father doesn't like it.'

'Anything to please you, me darling,' Tina said, and she stubbed out her cigarette with a martyred air. 'Though why Father should object to smoking is a mystery to me: he's always doing it himself.'

'And are you comparing a man smoking an honest pipe to gipsies and fast women puffing cigarettes all over the place?' her father enquired.

'What are gipsies and fast women like, Father?' Tina asked sweetly. 'Do describe them to us. I'm sure you know all about them.'

'Tina, how can you talk that way to your father?' Mrs Weldon cried. 'Will you keep your silly thoughts to yourself, if you've no objections. 'Pon me soul! Don't mind her, Tony,' she continued. 'God knows I don't believe she understands herself half of the crackpot things she says.'

'No, but it's all so interesting,' Tina explained. 'And talking of fast women, is it true, Maimie, that you are taking our future Beerbohm Tree to lunch with Maisie Maypole tomorrow?'

'Tina, you're the limit,' Deborah said indignantly, 'Yes, they *are* going to Maisie's for lunch. And if you want to know, she asked me too, but of course I can't go because of this rotten old telephone exchange. By the way, did you know, she wants us all to call her "May" from now: she's changing her name for the stage. May instead of Maisie and Minter instead of Hunter.'

'May Minter! Oh dear God! Pass the mint sauce please! Saucy Minter for everybody! And I mustn't even smoke a cigarette to calm my nerves.'

Lunch at May Minter's was a new experience for Martin. He and Maimie went upstairs at Buckingham Gate in a lift, not as big as the lifts at the Tube station but far more ornate, and Maisie-May herself came to the door of the flat, pushing an impressive-looking butler aside in an impulsive gesture that showed how happy she was to see them.

At lunch he found himself being waited on by two smart-looking people: the middle-aged gentleman, of grave demeanour and beautiful clothes, whom Maisie had pushed aside when the lift arrived, and another, younger gentleman, who was more plainly dressed, though he wore what seemed a sort of uniform.

'Oh, he's so tiny, do help him, Watson,' Maisie gurgled to the uniformed young gentleman. 'And give him some mayonnaise, Philip,' she commanded the other, and began to gobble up her delicious salmon. 'You can serve the wine, Watson, and only a teeny weeny dwop for Master Weldon, he's so tiny.'

Martin wasn't sure that he enjoyed these references to his so-called tininess, and couldn't see why this should cause him to be given such a stingy drop in his glass. But he smiled cheerfully and said 'Thank you,' and after a while began to contribute quite a lot to the conversation.

'Now why in Heaven's name,' Maimie said afterwards, as they rode home together on the top of a bus, 'did you want to tell Maisie – I mean May – all about Father taking you to Sir Herbert Tree to see if he would give you a job? A job! At your age! Why, you ought to be going to a good school, a really good one. But I've something to tell you: you know I've got a teaching certificate now. Well, that means you may not have to go back any more to that horrible school. It means that you can be taught at home for a little, anyway – by *me*! Now what do you say to that?'

'Sure, I'd love it of course.'

'And if you *do* get a . . . get a . . .'

'A job. That's what you mean now, isn't that so, Maimie?'

'An engagement, dear. That's the word I wanted. If you *do*, that's all the more reason for my giving you lessons at home. Because we'd start in at eleven instead of at nine, you see.'

'So late? But why, Maimie?'

'Well if you're working in the theatre you'll have late hours you see, and 'twould be easier for you to get your eight hours' sleep and be fresh for your lessons in the morning. Eleven until half one, I mean one thirty, then again from two thirty until five. Then your tea and a little rest, and then off you'd go to His Majesty's. Ah Martin, don't go dancing up and down like that, everyone on the bus will think you're crackers.'

'Ah, let them! But wouldn't it be wonderful, Maimie? Wouldn't it? Ha?'

The Minter luncheon party was swiftly followed up by an invitation to Maimie and Martin from May herself, to spend a week at Sir Nigel Brownloe's house in Kent.

'Who is this Brownloe fellow at all?' Father wanted to know. 'And why has Maisie Hunter a room in his house? Can you tell me that? I suppose she doesn't intend to marry him? Or does she?'

'Ah for God's sake, not at all,' his wife said, 'He's quite an elderly fellow, well into his fifties in any case, and sure Maisie's only a year older than Debby. I don't suppose the idea of marriage ever entered her mind.'

'Well I hope there's nothing wrong going on. After all, our children are going down to stay with them: is it a wise thing would you say to let them? There's Maimie now, pushing eighteen already, and she might easily get under a bad influence.'

But the week of high life in the county of Kent was luxurious and uneventful. Sir Nigel Brownloe, the children's host, was all that was kindly and courteous: he had silver hair, a silver moustache and a ruddy face, and no conversation at all. When he did speak, and he made the most strenuous and gentlemanly efforts to entertain his guests, it was invariably to ask them something of which they knew nothing whatever.

'Jolly fine – er – horses you breed in Ireland I hear. Do you go to many of the meets?'

'Not very many,' Maimie replied after a tingling pause.

'What are meets, Sir Nigel?' Martin asked.

'My father doesn't hunt very much,' Maimie said in a strangled voice.

'He doesn't hunt at all,' Martin informed his host. 'The only sport I ever heard him talk about was a bull fight.'

This was the general tone of the talk over several succulent meals. The food was always delicious: the house was charming and every room in it smelt of roses and pot-pourri; the drawing room was crowded with portraits and landscapes in gold frames, and little statuettes of Roman rather than Greek origin representing ladies with nothing but a little light drapery round their lower limbs. Sometimes even this was missing. Martin admired them all immensely, and made several copies of them in pencil in the sketch book that Maimie encouraged him to use wherever he went. But she was not at all sure that Mother would approve of these Italian Aphrodites.

But the happiest time during that week in Kent was when she and Martin walked together, not through the country (which was tamely pretty and mainly invisible because of the high, well-clipped hedges that bordered every road) but through the orchard of apple and cherry trees that seemed gently to flow out of the kitchen garden which, Maimie took care to inform Martin, was called *potager* in French: a much nicer name for it than the English one, Maimie said.

They passed out of the orchard and back to the lawn in front of the great half-timbered house where Sir Nigel sat waiting for them in a wicker armchair by a table covered with tea things. A smart young footman stood by ready to help them to hot buttered scones and honey and a large old-fashioned cake.

'I'm going to miss you two young people when you – er – leave me tomorrow,' he said. 'I suppose you couldn't manage to

– er – stay for a few more days?'

'I'm afraid not, and I'm so sorry we can't,' Maimie answered. 'We have to get home and get down to lessons together. But we're both so grateful to you, Sir Nigel, for giving us such a wonderful time. Aren't we now, Martin?'

'Of course we are,' he answered. 'I never was in such a lovely place in my life. I'll never forget it, never as long as I live.'

But that night the old bad dream came back again.

It began with the familiar sensation of walking arm in arm with Giovanni across the long bridge, the goodnight embrace at the doorway, the foreboding as he walked alone down the stone-floored passage to his room, the melancholy as he lay stretched out on his bed . . . And then – was it a dream within a dream? – this sudden violent activity, barbarous jostling, stabs of physical pain, hysterical shouts and angry curses and yells of terror that mingled with the rattle of gunfire to merge into a single storm of frenzied noise. Nothing like this had ever come into his dream before now, nor had he experienced the solitary stealing from doorway to doorway, hiding behind marble columns which formed a temporary shelter until, alternately rushing and hiding, he reached the bridge, crossed it alone, staggering and crawling in sharp pain on hands and knees under the brightening dawn, reaching at last the house on the corner and the safety of the old familiar room. And then numbness overcame him as he sat close to the shuttered window and waited for the inevitable. Thundering blows upon the street door, clanking sound of armed men tramping through the hallway, crashing blows on the door of his room . . . the door opening and the figure he was waiting for stumbled across the single step, the hat slipping down over the eyes . . .

Martin awoke frozen with fear. Daddy with the Hard Hat had returned, more terrible than ever.

Sir Nigel's chauffeur drove them back to their home the next day, and they arrived in time for the midday meal, which Maimie now referred to as lunch. The house was in an uproar

71

when they arrived, for Father and Tina were having words. Martin and Maimie listened in the hallway, entranced.

'And your imagination is morbid enough already,' they heard Father's voice saying, 'without making it worse reading the outpourings of a mad neurotic like Poe and the poisonous stuff of this degenerate . . .'

'You mean Oscar Wilde I suppose?'

'Who else? Who else, tell me that? The man was a disgrace. My God they had to put him in prison in the end. A most horrible scandal it was. Desperate!'

'Oh, it's so typical of the English to put a man of genius into prison. And for what? For leading his own life. As he said himself in that book you so kindly burned on me, "You seem to forget we live in the native land of the hypocrite!" And you admitted yourself just now, Father, that he was a most brilliant man.'

'And doesn't that make it worse? Sure if he was a dull mediocre sort of an individual it wouldn't matter so much. But there he was, a man of genius as you say – and that's what gave him the power maybe to corrupt others—'

'Well you'd no right to burn my book.'

'I'd burn it again if you had it again. Dorian Gray indeed! Oh no, I'll not have a book like that polluting my house or the mind of any of my daughters, let me tell you that much—'

'Ah me lovely pets!' Mother's voice came in high gleeful tones from the kitchen. 'Welcome now, welcome back home – God! will you hear the two of them in there?'

'What's wrong?' Maimie asked.

'Ah nothing darling, nothing at all – Father burned two of her books on poor Tina and she's raging – Martin, my lovely boy, come and give me a big hug and we'll soon stop their nonsense. And I've news for you, Martin – great news. Come in here, now. Follow me.'

Mother headed the small procession into the sitting-room: a courageous action for indeed the battle, though approaching the last stages, was at the moment in full swing:

'And whatever you say about being my father, which to me seems to have nothing to do with the question, you'd no right to burn my books.'

'You were lucky it wasn't yourself I burned. Openly defying me you are, and reading a lot of trash by a man who was rotten to the core.'

'Will you stop your blathering, the two of you, and look what's come back to this happy home, how are you?' Mother ironically enquired.

'My son, my son! Welcome home: a sad home you've come back to for the moment,' Father, always ready for a dramatic phrase, added. 'And welcome too my little Maimie: I think there's more colour in your cheeks, child.'

'Hullo, Maimie. Ah, my precious one! Ah, my sweet Martin!' cried Tina. 'The way I'm treated in this house is abominable, diabolical. But there, I'll be calm for your sake. Yes, I'll be calm.'

'I sincerely hope you will, you foolish girl,' her mother remarked. 'Such a way to be carrying on, and Maimie and the boy coming home after their grand holiday. Come on out all of you, and we'll have a bit of stew and I'll tell you the good news, Martin. And you too, me little Maimie, for you'll be as glad as the rest of us.'

'You'll not see Debby or Peg till this evening,' she went on. 'Peg brings sandwiches to the shop with her these days, and she'd eat up the house when she comes home for tea. And Debby's having lunch as she calls it with her new lover—'

'Hey, what's that?' Father said sharply.

'Ah, don't look like that, Tony,' his wife answered easily. 'He's a very nice young man, a young Welshman he is, I think, and didn't he ask her to marry him! Five times he asked her – I think 'twas five she said. But you know how fussy Debby can be. Wisha, I hope to God she'll accept him at the heel of the hunt. Tudor Jones, his name is.'

'Mrs Jones; most suitable,' said Tina crisply.

'Now you needn't twist your mouth about as though you

were chewing bullseyes,' Mother told her. 'You might do worse yourself, and so might she. He has a magnificent job, I believe, and his people have a mountain of money. They've a big house in Swansea, I think it was, as well as one here in Hampstead. A tradesmen's entrance and all.'

'Are they Catholics?' Father enquired.

'Ach, I wouldn't imagine so,' Mother answered him. 'Welsh Disestablished or something, I think she said. But what harm? Can't they arrange for a mixed marriage? Anyway, now for *your* news, Martin, I've a letter I want to read to you . . .'

'From Sir Herbert Tree?' Martin asked.

'No, dear, not from Sir Herbert Tree. From a Miss Field: Miss Lila – would you pronounce it Lye-la or Leela? God knows. Anyway, here we are, I have it in me blouse and here – it – is!'

She fished an envelope from her blouse, drew forth a sheet of writing paper with an impressive heading, and read aloud:

'Lyceum Club, Grosvenor Street, London W.1. Dear Mrs Weldon, Thank you for your letter of the seventeenth. We think the photograph of your little son is perfectly charming and are happy to hear of his audition before Sir Herbert Tree. Could you, I wonder, bring the boy for an interview with my sister and me on, let us say, Wednesday the twenty-seventh at 2.30 p.m.? If this is convenient, I shall so look forward to seeing him. Yours sincerely, Lila Field.'

'You see, there was an advertisement in the *Telegraph* under her name, that she and her company were preparing a children's play called *The Goldfish* and that she would be glad to interview any "pretty, intelligent children" – that's the way she put it – from eight to eighteen if their guardians – their guardians if you please! – approved of the idea of a stage career for them. So now! Wednesday the twenty-seventh, that's next Wednesday. Now what do you say to that?'

CHAPTER THREE
Enter a Very Young Actor

So Father brought his young son to the Lyceum Club for the interview with Miss Lila Field and her sister Bertha, and Martin was suitably impressed both by the Club's air of luxurious solidity as by the two ladies, who greeted them kindly and were very much alike with soft brown eyes and soft pink cheeks, dressed in the height of fashion with weighty hats like wedding cakes, only they weren't white but deep crimson (Lila) and pale green (Bertha), and these pretty hats were perched on rippling coiffures of dark chestnut brown. They both seemed enchanted to talk to Mr Weldon, and both bestowed friendly smiles and occasional encouraging remarks on Martin, though to his disappointment they did not ask him to act for them but seemed to take it for granted that he would be required for the play which they occasionally referred to as 'the Piece'.

'He will play – now which of the mortal boys in the first act is still free, Bertha? We've engaged quite a lot of boys and girls already – ah, yes, Charlie is not cast yet; splendid! Yes, then, Charlie in Act One, and what about Prince Mussel in Acts Two and Three – ah no, I forgot, little Noël Coward is engaged for that, isn't he? And for Jack in Act One. Wait: how about Prince Amethyst? in the second and third acts? Oh I think so, don't you? How well you'll look in the lovely purple costume. Now Mr Weldon, if you – and of course your little son – if you're willing, we will engage him for Charlie and Prince Amethyst. Professionally of course: no fees for rehearsals, but shall we say one pound a week for the run of the piece. Yes?'

Father gracefully inclined his head and the bargain was made.

'Of course he'll get a contract, and we'd like you both to sign it. And we'll take care of him for the licence, and bring him along to Bow Street.'

'Licence? Bow Street?' Father asked, but without dismay, though the phrase made his son feel that he was being turned into a puppy dog.

'Oh yes. You see, juvenile actors – and actresses of course – have to get a licence up to the age of fourteen. To make sure they're healthy and well taken care of and that their schooling is not being neglected.'

'I have lessons at home, Miss Field,' Martin explained eagerly. 'My sister Maimie teaches me.'

'Your sister? Oh how nice! But is she . . . I mean is she in a position, I mean, to teach? Qualified and all that?'

'My daughter has a teaching certificate,' Father said proudly. 'She is thoroughly qualified to teach elementary pupils.'

'Elementary?' Martin asked with disillusion.

'Oh isn't he charming?' Miss Field (Lila) cried. 'I think he'll be a great addition to our little company!'

Father did a most unexpected thing.

'Excuse me, Miss Field,' he said in his most elaborate manner, 'I believe it is fairly customary in the profession to take a different name?'

'Oh yes, but not invariable, Mr Weldon—'

'I have no wish that he should alter his family name, but I would be glad if he would change his Christian name and take mine. My name, Miss Field, my Christian name, is Anthony.'

'Anthony Weldon . . . well, why not? Anthony Weldon would be a very fine name for an actor.'

Father heaved a sigh and fixed his eyes on the speaker. He had often wondered why he had gone into the corn trade.

'And who knows?' Miss Field (Lila) was saying playfully to Martin. 'Who knows? One day you may be playing Antony with some future star as Cleopatra! How would you like that?'

'I'd love it,' Martin cried fervently.

It was decided that Maimie should accompany Martin to the rehearsals. The studio in Hanover Square was a spacious room and crowded with boys and girls and their older female relatives, all of whom were far more mature than Maimie and

76

more smartly dressed. Two big, blonde, pretty girls who were sisters were in a corner leaping up and down together and clapping their hands in their anxiety to start the rehearsal, and one tiny little girl in a pink dress came smilingly up to Martin and said, 'Hullo! I'm June. Are you going to be in the play? What are you playing?'

'I'm playing Charlie in Act One,' Martin told her, 'And after that I'm Prince Amethyst.'

'And what's your name?'

'Martin – no, I mean Anthony. What's yours?'

'I told you: June,' she said, pouting. 'June Tripp. And I'm going to be a dancer one day.'

'I'm going to be a singer, at least I hope so,' a much taller girl said in what seemed a deliberately honeyed voice. 'My grandmother was a singer and terribly well known, you know. Carlisle was her name, Rosa Carlisle, and she was known all over the shop. '

'All over the *world*, dear,' a stout lady corrected her from her seat on a chair by the wall. 'All over the shop sounds so frightfully common.'

Maimie was sitting on a chair by the wall in conversation with a lady wearing a fur coat in spite of the mildness of the September day. The lady was tall and imposing and had a wide smile that showed large, white and very even teeth.

'So this is your little brother, Miss Weldon,' she said. 'How do you do dear? What lovely curls,' she murmured *sotto voce* to Maimie. 'I wonder where Miss Field – ah there she is?'

Then everybody who was seated rose respectfully as Lila Field entered, carrying a large bunch of roses and followed by the faithful Bertha.

'Good morning, children,' she cried gaily. 'Good morning everybody. Now if somebody could find a vase for these – yes, aren't they perfectly beautiful? The last roses of summer! Ah, thank you so much. We'll put them over here I think. And now, what do you all think of my stage?'

Martin looked in all directions for Miss Field's stage,

77

presumably some structure raised high over the common floor, but there was nothing visible but a few chairs here and there. Some of them were placed back to back with a space between, others set two or three in a row.

'Oh wonderful, Miss Field,' they hypocritically cried.

'This,' she explained, darting towards the chairs with the space between, 'is the garden gate. Here,' she pointed to another, crescent-shaped arrangement, 'is the summer-house. And these of course,' indicating the three in a row, 'are just a bench where Dolly and Kitty will sit while Kathleen – she's Molly in the play of course – will sing her little "Love me, love my dog" number. Ah, there you are my little Clara Butt! All there? Capital! and you all have your scripts? Splendid. Now we open of course with Mr Ayre O'Naut's chorus, such fun! "School, school, goodbye to school!" Now all on stage, please. Bertha dear, start them off will you?'

The tune, a simple affair of the type known in 1910 as 'catchy', was played by Bertha, and then the song was sung, a little unsteadily at first:

> School, school, goodbye to school!
> Now we are always playing.
> By sea, by land, our games we've planned
> Everybody's playing!

('Sing up, June dear, can't quite hear you.')

> None of us care what clothes we wear
> It's holidays, please remember,
> Home again, home again,
> And we're not going back till September!

'Now all over again, dears.'

'God bless us and save us,' thought Martin.

After that they were placed in their correct positions in a half circle, and Miss Field taught them what she had called the

78

'moves'. Linking hands they threw out first the left foot to the right, crossing their legs to achieve the desired effect, then their right foot to the left.

'Coming beautifully!' Miss Field encouraged them. 'But more precision, dears, and much more voice. Some of you I couldn't hear at all! And remember, bright cheery smiles all the time: you have to create an atmosphere of Absolute Carefree Happiness! Now then!'

And School, school was gone over again and again.

Martin's opening line was: 'Well, I don't care where we have the picnic as long as we can have a jolly good bathe afterwards.' His cue for this was 'Crumbs, how exciting!', spoken in a crisp, determined voice by Jack, the part played by 'little Noël Coward', and in the break that came at about midday the two ten-year-old boys, Martin (now Anthony) Weldon and Little Noël Coward, held a brief conversation together. Little Noël was quite as big as Martin and seemed, with his straight, neatly arranged hair, his pale complexion, his small humorous almond eyes, and his clipped way of speaking, far more sophisticated and self-possessed. Yet it was Martin who started the conversation.

'What do you want to be when you grow up, Noël?' he began.

'An actor of course,' came the unhesitating reply. 'That's why I'm here. Why, what do you want to be? Surely an actor too, don't you? Otherwise, why are you here?'

'Oh, I don't know really,' Martin spoke in a melancholy voice. 'There are so many things to choose from.'

'What sort of things?'

'Well now, there's painting, and there's writing and there's . . . there's . . .'

'There's nothing as good as the theatre,' Noël told him with conviction. 'That is, if you're made for it. I should think you were you know, same as me. Don't you feel that yourself? You have some talent: I can see that already.'

'Can you now? Aren't you very quick?'

'Oh yes: terribly quick. But I'm not invariably right.'

'What's invariably?'

'Don't you know? How amusing. Invariably is another way of saying always.'

''Tis a better sounding word too.'

'Yes. I suppose that's why I use it. I like words. I enjoy words. You're rather like Bubbles you know. If your curls were a lighter gold and you had blue eyes. Have you ever seen Nellie Wallace?'

'I don't think so: who is she?'

'You never heard of Nellie Wallace? She's amazing. Hideously ugly, with a frill of teeth, like this: look.'

Noël withdrew his upper lip towards his gums so that his teeth seemed to protrude over his chin.

'She's a music hall star: Variety, you understand. And I know one of her songs: *I met a man, complexion fair, he put peroxide on his hair* . . .'

'Ah, go on, go on! Sing some more. Ah, do!'

'No, Bubbles. Not now. I don't like the idea of singing other people's songs to other people's music. Now this is going to be a song one day when I can write down the notes: I'll tell you the words of the first verse:

> I see you are bent on the stage:

(This is for you and me, Bubbles.)

> I see you are bent on the stage:
> All efforts to restrain you I fear would be vain
> You will fly like a BIRD from the cage
> And we may never see you again.

'Now you see, Bubbles, when I get a tune for that the word "Bird" will fly up on a sustained high note and that's what will get the laugh, you see?'

'Ah 'tis wonderful. Did you really make that up?'

'Course I did. There's lots more of it . . . but look! Behold

80

Miss Field looking like the Day of Judgement. So back we go to the Goldfish. "School, school, goodbye to school!" Not a *ter*ribly good song I'm afraid. All the same, back we go!'

And back they went, and continued until 1.30 when there came what Miss Field called 'Break for lunch, and back at 2.30 please!'

Maimie and Martin went to a Lyons' tea shop in Oxford Street, and both had Welsh Rarebit (pronounced Rabbit but tasting of toasted cheese): fourpence each, coffee with milk: twopence each, and Martin had his first chocolate eclair, also twopence.

'One and twopence,' Maimie said, 'I hope we weren't extravagant. And we must leave twopence for the waitress: that makes one and fourpence. Oh dear, isn't London the fright for expensiveness? With the bus fare there and back 'twill have cost two shillings. Never mind, we'll walk to Marble Arch when we go home for tea, that'll save twopence, and you'll be earning good money when the play goes on.'

Although the play did not open until after Christmas in the earliest month of 1911, there was great rejoicing among the Weldon family in October. It was then that Miss Field decided that the boy who played the leading part of the Goldfish was 'not really *up* to Shackleton, King Goldfish'. (The leaders of the Polar Expedition were the talk of London that year, so the topically inclined Miss Field had decided that King Goldfish's name in private life, so to speak, must be Shackleton.) 'And my sister and I both feel,' she went on to Maimie, 'that your little brother Anthony, who is a wee bit over-dramatic as Charlie in Act One, would be a splendid Shackleton. And Willy – he's playing Bobby beautifully in Act One and he can keep that of course – *he* can play Prince Amethyst and not be so noticeable. I'm so glad you are both pleased – dear little Bubbles, our little Beerbohm Tree I think we'll have to call him. And of course he'll get a bigger salary. Two pounds ten a week instead of one pound nothing, and I do hope your parents will approve.'

Her hope was fulfilled. The parents approved heartily, and Little Beerbohm Tree gave himself insupportable airs for a day or two until he was reprimanded by Maimie and Mother, who warned him severely about his 'notions', and Peg openly told him not to be such a swank.

So he calmed down and never tried any tricks of the sort again. Perhaps he realized how deeply unattractive they made him.

The Goldfish opened at last in the Little Theatre, where it ran for a whole week. No longer. But there were some pleasing notices in the press for Martin and the others, and after the week at the Little they had a fortnight at the Scala and another fortnight at the Court. The run came to an end at last at the Crystal Palace.

A memorable week or so marked the end of *The Goldfish*'s restless run: Deborah announced her engagement to Tudor Jones and a mixed marriage was arranged to the satisfaction of the families of both bride and bridegroom; Tina ran away with a young Englishman named Hawkins, but reappeared after ten days with the announcement that he was a crashing bore and totally unworthy of her; and Beerbohm Tree's secretary wrote a comforting letter with the offer of a part in the forthcoming production of *Macbeth*.

'Second Apparition: a Bloody Child,' Father proudly announced, 'and maybe another part if he does well in that: what other boy's parts are there in *Macbeth* for God's sake? Ah yes, Fleance I think, isn't that it, Maimie?'

'Well, there is another one too,' the well-informed schoolmistress told him. 'The little son of Macduff who's murdered by Macbeth's hirelings. But I don't imagine the scene is often played on the stage. Maybe they'll put it in for Martin.'

'Ah, of course, of course. I sincerely hope they will, Fleance isn't much of a part at all, and the Chief thought most highly of Martin, so he did. As I told you. And two pounds ten a week he'll be getting again: aren't you the great help to your family Martin?'

'He is of course. Didn't I always say he'd do well: and don't go strutting about like that, Martin, with that important grin on your face. Aren't there plenty of other boys and girls that do well on the stage? There's young Noël Coward, he's been engaged by Charles Hawtrey for a new play, an original comedy altogether, not an old bit of tragedy like *Macbeth*. So you're not the only pebble on the beach, let me tell you that, me darling.'

'And Deborah will be Mrs Tudor Jones,' Tina murmured, 'I suppose she'll imagine herself as a Tudor in future. You may be thankful your name isn't Anne Boleyn, Debby; your fiancé is not unlike Henry VIII without the beard, and you'd never be as clever as Anne of Cleves.'

'Well at least I won't be Mrs 'Enery 'Awkins is a fustclass naime!' Deborah snapped back in excellent imitation of Albert Chevalier, for Tudor had taken her to see the great cockney comedian several times and her ear was quick. 'Why didn't you marry your Mr Hawkins, Tina? Perhaps he never asked you!'

'Never,' Tina answered, 'Not even once. He had a wife already you see.'

'A wife already?' Deborah cried, 'What desperate people you get mixed up with Tina!'

'Such blather they talk, such brainless balderdash,' Father muttered impatiently. 'Come out into the garden with me, son,' he added to Martin, and they went out together as Tina was saying, 'Yes, he had a wife already. I, of course, was supposed to know nothing of her existence. But her name slipped out one evening when he was drunk. It was no surprise to me. Her astral body was always hovering about. It interested me for a while, but then it began to get on my nerves. Badly. But my reason for deserting Peter had nothing to do with that. It was because of the drink. I can't bear drunkards. Boring nonentities.'

In the garden, Martin fed the goldfish in the pond, while his father perused the contract which had just arrived from His Majesty's Theatre. It was a much longer and more elaborate affair than the Lila Field one, in small print on bluish-grey paper, and Father read it aloud in an impressive monotone to his son, who was scattering ants' eggs on to the water of the pond and hardly understood a word of it.

Rehearsals for *Macbeth* were very different from those for *The Goldfish*, and Martin was deliriously happy to be working with grown-ups. Real actors he told himself, and many of the actresses reminded him of his sisters. Miss Violet Vanbrugh however reminded him of no one but herself. Every morning she would arrive in a hansom cab, having no use for these silly new-fangled taxis, and from the moment when, script in hand, she walked into the scene on that enormous bare stage where the smell of size and dust and Leichner's greasepaint hung amid the shadows and the glitter of the air, and there was nothing but oddly painted flats leaning against the walls, a few chairs and benches here and there, and a maze of ropes and sandbags overhead, from that first moment she was no longer Violet Vanbrugh. She was Lady Macbeth in person, in spite of her smart modern dress and her hat, which now and then she would pluck from her head and hand to the young man who was known as Pickens the call-boy.

'Can't inspire one's husband to murder in a toque,' she would say, with a smile, once again in the role of Miss Vanbrugh, and then she would throw back her head, clutch the script in her left hand, leaving the right hand free for its delicate and terrible work, and lo! it was the pale fatal hand of Lady Macbeth once more, intent on regicide.

Ah, and the three witches! These were played by two actors and an actress who, true to the traditions of her sex, had decided – with the permission of the Chief of course – that the witch she played could overlook the reference to bearded ladies made by the author of the play through the lips of the leading man, and should be not only beardless but of a certain sinister loveliness. To this end Miss Frances Dillon wore a wig of silver-gilt, make-up pale as foam, blood-red lips, peacock green eyelids, and a gashed throat. The beards which had surprised Macbeth she left

84

to Mr Ross-Shore and Mr A. E. George, though she wore the same nebulously floating smoke-grey robes as they, and all three flew together on Kirby's wires through the worst of the Scottish weather among clouds as black as Acheron. And as they flew, strange bleak landscapes in silhouette seemed to pass far below them: bare mountain tops, black pine trees, a long flat space of heath, and the summit and the turning sails of a windmill. At the first dress rehearsal, which went on until 3.45 a.m., Macbeth's entrance was preceded not only by the blood-curdling spells of the Weird Sisters but also by the crashing fall of a pine tree struck by lightning, and the flight of a huge black crow across the stage. Then the Chief himself appeared accompanied by Banquo on the crest of a great rock, their cloaks and hair blown about by the wild winds. Sir Herbert raised a warning hand, and when the noise had subsided said in a piercing whisper, 'More light on my face. More light! . . . what do I say?'

He was prompted and the rehearsal proceeded.

It was all maddeningly exciting, and poor little Maimie, half dead with exhaustion on her seat on the bench just inside the stage door, was mercifully allowed to join her small brother in the dress circle where they both were given sandwiches and hot soup.

That was before Martin's entrance as the Bloody Child, which was effected from below stage on a trapdoor whence he had to emerge through the low circular walls of the cauldron, ringed with living flame. He obediently pointed his right hand at Macbeth ('More light on my face!'), and his drooping chiffon-draped sleeve immediately caught on fire, but this intrepid lad chanted his lines in the ominous monotone taught him by the Chief until seized by the three witches (still weird but kind and courageous) and successfully quenched, he descended whole and unharmed below stage. There he found the first apparition, Mr Frank Conroy, for whom the Bloody Child had a profound admiration, in a most acceptable (to Martin) state of agitation, and the third apparition (the Crowned Child, played by Master Charles Thomas) equally agitated, not for Martin's sake at all but for his own.

'I'm not going up,' he growled at them, and who could blame him? 'I don't see why we should all burn to death even for Sir Herbert: I'll shout my lines from here.'

And this he did.

Martin's next appearance was as Macduff's son, in a pretty scene with his mother (Miss Viva Burkett, as warmly motherly and charming off stage as on), and he was murdered at the end of it by Mr Edmund Goulding, with whom he became friendly. 'What, you Egg!' wrote Mr Goulding in Martin's autograph book, a present from Deborah's future husband, Tudor Jones, and all through the run of *Macbeth* he took an elder-brotherly interest in Martin, and presented him on the last night with Carlyle's *French Revolution*, which Martin, aided and abetted by Maimie, did his best to read, though in his heart he infinitely preferred *The Scarlet Pimpernel*, and thought Baroness Orczy a much more interesting writer.

So Martin found two friends in the traditionally unlucky *Macbeth*, his mother and his murderer, and after that first dress rehearsal he and Maimie went home at four o'clock on the top of a bus in the brightening August morning, and saw for the first time in their lives a new London: peaceful, wellnigh empty, new-washed, new-lit, it seemed as pure and untroubled as the river bank of Cork.

Martin was in for a run of luck, for his stage mother liked him so much as the child of Macduff that she wanted to play his mother all over again in *Peter Pan*.

'My dear, he'd be such a wonderful Michael in *Peter Pan*,' she told Maimie, 'Do ask your mother and father to consent and I'll have a word with Dot – I mean Mr Boucicault – we all call him Dot, you know, because he's so short. But such a charming man, and a marvellous producer: so wonderful with children. I'm sure he'll go mad over Anthony. And *Peter Pan*, you know – such a perfect play and lots of other children in it too. I played Mrs Darling in it last year and I know they want me back. Duke of

York's Theatre – oh, charming, fires in all the dressing rooms my dear, and everyone so friendly! Little Charlie Thomas – you know, Fleance in this show, the boy who wouldn't go up on the trap through the flames and none of us blamed him, poor boy – well, he played Michael last year: awfully good but I think that Anthony would be still better. Anyhow Charlie has shot up so much during the year, I'm certain they'd think him too tall for Michael, who's the baby of the family you know. Wendy – dear Hilda Trevelyan's playing her again I'm glad to say – and John are the older sister and brother. I wonder if Charlie could play John? I'll ask Mr Boucicault anyway. I'll suggest him. *Macbeth* will be in its last three weeks in November anyway, and *Peter* always opens on Boxing Day. Oh I do hope Anthony can play Michael. Do get your parents to say yes!'

And so it happened. Martin was on the pig's back, as his mother put it. He was having a marvellous time, what with the mid-rehearsal cups of tomato soup at 11.30, the pride and pleasure of playing with Pauline Chase (Peter Pan), Hilda Trevelyan (Wendy) and Holman Clark (Captain Hook), and his beloved stage mother, Miss Burkett (Mrs Darling). Also he was earning five pounds a week, and looked back on the two pounds ten days as being positively penurious. Best of all he flew, which ever since watching the three witches in Macbeth had been a raging ambition in his heart. Mr Kirby himself had fitted him into his flying harness and taught him how to fly. He counselled him to study Pauline Chase, who had been doing it for years and was as lovely to watch in the air as a ballerina. One, two, three positions to give the cue to the man whose unseen business it was to work each separate rope for each separate flyer: 'And mind you're careful to stand on your mark for each flight,' Mr Kirby warned Martin, 'or you may go bashing yourself to bits on a tree or a wing or a ship's mast or something, and we don't want that sort of thing, you know.'

But flying, with all its complications, was a source of weird and endless pleasure, and all the others in the cast agreed with him. Everybody in the play seemed to fly except the grown-ups:

Mr and Mrs Darling, Captain Hook and his sinister band of pirates, and the Red Indian chiefs and their men, all of whom, with the exception of Mr Humphrey Warden, unmistakably masculine as Chief Great Big Little Panther, were played by ladies.

In fact *Peter Pan*, from any point of view at all, was a hilarious and happy experience, and for Martin there were three consecutive seasons of it, 1911, 1912, 1913. He and all the other youngsters playing with him wept bitterly on the last night of each provincial tour that followed the three months in the West End, but the tears shed by Martin after the first tour were soon dried when, on a sunny, showery day in April, a letter came from Tree's manager engaging him for the title role in *Oliver Twist*. The Chief himself was to appear as Mr Fagin, Mr Lyn Harding as Bill Sykes, and Miss Constance Collier as Nancy.

Rehearsals were strenuous for the boy actor, for it was revealed to him that he didn't know nearly as much about the craft, let alone the art, of acting as he had imagined. This of course was extremely good for him, though the discovery caused a little wounded pride and a certain lack of self-confidence which, like the right amount of salt in a good dish, is necessary to the actor even when he is a child, but fatal if the quantity be too great. Yet everybody was kind to him, and the Chief was the kindest of them all, the most severe of his criticism being, 'You see, Boy Blue, it is perfectly clear to me that you can do it supremely well if you really want to *and* if you will act naturally as a natural if unfortunate boy, not pose in strange and beautiful attitudes as if you were appearing in the Russian – ah! I remember! You told me the other day that you had been watching that damned Russian Ballet! Ah! The great, the unbelievable Nijinsky! But acting is not dancing, Boy Blue, though dancing at moments may include the art of acting: a reversal of this leads to mannerism . . . posing . . .artificiality . . . Be natural, Boy Blue, be yourself and believe in what you are saying and what Dickens, adapted by Mr Comyns

Carr, has given to you to say. Your voice is good, your English passable, though you still say "hôsse" for *house* and "aboat" for *about* . . . still you are doing finely; continue if you must to watch the great Nijinsky – and the great Pavlova too – but do not let their art obscure your own. Now let us do the meeting with me again, little Holiver, and remember: "Dear Mr Fagin is vatchin' over you . . ." Mr King, call them all on stage please for the first thieves' kitchen scene.'

It was during the run of *Oliver Twist* that Maimie and Martin Weldon met for the first time a young actor who was to become one of the most important figures in both of their lives.

They were at Appendrodt's, the German restaurant in Piccadilly Circus which, in a setting of marble-topped tables and potted palms, specialized in the celebrated *Kaltespeisen* of the Fatherland, with Munich beer, *Kartoffelsalat* and the various sausages and pâtés of a highly national character, as well as in the innumerable elaborate cakes and iced coffees and sweets that all good as well as all bad Germans love so dearly; and in these Martin especially shared their taste. A party was being given by Geoffrey Leigh-Craig, a friend of the Weldon children, and consisted mainly of people who worked with Geoffrey at some important mysterious offices in Whitehall, together with a sprinkling of young English actors, all of them in hilarious spirits. They were all enjoying their talk and their feast when one of them shouted, 'There's Mac at last. Mac! How late you are!' Turning round, Martin saw a tall, golden-haired, absurdly good-looking young man in a pale grey suit. He swept towards them and sat down next to Maimie, crying out in one breath, 'Sorry to be late my darlings: how are you all in this divine June weather sheer heaven isn't it. And you,' he continued, '*you* are Anthony Weldon? Oliver Twist. Well, duckie, I've seen you in it at three different matinées and I don't mind telling you I thought you absolutely splendid. And somebody told me you were Irish. I'm so glad because I am too but from the *North* I'm sorry to say, such dreary pogs they are up there, and I was brought up as a Presbyterian, can you believe it?

But I don't think I've a Protestant expression, though me red-nosed aunt in Armagh has, she looks like *this*, so depressing isn't it?'

'Mac, will you shut up for one minute and let me introduce you?' Geoffrey Leigh-Craig said.

'But we all *know* each other, *don't* we dear? Except you and me: no, you and I, dear,' Mac murmured to Maimie. 'Sounds peculiar doesn't it? Tell me your name, dear.'

'Maimie Weldon,' she answered. 'I'm Martin's sister. I mean I'm Anthony's sister.'

'Are you really? Well, you're not a bit alike, are you? But I'm not like me brother George, thank God! He's red-headed and relentless with a moustache. Gone into the shipping business in Liverpool like me father in Belfast. Do you love the opera, Maimie? I may call you Maimie and Anthony mayn't I? Or Martin. Is that your real name, Oliver Twist? Suits you much better than Anthony I think. Do you both love opera? You *have* heard *Tosca*? Ah, wonderful. They say that musically it's better than *Butterfly* but I love *Butterfly* best of all. "*Suzuki, Suzuki, il te!*",' he sang with such vigour and such unexpected volume and power that everybody in the restaurant stared at him open-mouthed.

'So you're both Irish!' he went on after a pause that was filled with the conversation of the other guests at the table. 'Do you know Dublin? I adore Dublin: I'd love to live there, but what would one do for a *living*, dear? There's only the Abbey, and the other theatres are all for provincial tours from the West End or somewhere. Perhaps it would be better if one went back to Ireland to live, to do it in the country and have a farm in the mountains. I'm sure I could persuade me father to give me a couple of bantams to make a start. Could you ever bear life in the country Maimie? Could *you*, Martin? After all the parts you've played and all the things you've done! How old are you now dear? Twelve? Dear God, and you've done all those things already. You've even heard Caruso in *Tosca*, haven't you? "*Mario! Mario!*" But never *Butterfly*? Not that you'd hear

90

Caruso in that: he'd never dream of singing Pinkerton any more. But you must both come with me to *Butterfly*. Now promise, Maimie, promise, Martin, your first *Butterfly* will be with ME. Swear on my sword! And you never saw Sarah? Then that'll be with me too.'

His name was Alexander McMullen but nobody ever called him McMullen. None of his friends called him Alexander either, or even Alec. To his intimates, and there were hundreds of these, he was always Mac, and every one in London had decided long ago that Mac was a Lamb, though mad as twenty March Hares. At the moment, to his own distaste and embarrassment, he was playing a small showy part in *Everybody's Doing It* at the Empire, but he was soon to leave it to return to a revival of *The Scarlet Pimpernel* with Fred Terry and Julia Nielson. But his real ambition was to play all the leads in all the plays of Shakespeare, though it was years before this could be realized. At the moment he was drawing a respectable salary, keeping all his friends happy with his radiant personality, his passion for opera (especially Italian), his enthusiasm for the Russian Ballet, and his joyful, outrageous commentary on life in general and the theatre in particular.

The friendship between himself, Martin and Maimie grew steadily more intimate. There were wild luncheons in Soho when he had any money, hilarious teas at the Corner House when he had less, exuberant excursions to Hampstead Heath when he had still less, and delightful tea parties at the Weldons' when he had none at all. He was a great success with the whole family, though Deborah and Tina made fun of him after their contrasting fashions, and Mother simply adored him.

Mac was also a popular figure at the Leigh-Craigs' week-end parties, where he made frequent appearances on Sunday evening, his arms (during his prosperous periods) full of flowers for Maimie and sometimes for Katherine too. Geoffrey Leigh-Craig's wife Katherine was an Anglo-Indian lady of an avowedly Tory and Imperialistic view of life whose hero was Lord Kitchener, and whose favourite author was Rudyard

Kipling. She was a convert to the Catholic Church because her husband was a Catholic, and although she took exception to most countries which practised that faith – Italy and Ireland especially came in for a great deal of criticism – she found certain solid qualities in her adopted beliefs. 'A good, working religion to give to a child like our Peter,' she said, and had no objection to the framed reproduction of Cimabue's Madonnas that hung at various places on the staircase walls of their lovely Georgian house at Richmond, or the sanctuary lamp that burned continually in front of the picture just outside the dining room.

Mac went into ecstasies over this lamp. 'Little light: never goes out, dear,' he exclaimed, waving his cigarette in a series of rapid gestures above it. 'God! how I love it all!' he cried in melodious gustiness, and accidentally blew it out.

'Oh my God! Oh Kitty *darling!*' he shouted in anguish.

But Kitty was less put out than one might expect her to be. She took it all as a rather tiresome joke. Geoffrey, or 'Daddy', as she called her husband, was more upset, saying little and pretending valiantly to think it amusing. Geoffrey gently refused to let Mac light it again, and quietly arranged for a priest to come round next morning to perform the ceremony.

Katherine said no more about the sanctuary lamp, but the next day, when Mac had departed, she expressed her doubts about him at lunch time in what for her was a subdued tone:

'No doubt he is very good-looking,' she said. 'Wonderful golden hair. Do you think he dyes it?'

And from that time on Mac compared her unfavourably with the mother of Maimie and Martin.

'*Your* mother is so warm and relaxed, dear,' he cried, 'Kitty would be much happier as an instructress in the Girl Guides. Of course, she's English, poor darling.'

Mac kept his promise about *Madame Butterfly*, and took the brother and sister to hear Emmy Destinn in the role. But Martin unintentionally stole a march on him about Bernhardt, for later that summer, after the disaster of the *Titanic*, Martin was invited by Sir Herbert Tree to walk on as a page at the charity matinée in aid of the survivors and their relatives.

'Only stars will be on that stage on this occasion,' Father was saying impressively. 'So 'tis a good thing for *you*, me boy, that you played Oliver Twist this year, or you'd never have been invited. Stars as supers,' he continued, 'What an occasion! Phyllis Neilson Terry is playing the Queen of course, but Violet Vanbrugh and Laura Cowie will appear as ladies in waiting, and Ion Swinley and Donald Calthrop as courtiers. And Anna Pavlova will dance the *Swan*, and Caruso and Edvina will sing the second act of *Tosca*, and Nijinsky and Tamara Karsavina will dance in the *Spectre de la Rose*, whatever that may be. You'll be in great company, Martin. And, my God, will you look here!' he cried, passionately waving the *Evening News* in the faces of his family. 'Madame Sarah Bernhardt is appearing! Personal appearance of Sarah Bernhardt! What do you think of that? Such a galaxy. Do you think we could ever get a couple of seats, Mary?'

They did, and it was all as brilliant as they had dreamed it would be. The great auditorium was thronged with orders, and smartly pleated or delicately frilled shoulders, and smoothly groomed heads or startlingly modish hats, but no tiaras and no visible ringletted coiffures, for this was not an eight or eight-thirty affair, but a matinée, and there in the royal box against a suitably splendid entourage of *aides de camp* and of elegant ladies were the two unmistakable figures of King George and Queen Mary, and Her Majesty's hat was superbly smothered in sweet peas and her throat in a high collar of milky pearls. All this had a fatal effect on the stage Queen's horse, who lost control over his (or was it her?) bladder, and the contents trickled down the ramp to the footlights and caused terrible though muffled hoots of laughter among the stage courtiers. But Martin, who was in charge of the stage Queen's train, behaved like a perfect gentleman and seemed not to notice a thing.

Later on, as the perfect little gentleman was watching the show from the corner of the stage opposite the prompter, Nijinsky, dressed in the costume of the Rose, passed close by on his way to the other side, and Martin had just time to observe the long Mongolian eyes with their thickly beaded black lashes, and the hectic blush of rouge high up on the cheek bones, and then to watch the incomparable lightness and grace as the young dancer ran to greet Tamara Karsavina before he vanished into the shadows beyond the great window where he was to make his entrance. ·

When it was all over, and the celebrated performers were rushing to and fro in their dressing rooms, Herbert Tree came over to the boy in the corner of the stage and said, 'I see you changed your dress in the interval, and there you are, Boy Blue, in your nice jersey and ready to meet human beings again. Now, would you like to meet one who is not only human but a little superhuman too? No, I don't mean your friend Nijinsky, nor do I mean those great ladies Madame Pavlova or Madame Karsavina. I mean a greater still, for she works in your own medium and mine, though with a different tongue. Would you like to meet the greatest actress in the world, Boy?'

'Yes please, Sir Herbert.'

'Then come with me, Anthony, and meet her. You will have to bow very low. Can you bow, Boy?'

'I can, Sir Herbert.'

She was standing in the middle of the room, and had changed the draperies of her stage role for a clinging toilette of coffee-coloured silk and lace in which perhaps she intended to dine. A hat of the same colour and texture was drawn closely over a cluster of reddish-gold curls on her forehead, a high, filmy frilled collar hid the lower part of her chin and the sides of her cheeks. Her make-up was little different from what she had worn for her dazzling performance. With one hand held lightly to her cheek, she stretched out the other, glittering with jewels, and murmured some soft incomprehensible words. Hardly knowing what he was doing or why he did it, Martin bowed over her hand and lightly kissed it. It smelled of all the flowers of Eden and the fingers were warm and smooth, but the rest of her hand was covered with a frill of lace whose folds were

94

uncannily still; and Martin perceived that each fold was gummed to each separate knuckle, and all he could do was to mutter, 'Oh Madame!' as he gazed up into her eyes like the eyes of a cat, limpid and alive with humour, and coloured like emeralds. She laughed then and, stooping a little, for she was not a very tall lady, kissed him on the forehead and said something to Tree, who responded in the same language. Then, after a last low bow, he led the boy out of the room and said, 'You did that very well, Blue Boy, and Madame Sarah said charming things about you. Did you understand what she said, Boy?'

'No, Sir Herbert.'

'It is time you learned some more French,' the great man decided. 'And to my mind it is high time that Madame learned a word or two of something that wasn't French. Now run away home with your little sister, and tell your people that you have met the greatest actress in the world and that you kissed her hand most correctly, and that I say that you are a good boy.'

Tree engaged Martin in the following year, 1913, to play Benjamin in Louis Napoleon Parker's stage adaptation of *Joseph and his Brethren*, a colossal production which included a flock of sheep, several elaborate settings by three separate designers, Mr George Relph as Joseph, the Chief himself as Jacob, and a large and impressive camel called Nelly. It was on Nelly's back that Miss Maxine Elliott made her first entrance as Potiphar's voluptuous and unprincipled wife, in a howdah through whose red and gold curtains she peered with feline grace at the handsome youth she was so nearly to ruin later on in the play. All was luxury and ancient splendour, although the banquet in the last act, served on plates of gold and ivory encrusted with coral and turquoise, consisted mainly of chopped bananas, and the wine, served in jewelled goblets, was cold tea with no milk or sugar in it, and Martin's chief memory of the proceedings, apart from the few adolescent lines he had to say, was of being clasped to Jacob's breast and ticklingly embedded in the silvery locks of his beard. Harps were played, hymns both Hebrew and

Egyptian were sung, and in the final scene of all there was an elaborate ballet of twenty Egyptian ladies in lovely pleated robes and headdresses who floated through a series of sensuous rhythms and sudden static silences recalling the frescoes of Luxor and Karnak in their palmy days. But the true purpose of the scene, when the dancers and their lotus blossoms had vanished, the true ending of the story, of course, was the reconciliation of the brethren to Joseph: the brotherly embrace of Joseph (George Relph) and Benjamin (Martin Weldon) for whom, as Joseph had more than once during the scene declared, 'his bowels yearned'. This was a phrase that puzzled Martin, unused to biblical terminology, for he had always associated bowels with liquorice powder and not with fraternal affection, and he was too shy and too prudish to ask anyone for an explanation.

But he enjoyed *Joseph* very much indeed, and it had what was considered, in the West End of those days, a long run of over three months, and he was still playing it when the rehearsals of his third year in *Peter Pan* began, every morning in December.

As a result of *Oliver Twist* and *Joseph* Martin made many new friends, people who had become fans of the boy actor, and all through the years of 1912 and 1913 he would go, sometimes accompanied by one or more of these and sometimes with Maimie alone, to watch the Russian Ballet. During the summer he went as often as three or four nights a week, but in the *Peter Pan* seasons (when there were two performances daily, followed by three months of tour) and during the run of *Joseph and his Brethren*, there were no free evenings at all. Nor was there a moment for a matinée, but when the summer days came round again Maimie and her small brother attended the Pavlova matinées at the Palace Theatre in Cambridge Circus, and it was at one of these that Martin discovered that Tree had made a mistake about the Nijinsky influence on his acting. Nijinsky represented to the boy a matchless, inimitable supremacy of form and movement, a strange, sexless, ethereal quality that no other human being could endeavour to repeat. He did not seem to be a man: neither did he in the smallest degree resemble a woman. He seemed indeed a being far withdrawn from human life: he was a faun, a rose, a floating star, a tragic puppet, a dark and gilded personification of lust, an aerial abstraction of purity and grace that soared like a dream through the eyes and left the spectator breathless in some region of the spirit he had never known before.

No, it was not Nijinsky who had conjured up the boy's envy and led him to the imitative trend so rightly deplored by Sir Herbert Tree. It was the great Pavlova's partner, Novikoff, with his muscular build, his splendid virility, his joyful bounding grace. He it was who filled the youthful aspirant for the first time in his life with a pride that he too was of the same sex as this Russian dancer, that he himself one day perhaps could look like that and move like that, bounding so joyously through life and with such grace, such strength, such pride and authority. When Novikoff raised Pavlova aloft it was a man in adoration of the immortal goddess he held in his arms: when Nijinsky held the exquisite Karsavina on high it was the spirit of love and of death who carried an enchanted princess to secret places underneath the moon.

Yes, it was Novikoff who inspired a half unconscious desire to resemble him: not Nijinsky. Who could ever resemble Nijinsky? Nobody on the green earth, and but few in the heavens.

Every night, and at every matinée too, the players in *Peter Pan* were pelted at the end of the performance with little bunches of violets with a thimble attached, for thimbles, Sir James Barrie had decreed, were the symbol of kisses. Because, you see, when Wendy had told Peter that she would give him a kiss if he liked, Peter had said: 'A kiss: what's that?' and Wendy, in her childish confusion, gave the thimble she had used while she was sewing his shadow onto his feet, and he had worn it among the leaves of his collar for ever after. So they all got violets and thimble-kisses from members of the audience and Martin got his share of them, even in the last two years of his playing in the show, though as he was growing too big for Michael (just like Charlie Thomas) his part in the Darling family had changed to John, which he didn't really enjoy so much. It was a relief, however, not to have to be cramped, cribbed and confined in a cradle in the Underground Scene, and to be free to do the Pillow Dance with the Lost Boys, and to fight far lustier battles with the Pirates than Michael did in the Ship Scene. It was fun too to be with Noël Coward again, for in the third season Noël was engaged for the part of Slightly, for which he was quite unsuitable though he played with a clear foreshadowing of that brilliant crispness that was to be his own style and manner forever. In fact he was far too brilliant and too crisp for the poor, stupid Slightly because, as he explained to Martin, 'It really is unbelievably difficult to act like a moron when one isn't a moron. And I have very little sympathy, darling, with morons.' And then he had to explain to Martin what a moron was: 'Rather like you, darling, in your absent moments. These, fortunately, are few.'

For Martin *Peter Pan* ended with the completion of the annual tour, in Manchester, in the early April days of 1914. He and all the other children wept their usual tears, and Charlie Thomas remarked in a choking voice that it was 'like looking at and listening to the water running out of a bath, never to be seen or enjoyed again.' Back to their London homes they went with hope in their hearts that they would all meet again at Christmas time in the Never Never Land that Barrie had made them love so well, but Martin, and perhaps Charlie and Noël too, felt in their hearts that this would never be. Noël was the least sorrowful about this. He had never cared much for the role of Slightly and had already announced his intention, if he was free, of getting into *Where the Rainbow Ends* next Christmas. This the *Peter Pan* fanatics considered rather parvenu of him, and frankly told him so, but Noël insisted that A Change of Atmosphere was essential to an actor's development, and said that there were two superb parts in *The Rainbow*, William the Page Boy and the Slacker, either or both of which he was burning to play.

Rosemary Craig, who had acted as Second Twin in *Peter* and was the daughter of Gordon Craig's first wife, and the granddaughter of Ellen Terry, was the loudest and most abandoned of the weepers. She was certain, she moaned, that she would be too big for any of the Lost Boys by next Christmas, and her famous grandmother had agreed with her. The whole cast was mournfully sympathetic with Rosemary, and they were sad too at the thought of probably never seeing Ellen Terry again, for that fascinating lady had visited her grand-daughter between the shows on almost every Saturday evening, bringing the most beautiful little presents for the whole lot of them. Nobody was forgotten, and Carriage Grandma, as Rosemary called her, was looking old and fragile by the end of what was for all the children that last London season; though *Peter Pan* was to continue for years after their own day was done.

Yet somehow Martin settled down to idle days with his mother and father, his daily lessons with Maimie and with his other sisters again, though there were only three of the sisters at home now, Tina and Maimie and Scatty Peg, for Deborah was now Mrs Tudor Jenkins and living miles away in Chiswick.

Martin was so absorbed by his new interests, his visits to the Pavlova matinées and the delirious nights at the Diaghilev Ballet with Maimie and a host of grown-up friends (who as well as these treats kept taking him and Maimie to lunch at various Soho restaurants), that he was less affected than he otherwise might have been by the news that his eldest sister was expecting a baby.

It was Tina who told him of the coming event.

'Mrs Jones,' she announced, 'is about to replenish the earth. But I don't suppose it will have any great effect on history. Will it be a boy or a girl? Perhaps neither. One can be certain of nothing really.'

But the baby was a boy and Deborah decided that he should be called Brian.

'So we really are a London family now,' Tina observed one evening. 'An obscure London-Irish family in the depths of distant Suburbia. Can you imagine anything more sinister?'

And that same evening in some long conversation about Black Magic, her latest subject, she observed that Martin's voice was breaking.

'So is my poor heart to hear it,' she said. 'But breaking it certainly is, my poor adolescent, and you will find it more and more difficult to get little boys' parts in the theatre and continue as a blessing to your poverty-stricken family. For you are too large and too unevenly voiced to play at being a child any more, and you are not even remotely ready for adult parts yet, are you?'

And she fixed her darkly glowing eyes on the wretched Martin and made him wonder why he had ever been born. Then she murmured: 'Ah! what a tragedy life is for us all, my own darling.' And warmly embraced him.

CHAPTER FOUR
Spanish Interlude

The person who worried most about this hiatus in Martin's acting career was his mother. She had an instinctive, inborn love of the theatre and its people, though nothing in the world would have tempted her to pass through a stage door or to make any appearance, however brief, before the public. Her greatest pleasure, now that her family had settled in London, was 'a grand tea at the Corner House and then a seat in a gorgeous theatre and a play with a plot to it, something like, say, *Peter Pan* or *Within the Law*, ah, there's real excitement about a show like that, you could wish it would go on forever.' She had been thrilled by her son's progress, and it saddened her to think that it might be at an end. But Martin's father took another view altogether.

'The boy,' he pronounced, 'has other talents: he might turn out to be a painter or maybe a poet. Possibly even, he may turn away from the arts altogether and fix his eyes on a political or a – God forbid, but you never know – a business career. Now Mary, did I tell you I'd a letter from Seville the other day, from my aunt Luisa Concepción Fuentes, and you know how upset she was at the death of Domingo, her youngest boy. She told me how much she misses a lad of his age about the house and asked most affectionately after our girls and our only boy. She said she'd love to have him over there for a while, if we could spare him. She married well as you know – unlike my poor mother, God rest her – and has the best side on the patio of a fine house in the Calle San Fernando. Now Spanish is a most useful addition to any young fellow's knowledge if he's going to get on in the world. Supposing now, if Martin gets no more offers for the theatre for a couple of years and won't be working again until he grows to be a man, what would you say to his going out to

Seville and picking up the language and adding to his experience?'

'What?' cried his wife. 'Is it our Martin going to leave us and live in a foreign country for a year or more, and what do we do without him? God! the ideas you get into your head, Tony.'

But he persisted that Spain would be a splendid experience for the boy: he would acquire not only a second language but good manners as well and broaden his outlook on life, and at last Mother was converted to the plan.

So it came about that Martin, accompanied by his father, who arranged for a fortnight's leave from his firm, sailed away from Dover, where Mr Weldon waxed eloquent about the white cliffs, and they arrived an hour later at Calais, where the boy experienced an unexpected delight at everything he saw. All was strange and different from anything he had ever known, nothing was very beautiful, and yet it all seemed right and reassuring somehow. The shuttered houses, the clear pale azure of the sky, the refreshment room where he had the nicest coffee he had ever tasted even in Soho, the blue blouses of the porters, the liveliness of manner, the incomprehensible speech – though here and there were words he recognized from Maimie's lessons – the three high steps to be climbed up on to the train, the second-class compartment with its coarse white mats behind each head, everything he saw and heard enchanted him.

'This is France,' he told himself, 'I like France: I wish we were staying in France insted of going to Spain.'

He was asleep when they crossed the border, and when he opened his eyes again he was informed by his Father that he must wake up and be prepared to get into another train soon as they were approaching Madrid. He looked out of the window and saw a wild stretch of mountains, deserted and coldly tragic in the fast fading twilight. But the air was warm and pleasant, and presently a waiter passed by them in the long corridor ringing a bell and calling out that it was 'Diner, seconde série! Diner, seconde série!'

But when they arrived at the great station at Madrid and had to climb into another train with 'Sevilla' painted on the side, the boy was so tired that as soon as they were in the compartment he fell asleep again, indifferent to the hard bare wood of the seat, for he lay on a folded overcoat and his head was pillowed on Father's chest.

He was still tired when they arrived at Seville, though the beauty and the unfamiliarity of it all as they drove through the bright streets, the scented air, the sunshine and the answering black shadow, the white and yellow buildings, the tall gates of wrought iron, above all the flowering orange trees and the palms that seemed to grow in every open space, all these things enchanted him and made him open his eyes in wonder. They travelled in great luxury from the station in an open coach, for Father was in a gay, extravagant mood. He could not dream, he told his son, of travelling in a hot crowded bus and arriving at Great-Aunt Luisa's house on foot. After a while they followed the river, driving slowly past a great octagonal tower – the Torre del Oro, Father said it was, the Tower of Gold – then they turned sharply to the left past thickets of green trees and stopped in front of a house whose front door was not a door at all, but a tall archway and two open gates. While Father and the driver were pulling various bags and bundles out of the coach, two boys came flying out of a door on the right side of the house, which was built on three sides of a square with a fountain in the middle and two little flowering orange trees, one on each side. Both the boys embraced Father and chattered incomprehensibly to him, and then turned to Martin and shook hands and bowed their heads and continued their chatter, and Martin for the first time in his life was totally nonplussed and could do nothing but grin and say 'Sí, sí, gracias,' which must have seemed the funniest thing the boys had ever heard, for they both went into fits of laughter, and softly slapped Martin on both cheeks, and then they helped to carry the luggage through the tall gate and into the side of the house.

So it was all rather tiring, and Martin was glad to get into a cool white sitting room where he was greeted by Great-Aunt

Luisa. She was a small, handsome creature with two or three streaks of white in her dark hair. She was dressed all in black and held a black and silver fan in her hand, but she embraced Father warmly and, turning to Martin with a beaming smile, kissed him on both cheeks and on his forehead, and then she made the sign of the cross in front of his face. She was chattering all the time, and Martin felt more and more lost. But she was smiling at him so sweetly that he felt it ungracious not to say something, however inadequate, so he said 'Gracias, Tíabuela Luisa,' which his father had told him was the sort of relation she was to him and what he should call her.

But her smile vanished immediately, and was replaced by a frown from one of her finely drawn eyebrows only, leaving the other in its normal position, a habit of hers that Martin observed for the first but by no means the last time, and she then opened and closed her fan with a series of resounding clicks and said a thousand words in what seemed a severe tone of voice. Father said something soothing to her and she was all smiles on the instant, and kissed and blessed Martin all over again. Later on Father explained that what she had said was, 'Please do not call me Great-Aunt: I am Tía Luisa, your *Aunt* Luisa: I was fifteen years younger than my sister María del Carmen, your dear grandmother, may her soul be with God, and everybody in town agreed that I was much more handsome than she, though she too was a very pretty girl.'

Martin, who had not understood a word, grinned graciously and said 'Gracias, Tía Luisa,' and Tía Luisa laughed loudly and clapped her hands so that her fan fell to the ground, and Martin picked it up and gravely handed it to her, at which she beamed more than ever, swept him a bow, kissed and blessed him for the third time, and introduced him to the two boys who came into the room, the same pair who had helped Martin and his father with the luggage.

The older of the two boys was called 'tu primo Juan Sebastián.' The smaller one, who was thin and sallow, was 'tu primo Manuel,' and Martin's father explained that a *primo* was a cousin. 'He's really my uncle but who cares?' thought Martin in the jovial Cockney way he had picked up during the run of *Peter Pan*. Then a very beautiful girl with light brown hair and enormous eyes came into the room, and was presented as 'tu prima Teresa del Pilar,' and both parties gravely shook hands and bowed. Then they all giggled, for what else could they do?

So then it was lunchtime and they all sailed into the dining room and sat round a square table spread with a white cloth and having two carafes of white wine and two of red; and an elderly maid brought in a tray with six plates containing fried eggs garnished with red peppers and big green olives. After that came cutlets and fried potatoes, then a green salad, then some cheese and bread, and then mountains of fresh fruit. Martin had never eaten so much in his life or drunk so much wine, though Father, after a buzzing explanation from Aunt Luisa, told him that this being a day of celebration there was wine for lunch: in future there would only be water or orange flower water, and wine for the evening dinner. So after that they all went out to the patio where they sat in the cool shadow and drank coffee and then – good Heavens, what a strange country! – Aunt Luisa said it was time for bed.

'She only means for the *siesta*,' Father explained. 'An hour or two to get away from the hottest part of the day. They do it all over Spain you know: 'tis a good idea in its way: freshens you up for the evening.'

Martin saw that there were three beds in the room where he was installed by Tía Luisa and his father who, after endless incomprehensible chatter, explained that he was to share the room with Juan and Manuel. So at last, when they had all gone away, Martin undressed and slept for a long while, a deep sleep coloured faintly by dreams of flowering orange trees and tall white houses with yellow crinkled roofs. And when he woke up he heard two boyish voices talking away as fast as they could go, and a great deal of laughter, and saw that Juan and Manuel were pulling on their clothes.

Then they all went for a *paseo*, which Martin understood as meaning simply a drive but discovered, much later, that it could apply just as well to a walk or any sort of outing at all, and leaving the street and the elaborate amber-coloured façade of the cigarette factory behind them, they journeyed through a series of parks and gardens of such luxuriant beauty that it was as though he were still in a dream; and a dream of strange magic, for the air was sweeter than ever with the scent of orange blossom – 'Azahar, azahar,' shouted the helpful Manuel when he saw his cousin sniffing with such delight – and there was a curious strumming sound in the air at one point, as though invisible hands were plucking at the strings of guitars.

'It is guitars,' Father told him, and Tía Luisa sniffed, frowned with her left eyebrow only, opened and closed her fan several times and said in a superior sort of voice, 'Gitanos.'

'Sí, sí, gitanos,' the two brothers agreed with great enthusiasm, 'Escucha, Martín!' And Manuel put his hand behind his ear and rolled his eyes and winked at his brother. The carriages were stopped and they alighted at what looked like a plantation of tables and chairs in front of a pavilion among the trees. The place was crowded with people, but Father and Tía Luisa found two little tables with chairs set about them, and they all had orange-flower water, and then some tiny cups filled with what looked like rich brown mud but it turned out to be chocolate, exquisite to the taste and so thick that they drank it out of their spoons. And five strangely dressed people appeared, two young ladies and three men, one of the men carrying a guitar.

The men wore collarless shirts, rough trousers of dark blue linen, short jackets and round flat hats, but the girls were gorgeously dressed in tight flower-patterned bodices with small fringed shawls knotted over their breasts, and carnations in their smooth black hair. Their frilled skirts were as brilliantly coloured as the rainbow, and as thickly spotted as the leopards they strikingly resembled, and they and the two younger men began to dance while the older man, seating himself on a chair and striking the strings of his guitar with his brown fingers, accompanied them.

The dance was watched with wonder and enthusiasm by Juan, Manuel and Martin, all standing up on their own chairs and shouting *Olé* when everybody else did, but when poor little Teresa del Pilar tried to follow their example she was tapped smartly on her bottom with Tía Luisa's fan, and made to sit down again so that she could see nothing at all over the heads of the intervening rows of chocolate drinkers; and Father whispered to Martin, 'Young ladies in Seville are not supposed to stand on chairs. What would your sister Tina say to that, I wonder?'

At last the dance was over, and the two gipsy girls placidly dealt with the long strands of black hair that had fallen loose in the frenzy of their movement, and they sat together between their partners and clapped their hands at various moments, and shouted occasional rapid encouragement to the musician who sat a little to one side and, still plucking and strumming the strings of his guitar, presently began to sing.

What a weird, incomprehensible sound, was Martin's reaction: it was like listening to the half-human crying and calling of cats under the moon. After a little it began to fascinate his ears, and he listened with a rapt and growing pleasure to this uncanny performance. Three more dances followed, and four more songs, and then a collection was made with the two gipsy girls shaking tambourines with brilliant smiles, laughter and talk that Martin perceived was obviously of a coaxing, seductive nature. They were extremely successful, and soon the tambourines were clanking with pesetas and centimes, and even a few paper notes were presented which were received with passionate gratitude and kisses on the hands. Father was among these, giving a five peseta note to one of the girls, who not only kissed his hand but her own fingertips, with which she touched his moustache and murmured something that made Tía Luisa's eyebrow busier than ever.

Life was pleasant and monotonous in the Calle San Fernando, and Martin easily slipped into its ways. He made astonishingly swift progress with the language because he could never endure the thought of being left out of things. His father and the two brothers helped him nobly, and his ear, like his emotional reaction, was swift and responsive. Quite soon he was chatting away with a brazen indifference to the mistakes he made and the occasional hoots of laughter from Juan and Manuel, and he was feeling quite happily at home until the day when his father announced his departure for London.

'Tomorrow?' Martin demanded in horror. 'You're going back tomorrow? Ah, but Father you can't leave me here alone!'

'Your pleas are useless, my poor boy. You came here to learn Spanish and that's what you're going to do. Comfort yourself by remembering your past triumphs – Tree, and *Peter Pan*, and *Joseph and his Brethren*, and all the rest of it – ah, what memories for a boy of fourteen! And think about your future too. When you know Spanish well, and I think you will, there'll be wonderful worlds waiting for you. Spain, South America, as well as the great English-speaking world. Aren't you the lucky boy! So be a brave boy too, and if you're not happy with Tía Luisa and her family you've only to let your mother or myself know and I'll come out again and fetch you back to London.'

Martin didn't cry when his father drove away from the house in the Calle San Fernando. The tears did not come until that night when, after a lot of shouting and tricking and dancing and praying on the part of Juan and Manuel, he got into his small white-sheeted bed in the corner, and when the candles were blown out and the last 'Buenas noches, Martinillo!' had been said, he lay shuddering, and then the tears came. He wept and wept, thinking of Mother and of Maimie, of the dressing room at the Duke of York's Theatre, of Tree, of Maxine Elliott as Potiphar's wife, of Scatty Peg, and then, inconsequently, of Jack Hunter and the bedroom in Cork – oh, a hundred hundred years ago – and the tears came faster and faster . . .

What was this? Juan, whispering in his ear words that he could not hear, was climbing into bed beside him.

'Pobrecito mío,' he was saying, 'Porqué las lágrimas? Porqué? Ánimo, ánimo, Martinillo!'

But Martin didn't really understand. He murmured: 'Sh! Juan, Sh! Manuel—'

'Manolito is asleep,' the other whispered reassuringly, and Martin understood that, and after a few sniffs he stopped crying, because Juan was behaving so strangely. Ever since *Oliver Twist*, and increasingly often after the opening of *Joseph and his Brethren*, his life had been full of grown men who would ask him for autographs at the stage door or, meeting him at the house of some mutual friends, would make a great deal of fuss of him, and often when left alone with him would kiss and embrace him. He had taken it all for granted and had even wondered, when such favours were neither offered nor begged for, what was wrong with the poor gentleman? Was he ill? Was he afraid that Maimie might suddenly appear: a habit which she had frequently practised? For he understood dimly that the kisses and caresses were of a strictly private nature. But never before had anything like this occurred. Never had any of these admiring and affectionate gentlemen got into bed with him, and they were all older and more authoritative than the sixteen-year-old Juan, however much he boasted of having to shave every day. Never before now had anyone burned his mouth with kiss after kiss until it hurt, or done what Juan was doing now. For Juan, already divested of his own shirt, was alternately stroking and kissing his face and his body, and gently pulling off his pyjamas. Ah no, nobody in London had ever gone so far as this, and for a few moments Martin, in whose nature passion and prudery was so often at war together, put up a struggle. But his cousin was too strong for him and too resolutely determined, and at last the younger of the partners yielded. He was too tired and too miserable about Father's leaving him to resist. Besides, the truth was that this display of passionate affection gave him a feeling of comfort, although the panting frenzy of the older boy as he worked up to his climax frightened him a little, he confessed frankly to himself that he was enjoying it. 'Did you take pleasure in it?' he heard an imaginary sacerdotal voice ask, and he wondered vaguely what would result if he answered,

'Oh yes, Father, 'twas marvellous.'

When it was all over he felt at once relaxed and regretful. Not guilty. Why should he feel guilty? He had done no harm to anyone. But when Juan, after a breathless embrace and a stern warning to tell nobody what had happened, had returned to his own bed, he knew that childhood was over. He was a child no longer.

Next day Juan and Martin met in the most friendly fashion, and both of them behaved as if nothing at all unusual had happened the night before, though at one moment, alone together in the patio, Juan with a charming smile but a dangerous sparkle in his dark eyes, took both of Martin's hands into his own, and beginning with the endearing address *Amor mío*! went on to a rapid speech whose ultimate meaning was clear enough although many of the words escaped him. The message, briefly, was, 'If you are silent I will always love you, and I will be kind to you and protect you. Always, always! But if you say one word to Manuel or to little mother I will kill you. *Me entiendes, Martinito de mi vida?*'

And Martin said, 'Sí, sí, Juan,' and they embraced and shook hands, and Juan with the forefinger of his right hand pulled down the skin under his right eye and barked out, 'Ah! Cuidado, amor mío, cuidado!' Then he laughed, slapped his young cousin on both cheeks, and went out into the street.

Life went by pleasantly enough, though that night in bed Martin was restless and wondered if Juan would repeat the amorous performance of the night before. But no, there was no sound or sign from him, and sleep gently invaded the peaceful room. In fact it was not until a week later that the experiment was repeated. When all was over Juan, springing with great agility from the bed, went over to his own bed and, returning with a packet of cigarettes, gave one to Martin who accepted it as well as the lighted match his cousin held out. They lay down together, contentedly smoking, when presently there was a stir at the other end of the room and little Manuel came over to them.

'For me too, Juanillo,' he said in a conspiratorial whisper. 'Give me a cigarette. I implore you, brother.'

'You are too young, my child.'

'I am only a year younger than Martinito,' objected the other. 'And if you don't give me a cigarette, Juan, I shall tell Mamá that you made Martin smoke and also that you were both naked.'

Juan shrugged his shoulders. 'What is more natural?' he enquired in a bored important voice. 'The nights are getting warmer. Summer is on its way.'

'It is not so warm,' cried his brother. 'Not so warm at all. The night is fresh. Do you want me to tell Mamá that you were naked and smoking together in the one bed? Yes? Ah, you would enjoy that, no doubt.'

'You little fool,' his brother growled. 'Be careful. *Cuidado*, I say, or I will kill you. Yes I will. And this is how I shall do it.' He leapt to his feet and took his brother by the throat: 'Like this, do you feel it, little brother? Like this! Ha ha! Ha ha! But as you know now what your destiny will be I will show you how kind and good your brother can be for you. Here is a cigarette, you see it? But – no, don't move yet – give me your word, your sacred promise. No syllable to Madrecita. Say it.'

'God in Heaven, I hate you Juan! I hate you, you foul toad! I hate you because I must obey you. Though you will never kill me, because if you did they would kill you! And you are a coward. You are afraid of the law as you are afraid of Mamá. Yes!'

'I afraid of Mamá? Why should I be afraid of my beloved Mamá?'

'I do not know, Juan. But you must be afraid of her, or why must I promise not to tell her what you do? Smoking cigarettes and lying naked in bed with our pretty cousin. Ha! Why are you afraid she should know your habits – no, do not threaten me again, Juan! I beg you, I implore you! *A rodillas*!'

And he actually went on his knees before his brother, whom the action somehow seemed to satisfy.

111

'I forgive you, miserable one!' Juan chanted magnanimously.
'I forgive you. Back to your bed, foul viper.'

And Manuel, rubbing his throat, went to his own bed, the
cigarette Juan had thrust between his fingers still in his
possession. Presently he came tripping back.

'May I beg for a light, *señorito*?' he asked in mock humility.

He got it, and with a solemn and, to Martin, ludicrous
dignity, they both said, 'Goodnight, my brother,' and all was
peace.

But that night the old black dream came back again. It was
the night at the theatre and all the friends of the Revolution
were seated together in the box, and the man who once had been
Martin was as usual on his feet and hiding from the audience
behind the heavy curtain. And the swallows – or were they bats?
– were flying round and round in the dusky air below the central
hanging chandelier. And the woman's lovely voice was floating
above the music of the orchestra as she sang of flowers and of
Margherita . . . and now he was walking over the bridge with
Giovanni, watching the moonlight rippling on the water, and
crossing the road and parting at the door of the house on the
corner, and then . . . then there was nothing but darkness for a
while until the morning light came into the room and he was
sitting fully dressed on the sofa by the window, and the same old
terror was in his heart and the same thundering *knock! knock!* and
the same marching feet of armed men on the stone floor outside,
and then the door flew open and *he* stumbled across the step that
led down into the room, and his hat fell down over his forehead
and he pushed it back, revealing those merciless eyes close set in
the dark pallor of the face. And Martin woke, screaming.

The room was still dark but across it came a figure: his cousin
Juan in his nightshirt, and gently, soothingly – so there was
another side to Juan's nature, was there? – he lifted the boy and
carried him over to his own bed, murmuring words that Martin
only half understood. He found himself wondering what the
words meant and at the same time thinking of Jack Hunter long
ago, and then Juan, his arms still around him tenderly, not

112

amorously, began to sing a little song:

> *Duerme, duerme,*
> *Niño mio,*
> *Sueños dulces,*
> *Duermete!*

With the words reassuringly in his ears Martin fell into sleep, and was hardly surprised when he understood gradually that the tune, not at all a typically Spanish one, was familiar to him. It was the tune that Father used to sing to him when he was a little boy, years and years ago:

> I'se a goin' to bite you
> I'se a goin' to bite you
> I'se a goin' to bite you
> All down here . . .

So Martin Weldon, writing from Seville to London one fine day in April:

'My darling Mother,

A thousand thanks for your lovely letter. I was so glad to get it. I suppose you must be up to your two eyes with Tina's getting married to this what's his name at all? Father said something about it before he went back to London but seemed not to have met the young man. You didn't say much about him in your letter, but I hope he'll be all right and make our Tina happy, if anything could do that.

The Semana Santa is nearly over now – today is Good Friday – and God forgive me I am glad because though it was wonderfully beautiful, yet to me somehow it was a bit overwhelming with the constant processions and the singing and the music, and those frightening fellows dressed in long robes and tall pointed hoods with two holes cut out for their eyes, and the *pasos* going past with holy images of Our Lord and Our Lady and all the rest of it, and all blazing candles and jewels. Everyone going mad all over the town singing and dancing, and now it is nearly over and they're waiting already for the *Feria de Abril*, when all the country people come in dressed in the national costume, and the gipsies too, hundreds of them, coming out of their caves. On Easter Sunday I am to be taken to a bull fight with Aunt Luisa and the boys and an old man called José María Something, Dacosta I think, and he is supposed to be a relation of Father's. Poor Teresa is crying her eyes out because Aunt Luisa won't let her go. Bull fights are for men and boys and grown-up ladies, she says, but not for young girls.

I am making a lot of progress with my Spanish so tell Father won't you darling when you give him my love. And love too to beautiful Debby and to Tina the Terror and to my dear little Maimie and Sweet Scatty Peg. And most of all to yourself my own darling Mother.

Your loving son, Martin.'

At the bull fight on Sunday afternoon, Martin was fascinated by the unreality and splendour of the picture before him. The amber-coloured arena was cut in half, one of cool shadow where they and the other favoured ones were expensively sitting, and the other, sunny side a blinding glitter, where the poorer people were sweating and shouting as the entrance of the combatants began. Marching in to the emphatic rhythm of the band came the picadors on horseback, the banderillos and the matadors on foot in their brilliant coloured jackets, white shirts and narrow scarlet ties, close-fitting satin breeches of apple green, gold, wine-purple and silver, rose-pink stockings and brave black hats and low-heeled gleaming shoes. The president, dressed in black, stood proudly in his box and was saluted silently with a flourish of their hats by the band of heroes as the trumpets rang out with so ominous, so celestially final a note. Death and victory together hung in the quivering air as the key to the *torril* – the bull's den – was thrown down, and the howling

114

of the thousands who watched and waited dropped suddenly into the deepest silence in the world, a silence of the tomb as one of the men, after running across the sand and disappearing into an archway, reappeared in the wake of the black sacrificial beast which came rushing out into the light, his horned head bent low, then tossing back and plunging low again, and a long faint *A-a-h*! came back from the spectators, and then the deadly silence fell again, and the first movements of the combat were begun.

It was a dream to the foreign boy who sat watching, this huge circle of shadow and blazing sunshine, this calm, indifferent azure hanging motionless above, these alternate bouts of silence and their sudden breaks when three thousand voices yelled *Olé*! and were silent again. The dream went on until the first thin stream of blood came trickling down over the black hide of the bull's neck, quite close to their party. The blood was real enough, and from that moment all was reality again, bright, sharp and unendurable. Eight times the pain and the excitement waxed and waned through the afternoon: the plunging horns, the staggering blindfolded horses, the yelling and the silences, the lightning lethal grace of the matador, the final thrust over the small red flag into the thick black head and throat and shoulder, the rushing forward of the chulos to harness the horses to drag away the carcass and sprinkle fresh sand over the places where the gouts of blood had spilt, and the making ready for the next sacrifice. Eight times the show was repeated, for today was Easter Sunday. The last bull was the biggest and most ferocious of all, and he gored three of the horses and one of the picadors before he knelt for his own last agony.

Martin, like most (though not all) non-Spaniards, could never become a true *aficionado* of the bull fight. It was too bloody and too cruelly realistic in style to appeal to a taste that had been shaped so early by the Russian Ballet, the productions he had worked in with Tree, and by the fantasies of James Barrie, given form in the stage production of *Peter Pan* among the floodlights and the flying wires of the Duke of York's Theatre. But he returned on many a blazing Sunday afternoon to watch the splendid horror, sometimes with the family, sometimes accompanied only by Tío José María and the two boys, and once in the conspiratorial escort of Pepe Gutierrez, a rather fearsome character who more than once, through sheer mischief, had got Martin into trouble.

'I dare you, little Martin,' he said, one dazzling noonday in May, 'to walk slowly – slowly, mark you – without a hat across the Plaza Nueva from the corner of the Sierpes to the centre and back to the Apartamiento. Aha! you will never do it of course: you English – no, do not interrupt me – you English are all brag and swagger and at heart you are cowards. Yes! So now, my bold – all right, I will say *Irlandés* as the magnificent difference appears to you of such importance – my noble *Irlandés*, you will do it! No? Yes – you will – *Olé, Olé*, Martinillo, away then let us go!' So that evening Martinillo had a bad headache, a high temperature (Aunt Luisa's left eyebrow had never been busier than when she surveyed the family thermometer), and was violently sick in the lavatory.

'*Nuestro médico*,' cried Aunt Luisa, 'Juanito, take a note *at once* to Doctor Lopez: tell him that out dear Martin is suffering from an *insolación*: no, say nothing of that, I will put it in my letter, but tell him to come soon, soon, as soon as possible!'

By the time that Dr Lopez arrived it was ten o'clock and Martin was still feeling ill, and lay in bed shivering with alternate waves of heat and of icy coldness.

'Una insolación' agreed Lopez, wagging his bushy head up and down and plucking at his beard. 'You have – how you say? – one *ajajá* from the sun, you understen, ha? Bang! From the sun, oh no, not dangerous, boy! No. Here we give you—'

He took a small tin box from his bag and daintily extracted something that looked like a well-sucked date. Then, between the fingers of his left hand, another.

'Sanguijuelas,' he announced, smiling.

'Que son? En inglés?' Martin enquired.

'En inglés? Ay do mi, no lo sé. Pero chupan la sangre. Muy

sano, muy saludable. Sí!' He made a sucking sound with pursed lips, and placed the 'dates' (which were, of course, leeches) on each side of the boy's forehead.

'Make again healthy!' he said, and turned aside to write a prescription which he handed to Aunt Luisa.

That night Cousin Juan, in his white and blue shirt, knelt by Martin's bed in a condition of great emotion and said, 'Thank God, you will not die, Martin *de mi alma*. But when I see that poisonous toad Pepe Gutierrez, I will kill him. It was he who made you ill, who tried to kill you. I know this wolf, this pig, this Gutierrez; he was at school with Manuel and me: he was always trying to kill people, he is a poisonous – ach! I don't know what he is, but I will kill him one day, I will strangle him like this, look! No, no! Calm: we must be calm. Be calm, Martin! Be tranquil! Sleep, my heart, sleep!'

And at last Martin was left in peace.

The next and last unfortunate adventure Martin was to undergo at the hands of the fell Pepe Gutierrez was when, in spite of Juan's warning, he went with the young villain to swim at the *Piscina del Pilar*. Or rather, to pretend to swim, for whereas young Gutierrez could swim like any fish, young Weldon could not, though he gave an impressive performance so long as his feet were firmly planted on the marble floor of the *piscina*. Pepe swiftly discovered this and made several comments of a heavily satirical nature about fish with feet and curly hair who gave unconvincing performances which wouldn't deceive a child in arms. When they had both had enough of the water they climbed out and dried themselves, and Martin discovered he had no comb, so he asked Pepe for a loan of his. But his Spanish, though comprehensible and shamelessly fluent, was far from being perfect, so when he asked Pepe to lend him his comb he overlooked the 'i' which comes between the 'e' and the 'n' in the Spanish word, and pronounced *peine* like *pene*, which has quite a different meaning. Pepe regarded him with brief mockery for a moment, suppressed an obvious desire to laugh, then assumed an expression of lamb-like innocence and, shrugging his shoulders, replied sweetly, 'I haven't it with me; ask that chap over there.'

So Martin did, and wondered vaguely why 'that chap', who was a youth of about sixteen, started violently and snorted? And why did he look over at Pepe who was making signs at him behind Martin's back? But he sent the poor bewildered foreigner to another youth, and the same performance proceeded. The other youth sent him to yet another, and this went on until nearly half the bathers, all of them drying themselves busily, wore contorted, mysterious smiles. At last one of them said: 'You see that fatherly old gentleman who has already dressed himself? Go to him, for surely he will give you what you want.'

Poor, silly unsuspecting Martin approached a fine-looking gentleman with grey sideburns and smart upcurling moustache, and made his request. The result startled him.

'Pero con mucho gusto, muchachito mío,' said the gentleman, and unhesitatingly, with a lurid smile, he began to open the front of his trousers.

'Perdóneme, perdóneme, señor, no es para eso!' Martin managed to gasp, and rushing back to where Pepe, in highest spirits was pulling on his clothes, he fell upon him and they had a ferocious battle, rolling together on the floor and dealing blows and kicks with unabated savagery. It all ended with Martin sitting on Pepe's chest and threatening him that he would tell Juan unless Pepe explained the whole affair to the bewildered and disappointed gentleman with the smart moustache.

Pepe promised faithfully that he would do this, but when he got to the other side of the baths the gentleman had vanished, and he contented himself by calling Martin a fool and a *bobo lugareño*, which Martin understood to mean a provincial halfwit, and they walked homewards together as far as the Alcazar Gardens, where they parted with sad and dignified expressions of disgust on both sides.

And that was the last time they met. During the rest of his stay in Seville Martin saw Pepe Gutierrez no more.

* * *

The time went rapidly by and the days grew warmer. Martin was royally entertained by Aunt Luisa and her children, and on one occasion was taken by Tío José María and the boys to a theatre in the Street of the Love of God to see a programme of dancers which included one voluptuous lady called *La Tortojada*, resplendent in a series of gorgeous dresses and embroidered shawls of Manila silk hung about with fringes that shone like the rainbow as she tossed them passionately from side to side, and whirled her hips, and gave dazzling smiles or closed her eyes and set her lips together as if she was suffering excruciating pain. And then she would glide away with sad alluring smiles and nothing would happen at all for quite a long while, until she reappeared in a red velvet riding habit and a flat broad-brimmed hat, and sang in a low nasal tone and tapped with her high-heeled boots on the stage until she seemed to make it speak of a thousand passionate messages of love, a thousand idiotic, rapidly passing dreams. Then, when the evening was almost over, a clown came jumping into the light, waving a flag of many colours and shouting '*Niña del Albaicín, la grande estrella frívola!*' and the audience began to cheer and Tío José María rose to his feet and said: 'Enough, enough. This is the last number. We go! Juan, come Manolito, Come Martín.'

'But why, Tío José? We have not seen *Niña del Albaicín*. Please let us stay.'

'No. I say, no, no, no!' came the pitiless voice. 'Your dear and beloved Mamá begged me to be sure we returned before the last number if it was . . . well, if it was of an immoral tendency. Usually, as she reminded me, this is the case with the ultimate spectacle. Ah, these *estrellas frívolas*, they are quite shameless. We go! All of us. We go!'

And off they went. But Juan discovered when they had passed through the door to the street that he had left behind him the circular comb he wore to keep his hair from blowing from side to side in the wind, and made this the excuse for returning to the auditorium where he stayed, searching for it for so long that he received a severe lecture from Tío José on his return, with

119

flushed cheeks and sparkling eyes, to agree meekly with his uncle that *Niña del Albaicín* was indeed a *sin verguenza*, a shameless one and a disgrace to her sex and her nation: 'If that is what they are like in the Albaicín, Tío José María, no wonder the gipsies there live in caves: they are not fit for good houses. Oh, shameless! Shameless!'

Then he added in a brief aside to Martin: 'But I saw her! I was quite close to her! Ah! what beauty! But coarse, little cousin: terribly coarse and *ordinaria*.'

And so it glided away, 'the Spanish year' as Martin was to call it for the rest of his life. But it did not last for a whole year for suddenly, in the first week of August, it came to an end. One day Tío José María came to the house, white in the face with emotion and fear, and shut himself up for a consultation with Aunt Luisa in the dining room. At last the two of them emerged together and Aunt Luisa summoned Martin to their presence.

Three days ago, she told him, on the fourth of August, war had been declared between England and France on the one side and Germany on the other, and that before one could count many more days Spain too might be at war as well, though Heaven only knew, Aunt Luisa cried, opening and closing her fan with a series of agitated rattling sounds, which side she – meaning Madre España – would be fighting on. 'We may all be killed, my little nephew,' she went on, 'but you must be with your own Papá and Mamá and sisters. My dear child, we shall miss you, we shall all shed tears, especially perhaps I myself and my poor Juan, who loves you more than a brother! No no, I must not cry! No . . . tranquillity! Calm!' And she sobbed and sobbed, and Martin put his arms around her shoulders and shed a few tears too, and when Teresa del Pilar came in with the two boys and they were told that war had broken out and that Martin had to return to London they all wept and howled together, and perhaps it was only Martin who realized as the tears came at last to a staggering halt, and were replaced by sniffs and sad, sad waggings of heads and rollings of eyes and exchanges of wet handkerchiefs that they had been having a perfectly glorious time.

120

Now a quietness and reality settled on them all for a few days of packing and preparation as the foreign cousin's departure drew closer. A telegram from Father arrived from London, written in Spanish for Aunt Luisa with some words in English from Mrs Weldon to her son: 'We are worried and hope you come soon darling, send a wire and Father will meet you Dover your loving Mother.'

But on the day of his departure with his one small suitcase in his hand, the storm of emotion broke out all over again when Martin, with hearty *abrazos* all round, mounted the train that was to bear him northwards to Irún, the frontier station. And Martin, sitting alone with his pockets full of ten and twenty peseta notes, and with several packets of his favourite homemade *carne de membrillo* or flesh of the quince from Aunt Luisa, of a paperback copy of Cervantes' *Novelas Ejemplares* from Uncle José María, and a photograph of Cousin Juan signed *còn mil abrazos cariñoses par mi querido Martin de su almo Juan XXX*.

The journey through France was a nightmare, with uniformed men, armed to the teeth, invading the train at every stop and searching the passengers and asking incomprehensible questions. The fields of France looked flat and desolate once the Pyrenees were left behind, and the whole countryside seemed stricken and deserted. It was war, there was no doubt about that, and even though the night was so silent it seemed to Martin's ears that there were explosions in the air far away, as though all the thunders and all the cannons in the universe were crashing their way through life and leaving catastrophe and emptiness behind them. Then, as they drew up at some great station, a throng of soldiers in uniform, their rifles slung over their shoulders, invaded the train. Baskets of sandwiches and rolls and cheese appeared, and bottles of wine and beer. One of the soldiers, grinning like a madman, forced Martin to open his mouth and be fed with food and wine, and Martin, not to be outdone, offered him a slice of the flesh of the quince which he bit into and then shared with his mates, and they all began to

121

sing in loud and raucous voices. Martin tried to sleep for a little, closing his eyes and pillowing his head on the nearest shoulder to him, and his eyelids became luminous and he saw black empty spaces of air through which plumes and blooms of fire flared and exploded.

All the while the husky voices went on singing, a tune that in the massed choir merged oddly with the rhythm of the train, and its seemingly limitless verses lilted and mingled into almost visible patterns of surging darkness and flame, jagged and broken into clouds of laughter, and faded slowly and died into oblivion until at last, with a grinding crash in his ears, the boy woke and found that it was bright daylight and he was lying on his back in an empty carriage, and the train was slowly shunting into a station. They had arrived at Calais, and everywhere French and English people jostled together, shouting to the officials about their luggage and their tickets, and when at last Martin found himself on the steamer he felt he was a hundred years old and that life had fled far away from him and disappeared into space.

England, once the bewildering ordeals with customs and police officials at Dover had been endured, did not seem at all like home. Martin understood suddenly and for the first time that Spain had changed him incurably. He would never be quite the same person again, but it was not a transformation of human love that he felt, for not one of the members of the family in the Calle San Fernando could ever take the place in his heart that his mother and father and his four sisters held. The intimacy between himself and Juan left nothing behind but a consciousness of his nature that he both resented and accepted as being inevitably within himself. Juan had revealed to him that he was growing up and that he must accept himself as he was, but this was merely a development, not a revolution. What had changed him was not Juan or the understanding of that side of his own temperament which he knew had been foreshadowed in his early childhood when Jack Hunter had saved him from his nightmare terror. That had always existed in the depths of his

122

being, and Juan had merely thrown a light onto it.

What Spain had done was to create in him a desire to draw, to paint, to make pictures of things he had seen under those limpid skies and in that burning light, things beautiful and hideous: the piles of fruit and flowers in the markets, the gipsies dancing like flames in the dim reflected lights of gloomy cafés or under the archways of bridges by the river, the sellers of delicacies in the parks calling out their wares, the heroes of the bull fight marching in their brilliant clothes, the blood streaming down over the sand, the dead black carcass being dragged away. Things he saw with his inner eye, fantastic images, unearthly lights and shadow, and a secret invisible world, that somehow, one day, he would reveal. It was Spain which had set him dreaming, something in the air of Seville that was born of sound as well as of sight, of music as well as of colour and form, of a heavenly radiance and of a dark eternal night. Yet while he was in Spain he had hardly been conscious of it.

Meanwhile, here was Dover, pallid and slate-coloured under the timid sunshine, and a cold breeze blew firmly from the sea. Presently Father was embracing him, taking his suitcase in his own hand and leading the way to the Customs House.

'All the way from Spain, eh?' said the official as he rummaged through his things. 'Sunny Spain. Oh well, it takes all sorts to make a world. Well, none of your traps is smelling of garlic, that's one good thing. Very fond of garlic the Dagoes are. Swallow it down like toffee. Supposed to be remainin' neutral in this war, I'm told. They would, the dirty dogs. Not that they'd be much of an 'and against the 'Uns, I don't suppose. Land o' mananer, as the sayin' goes.'

But when at last they were seated in the train Father said, 'You'll be seeing your mother and Peg and little Maimie in a couple of hours now. But you'll not see Deborah until tonight: she'll be coming in to supper and I suppose she'll bring her husband with her. They're all well, thank God. And tell me now, how are the cousins and the sisters and the aunts in Calle San Fernando? *Y como va el castellano? Has adelantado mucho?*'

Martin provided a vivacious, not grammatically impeccable report on the Familia Fuentes y Moreno, discreetly leaving out certain incidents, and fell back into English to ask about Tina and her husband.

Father's face darkened a little.

'Tina?' he repeated. 'Ah, the devil knows where she is or what she's doing. Your mother and I are worried about her. Ran away from that fellow she had the audacity to marry in a registry office, God forgive her, a couple of days after what she'd the cheek to call the nuptials, and we've only seen her once since then. Blew in suddenly one evening to collect some of the things she'd left behind her, and frightened the life out of your poor mother. Upon me oath, Martin, she's a holy terror. Ah, let's not talk about her yet until we see how things will turn out for her, the creature! You'd be sorry for her in a way you know, she has so many fine things about her, but sometimes I think there's something, mind you, something radically wrong in the depths of her soul . . . And little Maimie is a governess, now; did you know about that? Oh yes indeed, she's teaching the young son of an old friend of yours – what's this his name was? Leigh-Craig, that's right, Leigh-Craig. Living out at Richmond with them she is; they're rather grand and that suits Maimie of course.'

How wonderful it was to be at home again. To see Mother especially, and to eat her specialities of scrambled egg and fried rashers of bacon for tea, her seed cake and homemade raspberry jam, and to hear her say, 'You didn't change a bit, God bless you, boy, though you're a little taller, isn't he Tony? Oh isn't it desperate about this rotten old war, please God it'll soon be over, why in heaven's name do people want to go fighting each other? For what? And all for Brave little Belgium, how are you?'

For Mother had an unexpected streak of cynicism in her nature about Causes and Taking Sides, when it came to people killing each other merely because they were encouraged to do so by what she slightingly referred as 'governmental busybodies and bloodthirsty fanatics in both camps'. 'Why can't they let each other live their lives in peace? Tell me that. Tell me that!' she repeated, herself looking quite ferocious as she poured out the tea.

'We can't tell you, darling,' Scatty Peg replied in her most reasonable manner, for she was the one to whom the challenge seemed to be directed.

'The world has always been that way,' Maimie said in her quiet little voice. 'Read your history books, Mother. Nothing but wars and invasions, wars and invasions. Adam's curse, I suppose. But I love to hear a point of view like yours that longs for peace. What a contrast to the atmosphere I'm living in at the Leigh-Craigs. There's Kitty now – my dears, 'tis like living with a recruiting sergeant in woman's clothes. She's driving every young man that ever visited the house into khaki: there's Roy Pennant and dear little Foxy – Geoffrey Fox the dancer, you remember them both, Martin – well, she practically pushed them into the recruiting office and they're both in khaki now and Foxy expects to be leaving for France next month.'

'Don't speak of it!' cried Deborah, as beautiful as ever as she reclined on a sofa in the sitting room, nursing her baby, Brian. 'Don't speak of it!' she repeated with a shudder. 'My poor Tudor has got it into his head that he ought to join up. "What has it to do with you?" I asked him. 'There's no need to go; let the younger men do it. England isn't a conscript country, thank God. And anyway you're a Welshman, you're well over thirty and your place is with your wife and child." Isn't it, my angel?' she continued, holding the baby up in her arms and kissing him as fast as a sewing machine pursues its busy course. ' "Oh well," says Tudor,' she went on, the kissing over, ' "all the chaps I know seem to be going. I just feel . . . maybe I ought . . ." Well, you know what men are. Weak as water where "all the chaps they know" are concerned. Silly asses. Let's forget about the war for God's sake! Here's Martin back with us again. Tell us something beautiful, Martin. Tell us all about Seville. Are there really orange trees growing in the streets? There's a sensible country for you. *They're* not going to get mixed up in this infernal war.'

But the sensation of the evening undeniably was the sudden arrival of Tina, who after much loud knocking on the street door swept into the midst of the Weldons and cried, 'Here's the Bad Girl of the Family!'

She was dressed in black, with a long cloak and a three-cornered hat that caused Peg to say, 'My God, will you look at Dick Turpin?'

'On the last ride to York? And so I would be if I'd a broomstick,' Tina answered evenly. 'My own darling Martin, welcome to this hateful town!' she continued, having covered his face with kisses and tugged so hard at his curls that it hurt. 'You at least may be glad to see me. Or are you?' she added after a pause during which she gazed at him with her sombre eyes.

'Don't worry,' she said lightly, and went over to greet the other members of the family, talking easily and naturally in her low voice. Yet Martin and the rest of them felt, somehow, somewhere in her there was a change.

Presently she took off the three-cornered hat and threw it over to Peg.

'You can wear it if you ever take a notion to ride to York. What do you all think of my hair?'

'God forgive you: your lovely hair!' cried Mother indignantly. 'She's had it all cut off, look at her, will you look at her? Her gorgeous hair. All gone with the wind. What in Heaven's name will you be up to next?'

'It isn't *all* cut off, my pet: quite a lot left. Somebody at the Circle said I looked like the Sphinx, so I thought I'd live up to it.'

'Mind somebody wouldn't shoot the nose off you,' warned her father. 'For that's what happened to the real Sphinx.'

'It lost none of its power,' Tina replied. 'The modern Egyptians call it Abu el Khol, the Father of Terror. Is anyone going to give me a cup of tea? An idiotic drink but it can help to calm the nerves.'

'Ah, my poor pet, you're too young to be talking about

nerves,' cried Mrs Weldon, but she gave her daughter a cup of tea and laughed.

'I'm twenty-four and unfortunately married, and if you had chosen a husband like Rupert Wilson you'd know everything about nerves, my darling. A detestable individual who is Welsh like your Tudor, Deborah, but far less reassuring. Is that divine baby Tudor's by the way?'

'Such a question!' Deborah said with indignation. 'Whose else would he be?'

'Ah well, "it's a wise mother," as the saying might just as well have gone. So it is a boy? I knew it would be. I know most things before they're told to me. I knew Martin would arrive today: that's why I'm here.'

'How can you know things before they happen?' asked Maimie with her severe governess expression.

'You're so well educated, Maimie,' her sister said. 'Surely you've heard of training in divination, haven't you? There are courses in it at the Circle.'

'What is this Circle, Tina?' her father demanded. 'You never said a thing about it to anyone. When did you join it? Sort of a club I suppose?'

'I said nothing because I thought if I did you might not approve. And then I would have been obliged to disobey you, and I don't want to do that. It is headed by a Beast.'

'By a which?'

'By a man who calls himself a Beast. The Beast. But he is a very great and very singular creature.'

'What's his real name?'

'Crowley.'

'An Irishman?'

'No. Maybe his great-great-grandfather was. The name's Irish of course.'

'And what is the idea, I mean the central idea, the aim, the subject of this Circle? What do you do there? What do you talk about?'

'Magic.'

127

Mother had been listening to her husband and her daughter uneasily, for there was a faint hostility in the air between them, but now she clapped her hands with relief.

'Ah, like Maskelyne and Devant,' she cried. 'Isn't that grand now? Wonderful tricks they used to do – we saw them here in London years ago, do you remember, Tony? Before Martin was born, and even you couldn't make out how 'twas all done. But Tina, do you mean to tell me—'

'I don't mean to tell you anything at all, my pet, because you're far too sweet to be told things,' Tina half whispered, and she put her arms round her mother's neck. Suddenly then, to everybody's consternation, she broke into a flood of tears.

'Ah, me poor little girl,' her mother was whispering to her as she stroked her while the rest of the family looked aghast at the spectacle. 'Come on now, Tina, tell your mother all about it; you'll feel better when you get it off your chest.'

'It isn't on my chest, but on my soul,' Tina gasped. 'My soul, that's where it is. Is it the storm, is it the stars, is it their fire or am I in the mire? My mind changes every five minutes . . . no you can't do anything for me, my darling. Nobody can. I'll have to go through or go round it, and where will I go then? Where? No. No! I'll go round it and escape somehow. I'll be alright. I will. I'll be grand, I tell you. I must go. Goodbye my dear Mother. Goodbye my precious Martin. Goodbye to everyone. Believe you haven't seen me tonight. You haven't seen me.'

And she fled away through the door, leaving her family bewildered and uneasy.

'She's up to something,' Mrs Weldon said with the air of one who makes a remarkable discovery.

'She always is,' Deborah answered her lightly with a touch of scorn in her voice. 'Last year, just before she encountered her wonderful Rupert it was a Man: now it's a Message. A magical message, of course: it would be. She tried to get poor Tudor in her clutches last year, but 'twas no use. He just laughed at her, the creature. He's no interest at all in the uncanny and here was Tina trying to hypnotize him and telling him I was just a pretty

128

piece of nothing and the soul – no, 'twasn't the soul for she said I hadn't any – the essence, that was it, of the commonplace. Now at this moment she's wallowing in some sort of mystical blather. Up to her eyes in it, but she'll get over it. Of course she will. She's nothing but an old sensation seeker. You wait now, in a few weeks' time she'll go all political: she'll be urging young men into the army or else starting a revolution. Ah, forget about her. Martin darling, tell us all about Spain.'

CHAPTER FIVE
Irish Awakening

Two events happened in Martin's life in that first autumn of the war. The first was his discovery of a book left at Richmond by a friend of the Leigh-Craigs. It was called *Ideas of Good and Evil*, by William Butler Yeats, and as Martin read it, wading at first through the dense, mysterious pages, and later wandering through them in a rapture of joyful revelation, he knew that his life would be changed henceforth. For the first time since the age of seven, when he gazed out of the window at the London street under the falling rain, and felt a stranger in a strange and hostile land, he was conscious of Ireland once more.

Of Ireland. That was where he belonged. That was where he would return. Everything he had to do in life would be fulfilled if he could only get back. But what was there in Ireland for the likes of him, who wanted to paint and write, and maybe act again one day? What was there in Cork or Limerick, the only cities he knew, for someone who had worked with Tree and flown on a wire through the magic air of *Peter Pan*, and seen Nijinsky and Bernhardt, and watched gipsies dancing in Spain, and endured the ardours of bull fights, and had been loved by his cousin-uncle Juan Fuentes, and desired by an endless cortege of distinguished Londoners, and heard Caruso and Edvina in *Tosca*, and gazed on Murillo and Zurbaran in Seville?

Maimie had no dreams of going back to Ireland; nor had Deborah, or Tina, or even Peg, and yet here was Yeats pleading with all young Irish artists to turn their thoughts back to this land that might become 'a holy land to her own people,' back to Ireland 'where the soul of man may be about to wed the soul of the Earth.'

Mother and Father were quite happy in London where, as they pointed out, there were all the opportunities of the world waiting for young men and women of any talent or personality. No, he would be alone in his adventure if he did go back, if he followed where Yeats's finger pointed.

But the finger was pointing inexorably, and he knew that he would follow it. Yeats had said that he might have found more of Ireland if he had written in Irish, so poor Martin, his head on fire with his new-found prophet, asked his father if there was anywhere in London where he could learn the Irish language.

'Oh yes indeed. There's the Gaelic League. I know two of the members in the City – I'll introduce you if you really want to learn it. But why do you, son? My own father spoke Irish before he spoke English – he was from Clare as you know, and Clare was Irish-speaking in his day – but he never had any regard for it. Nor had anyone else as far as I know: a half-dead language for God's sake, sure what's the use of trying to blow new life into it?'

But Martin insisted, and by the following month he was attending classes at the Gaelic League in Ludgate Circus and ransacking Father Dineen's Irish-English dictionary in the Finchley Road library in order to add to his vocabulary. A complete wild-eyed fanatic he became and, with Spanish as well as English in his head, he was soon making great progress.

At the same period he joined an art school, and this was the scene of the second event of importance in his life at that time. In the studio where the first year students drew from plaster casts of classical sculptures he saw on his second day a tall dark girl with dark brown hair, a longish face, and up-slanting, luminous, green-blue eyes that watched him for a moment or two over the corner of the drawing board she held in front of her and then looked away to concentrate on her work. Presently she looked at him again, and he said:

'I've seen you before somewhere, haven't I?'

He really thought he had.

'I was thinking that about you,' she answered him. She held her drawing board at arm's length, gazing at it critically, and later on he noticed that she was looking at him from time to time

131

over the top of her drawing board.

When the morning class was finished, he and she lingered in the studio when the others had gone.

'Are you coming back to the afternoon class?' she asked of Martin.

'I suppose so,' he replied. 'But I'll not be afternooning tomorrow I think, because I want to come back to the Historic Design in the evening.'

'That's funny, I am too,' she said. 'And I can't come in the afternoon tomorrow either. Mother wants me to go shopping with her. Anyway, on we go with the pears and the bottle and glass today, I suppose. Still-life isn't madly interesting, is it? A wine glass and a bottle with a label and no wine in it, and two pears going slowly rotten. You'd want to be a Van Gogh to get anything out of that. And I'm not a Van Gogh. Are you? May I see your drawing? . . . Oh! Oh well, you may not be a Van Gogh but you've quite a touch. Quite a touch. Much better than mine, no, I'd rather you didn't look if you don't mind. What's your name?'

'Martin Weldon. What's yours?'

'Maeve Kelleher.'

'Kelleher? Then, you're Irish?'

'Half and half. My father's Irish, my mother's English. Why do you ask?'

'Oh, the name of course. Besides, you look Irish. But you sound English.'

'Yes I know. I was born and brought up here in London. Never was in Ireland in my life. But I'm going there some day. To live, I hope. Weldon . . . are you the same boy as the actor? No no, that was Anthony, wasn't it? Are you a relation?'

'A very close one. I'm him, I mean, that's me. You see, Anthony's my father's name; I took it when I went on the stage.'

'Aren't you still on the stage? No, I suppose not. You wouldn't be here if you were.'

'My voice broke you see, but it's getting all right again now. But I don't know whether I'll ever go back to the stage. I don't think I will. I don't know that I want to. I want to be a painter – maybe a writer too, maybe both – and I want to go back to Ireland.'

'Oh, so do I. It must be wonderful. My father took my mother there for their honeymoon. I long to live there. And I'm not enthusiastic about London. Are you?'

'I adored it while I was working in the theatre,' he told her. 'It seemed the centre of the whole world to me. And there are marvellous things here: the Russian Ballet and Anna Pavlova and—'

'There's no more Russian Ballet: the war has chased them all away . . . Anyway I never saw anything like that. I'm fated to be a daughter of Suburbia with no brothers or sisters and no interesting friends, until I met you.'

'But we've only just met.'

'So we have. Or have we? Is this really the first time? I feel as if we'd known each other for ages. Ages and ages! Curious, isn't it? Oh well. I'll see you this afternoon. I have to go home for lunch now or Mother will go out of her mind. Look, today's the last day at this still-life. Tomorrow it's plaster casts until the evening historics. If those pears are still extant at the end of today why don't we eat them up? Much better fate for the poor things than just being chucked into a rubbish bin.'

So that evening, after the day's work was done, they ate the still-life together, one large, overripe pear apiece, and felt, as Martin put it, 'exquisitely guilty', for under Tina's influence he had been reading a good deal of Oscar Wilde lately, and admired indiscriminately his best and worst phrases.

The night after the eating of the still-life pears, the historic ornament class came to an end at nine-thirty. As Miss Mortimer, the design professor, prepared to leave, there was an ominous flash in the dusky twilight of the sky, and presently a distant growl of thunder.

'My goodness me,' cried Miss Mortimer as she put on her hat and her new autumn coat. 'We're going to have the most frightful storm! If any of you young people want to wait on here

133

until it's over it'll be quite alright: I'll tell the caretaker not to lock up till the last one has gone. Perhaps it would be better to make a dash for it, of course; that's what I'm going to do – I'm lucky, I live only just around the corner – and it's not raining yet but I suppose it will. Goodnight to you all, and good luck!'

She hurried away, and most of the students followed her example. Soon Martin and Maeve were left alone.

Another blinding flash of lightning ripped the skies apart and suddenly the lights went out all over the room.

'Are you afraid of thunderstorms?' Martin asked.

'Not a bit, I love them,' she said. 'Let's watch it.'

Presently he saw her figure silhouetted against the bay window. She was standing at the right side of the bay and she pushed the window up with a jerk.

'Oh, listen!' she said as the lightning flashed again, and again the thunder pealed. He joined her at the open window and they leaned out into the night.

But although the rain was pouring down into the gutters with the tumultous music of invisible legions tumbling from the skies, yet all the world seemed for a moment caught up into a mysterious stillness, and there they were, the two of them, journeying slowly through wooded valleys among great mountains under a golden light of the sun.

In a vision of beauty and peace they wandered together through the forests that were filled with flickering lights and shadow; they would pause now and then to pluck fruits from the low branches, to break them apart and drink their juices; and as they looked at each other they laughed and broke the fruits and drank again.

'It was the Golden Age,' he heard her say, and then all was dark again, and they were back at the open window in a darkened room and the rain was pouring down over the London streets.

'Why did you speak?' he asked her, and she replied that she had said no word she could remember but had only thought, with a pang of regret, as they wandered through the forest, of the age of darkness and iron that waited for them, it might be, in a

134

future life when they would be banished from the valley among the mountains.

'It was sad somehow to think of that,' she added. 'But I didn't think I had said anything.'

'Was it a dream or a vision we had?' Martin asked her, and she answered: 'You saw it too, did you? Oh well, I suppose that's why we seemed to have known each other before this time.' And presently, when the storm was over, he walked her home to Willesden Green, she wheeling her bicycle beside him through the wet streets and speaking of everyday things. When they reached the garden gate of her home she asked him if he would like to come in and meet her mother, but he wanted to get to his home and walked back alone through the long suburban streets that still were filled with the invisible magic of that golden valley where he had wandered in a dream with this girl he had known in fact only for a couple of days, and who yet seemed to have shared his life in some distant country, at some remote bygone time.

'You did see it too, didn't you?' Martin murmured at the garden gate, just before leaving.

'Yes,' she answered, 'I saw it and remembered it. Because that was where we first met. Oh, thousands of years ago, I suppose.'

'I'm glad we both saw it,' he said. 'Like a memory really, wasn't it? I wonder why it came through a thunderstorm?'

And he left her without another word.

It was a strange friendship, the only real friendship Martin had known with a woman who was not his sister. Strange perhaps, because it was so passionless. There was no hint on either side of any romantic excitement, of any sexual curiosity. Yet this background of some remote and beautiful past clung often about them as they sat together at work before their easels at the school, or walked together through the streets or over Hampstead Heath, or when she visited the Weldons' home or he the Kellehers'. Maeve had no brothers or sisters, but lived alone with her mother, a tall, silver-haired lady who, although separated from her husband, was deeply Victorian in type and dressed in the nurse's uniform she had worn in her professional days in the last decade of the nineteenth century.

'I like to remember my happy days in Weymouth St,' she would say. 'Of course I was very independent according to ideas of the times. Thought nothing of riding about London in a hansom all alone. But I didn't care a rap about Mrs Grundy. Oh no. Downright old Flo me dear father used to call me. Of course, things were different in those days. None of us made up: it was considered fast. Not like your sister Tina whom you brought to tea the other day, Martin.

'I wasn't bad-looking myself as a girl. Nice fresh colour, and it was natural too. Though why I ever married Jim Kelleher I can't think. My dear mother was against it from the first. He was Roman too, or supposed to be. Never bothered his head much, though. Of course I'm Anglican. All the essentials just the same as in your Church, except that we don't bother our heads about that silly old man in Rome. Now don't frown at me. Maeve. You said yourself that Martin didn't go to church very much. Of course I knew he was Roman originally, most Irish people seem to be, don't they?

'Poor Jim. What a mistake I made. Faithless to me. Some snake-woman got hold of him. So I walked out of the house holding my child by the hand. Out I walked. But I've got over it all, and I'm very happy really doing what I can for the needy in the parish. Kelleher was your great-grandmother's name, wasn't it? Funny if you turned out to be relations, wouldn't it? From Co. Tipperary too? Ardfinnan? No! Then we must be related. You call me Aunt Florence if you like. I've always craved to have nephews and nieces. Never had any. All my dear sisters married. Except one who's a nun in Africa – Anglican, of course, not Roman – but they're all childless except me. I thank God every day for Maeve. I always craved for a daughter. And now perhaps I have a nephew. Do call me Aunt Florence. I've always craved for a nephew or a niece.'

'You're always craving for things, dear,' Maeve said. 'I think we should call you Craven.'

And from that moment Aunt Florence became Aunt Craven, and a little later, simply Craven.

Martin's life had taken on a number of aspects as deeply contrasted and as many-coloured as Joseph's coat. Maeve Kelleher and the art school absorbed his days, and the house at Richmond with Maimie and the hospitable Leigh-Craigs and their friends almost always filled his weekends. And then, on those weekdays when the arduous studies at school were done and he had walked Maeve back to her home, or entertained her at tea with his mother and sisters, or gone bicycling with her to Hampstead (for she had persuaded him to let her teach him how to manage a bicycle, to the astonishment of his family), he would meet various friends in town to see a play. Or sometimes it would be to a revue with a title characteristic of those feverish days of the First World War, *Business as Usual* or *Tonight's the Night*, starring Ethel Levy who thrilled him with her husky voice and her dresses designed by Leon Bakst, or *The Bing Boys*, in which George Robey sang 'If You Were The Only Girl in the World' to Violet Lorraine's 'If You Were The Only Boy.' Martin admired them both although Robey, unquestionably the greatest English comic of his day, never made him laugh, and this fact brought the boy back to his newly awakened sense of his own nationality, and caused him to decide that English and Irish senses of humour were of a different breed.

Sometimes there would be no show, just dinner in some restaurant in Greek or Frith or Old Compton Street; and on those warm moonlit nights, surrounded by the friends he had met mostly in the house at Richmond, some of the younger men in khaki, Martin felt he was growing up in the most select and cultivated surroundings, and learning a great deal about life. And then, to stress the violent contrasts between his amusements and occupations, there were the nights at the

Gaelic League, ironically housed in Ireton House in Ludgate Circus, where in a setting of feverish enthusiasm he would sit among young Irishmen and girls, most of them in commercial jobs in London, a few of them Londoners of Irish origin – often the most ardent among the enthusiasts, these – and study the elements of the Irish language from one Seán ó Cochlainn, a hearty fellow in saffron kilts, and later from a charming young lady, a native Irish speaker called Bríd ní Uallacháin who hailed from Ballyvourney in West Cork. Both she and Seán ó Cochlainn were delighted with Martin and his swift grasp of the half-forgotten tongue. His knowledge of Spanish made it easier for him to learn a third language than for many of the others, and all through the year of 1915 he made rapid progress, feeling completely at home in this atmosphere of fanatic Gaeldom, and he kept the paper-covered textbooks as precious possessions for years. They were called *Ceachta Beaga Gaeilge* – Little Irish Lessons – and were the work of Miss Norma Borthwick, with superb, roughly drawn illustrations in black and white by Jack B. Yeats. They were deeply admired by Martin's father, though he could never quite understand his son's passion for the language. 'My father was no enthusiast about it,' he would say, 'and of course 'twill get you nowhere. Still, as you love it so much, go ahead. It won't do you any harm. Get all the fun you can out of it.'

Travelling to and fro between his own home and the Gaelic stronghold in Ludgate Circus, Martin, seated on top of a London bus, would mouth columns of verbs and scraps of poetry from the Love Songs of Connacht as he rode through the streets darkened every night against the German bombs. For the air-raids were beginning in earnest now, and everywhere one heard talk of the Zeppelins and of the brutal Huns and of how, in the words of one of the most popular songs of the day,

When we've wound up the Watch on the Rhine,

You and I – Hurrah! we'll cry! –
Everything [*bang on drum*] will be Potsdamm fine!

It was a curious time for Irish people living in London.
Martin and his family were characteristic of their kind: united
in a deep mutual affection, but divided in their outlook on the
world situation that whirled and swayed and marched and
cheered and wept and sang about them. Tina, Peg and Martin
were the least enthusiastic for the side represented by
England and her Allies, while Father and Maimie were
decidedly inclined to it, with an eye always on what they
called Home Rule as a reward for Ireland, if Ireland played
her part as a supporter of the Allied cause. Mother and
Deborah both remained delicately aloof from the passions
that seemed to be sweeping everybody else along. Deborah
seemed to sum up this cosily domestic neutrality, when she
said one day, 'Of course I'd be delighted to sit like Susie in the
song, you know, "Sister Susie sewing shirts for soldiers". I'd
be delighted to be doing something for the poor devils out
there in France, fighting to keep us all safe, but what can I do
with Tudor wanting my entire attention about himself and his
shirts and his everything else, you see, and Baby Brian
beginning to talk. At such a rate too! You never heard
anything like it.'

And then Tina suddenly reappeared in the family circle
and drove all other thoughts aside. She had, it seemed, passed
the first initiation in her Circle, and was embarking on her
studies for the second and third when, in the midst of her
absorption in Hebrew and astronomy and casting of
horoscopes, she was suddenly seized by fear and remorse, and
decided to resign.

So, screwing up her courage to the sticking-place, she
approached the chief who was known in his own sphere
alternatively as The Great Beast or Brother Perdurabo, and
elsewhere simply as Mr Crowley, she unfolded her tale and
informed him of her decision.

At first he said nothing, but sat there smiling at her. Then at last he rose, and with a sigh stood in silence at her left side.

'So you wish to leave us?' he said slowly. 'Well . . . well, well. Beware in the future, will you not, of darkness, of blackness that will follow you everywhere and may stretch forward to follow your children. Above all and below all, my dear Suor Tina Weldon who are going to desert us – beware of monkeys.'

Suddenly he raised his left arm, brought it swiftly down, and dug the index and little finger of his left hand into her shoulder. 'I fear that monkeys will betray you and you will die in terror,' he added gently. 'Good evening, Mrs Wilson.'

Tina had a bad time for a long while after that, and her family saw little of her. She retired to her flat in St John's Wood, where she was cared for by two kindly Scottish ladies, two sisters to whom she was devoted, and where she was paid for by her despised and rejected husband Rupert who, as Mother said, turned out to be 'not the worst of all, God help him. Although 'tis the least he could do for her, the poor child, for wasn't it he introduced her to all that nonsense? Devil's work, that's what I'd call it.'

So throughout the rest of that year of 1915 little was seen of Tina by her family, and Martin more than the others missed her badly. So did Maeve Kelleher, in whom Tina had taken a great interest.

'A remarkable girl,' she had pronounced. 'Quite remarkable. Stick to her, Martin.'

He stuck to her. As long as she lived he stuck to her, and though nobody seemed able to understand this odd, fervent, unromantic friendship, it was the simplest and most natural relationship to the two people concerned, both of whom were firmly convinced that it had its roots in some former chapters in the history of their souls.

Yes, it was in their souls that the attachment lived, far more than in their hearts and far, far more than in their bodies; and the consciousness of this came from Martin's growing

140

awareness of his own temperament, and from Maeve's complete understanding and acceptance of this; perhaps, too, from an equally complete coolness and indifference to what she called 'that side of life' in herself. At eighteen she was two years older that Martin, sixteen now, in the spring of 1916, and they spent so much of their time together that people would sometimes ask, 'Do you ever think of getting married in a year or two's time, you two?' And while the question was embarrassing to Martin, it gave the girl no trouble at all, and she would answer simply, 'No, it has never occurred to either of us and it never would.'

But they both were conscious of a long and varied series of encounters that had passed centuries and centuries before this present one, and when a distant family connection between them was traced – their great-grandmothers had been cousins – and Maeve's mother, all excitement at the discovery, had cried, 'Then I really *am* your Aunt Florence, I mean Craven, and that must be why you're such chums: it's family feeling you see, and isn't that lovely?' her daughter had answered, 'I don't think it's that sort of family at all, dear.' Not exactly coldly she had spoken, but very decidedly.

'And yet,' Martin observed one day in a discussion with his remote cousin, as Maeve called herself, 'I don't believe you were in that last life. The Italian nightmare I mean, when Giovanni and I walked to my home across the bridge and Daddy with the Hard Hat arrested me on that ghastly morning.'

'No, I don't feel I had anything to do with that,' she answered. 'Our encounters I think were all much earlier. And the one in the great valley that we relived in the thunderstorm that night, perhaps that was the earliest of them all.'

Meanwhile Martin went to the Slade every day – the youngest student ever admitted – and he drew, like the others, sitting astride a structure known in that famous school as a Donkey, a drawing board propped up on what seemed the back of a donkey's neck. Drawing daily from the nude: one day a male model, the next a female. And some days the professors, Tonks and MacEvoy and Rees and 'dark W. W. Russell' inspected his work and were kindly and helpful but never, he felt, wildly impressed. The truth was that his mind was too cluttered with other passions: the reading of Yeats and AE, the study of the Irish language, the growing determination to live for the future in Dublin.

And he had already started, when the hours at the Slade were over, on a series of drawings in black and white, water colour and gouache, that expressed more of himself than any drawing, however faithful and meticulous, of the male or female body. They were fantastic in concept, these pictures he was making almost in secret, although he would show them from time to time to Maeve or to Maimie or Peg, who gave him what his nature most needed: encouragement. There were pictures of Irish mountains in moonlight or twilight or dawn, and they are alive with unearthly creatures of the underworld, of faeries and satyrs and the half-human forms of cloud and storm, and the veiled faces of forgotten gods. That was the world Martin loved and wanted to love wholeheartedly, though his life was already torn between it and the hilarious, sentimental and often sensual hours he spent with his admirers, all of whom were much older than he, far more worldly wise, far less mystically ambitious. Perhaps that was why nothing he did was completely itself, why there always seemed some other alien quality in everything he touched, and why, in later years, he was to describe those early pictures and many later ones as 'a rollicking compromise between William Blake and Aubrey Beardsley'. There was perhaps a little of Arthur Rackham too, although he never attained that dim and foggy monochrome of subtle colour that broods over Rackham's work, any more than he ever achieved or even endeavoured to achieve the essential ecstatic holiness of Blake, or the exquisite leering corruption of Beardsley.

* * *

Deborah's prophecies about Tina and the violent contrasting phases seemed on the edge of fulfilment during the spring days of 1916. She had recovered from her nervous breakdown and was a frequent visitor to her family, and there was no more discussion of magic, of the study of Hebrew, of dark hints about demons or apparitions with wings and eyes of flame. Irish nationalism was her latest and most vehement obsession, and although she expressed no desire to join the Gaelic League (for she had, she said, little faith in the language movement) she blazed like a furnace when the news came through in the London papers of the Easter Week Rising in Dublin, and defended it with passionate eloquence.

It was Tuesday evening when Father burst into the kitchen where Mother, Martin and Peg were sitting together.

'The madness of it! The madness of it!' he cried, in despairing tones. 'Dublin all in flames and British troops being sent over in their thousands, ah, God forgive these young hotheads. They'll ruin us all yet. Well, there's the last hope for Home Rule gone, in my lifetime anyway. Lost forever maybe. Listen to this now . . .'

And there followed a lengthy reading of the English view of what was called 'this stab in the back' with a peppering of emotional comments from Father: ' "Stab in the back" is what they call it. Well, could you blame them in a way? Getting in German help too, or trying to: listen to the Proclamation, you see, here's Pearse's signature – I thought he was a poet or a schoolmaster or something – and James Connolly, he's a labour leader of course and Joseph Mary Plunkett and Tom Clarke – my God, that's the old Fenian lad, I thought he was dead years ago – and a reference – did you hear it? – to "gallant allies": that's the Germans you see. My God what a tragedy: what a tragedy!'

Maimie, who had come home for the Easter holidays, was the next to arrive, and she too had newspapers in her hands and was overcome with a sort of sad indignation, and convinced that the Rising was a terrible mistake.

143

'Ireland's gone mad,' she said, 'don't you agree, Mother? What a crazy wicked thing to do.'

'The whole world seems to me to have gone mad,' her mother answered sadly. 'I can only hope to God the trouble doesn't spread to Limerick. I'd be very worried about my sisters. Poor Ellen, poor Kate!'

'Mother! What a personal, domestic point of view!' Peg cried. She was speaking for the first time since the news had broken through, and the attitude she took surprised them when she added, 'I don't know – I may be wrong – but I think it's a wonderful thing in a way. Wonderful! A little handful of men up against the greatest power in the world to take what their conquerors wouldn't give them. Why can't the English understand? With all their talk about brave little Belgium standing up against German occupation wouldn't you think they'd see it's the same thing with Ireland? But of course as it affects their own interests they won't see, they just won't see.'

'The case is different,' her father retorted. 'The Germans brutally invaded Belgium only two years ago. The English invaded Ireland – at the invitation of an Irishman, remember that – more than seven hundred years ago. It goes back in history, and there are certain advantages – not many, but there are a few – that Ireland has gained out of that long occupation. This is not the moment to strike at England.'

'I think it is exactly the moment,' Tina's deep voice proclaimed as she swept into the kitchen. 'I think it is a magnificent gesture of Ireland's at last from what was rapidly becoming a little sad, beaten, tamed, conquered, submissive rabbit. Pearse has said it all: "It is Easter Monday! Christ has risen from the tomb! Ireland had risen from slavery." '

Tina went on for a long time, with fierce gestures and flashing eyes, and in their hearts Martin and Peg found themselves agreeing with her.

'I wonder what Mac thinks about it all?' the boy said suddenly. 'He's back in Ireland, you know.'

'Yes, but he's not in Dublin, thank God,' Maimie assured

144

him. 'I'd a letter from him yesterday, he's touring with a little theatre company, he's in Westport in County Mayo.'

'Now there's a lovely boy for you,' Mother said. 'And wasn't he very wise to get out of London before conscription came in, for everyone says it's coming in now? Thank God you're past the age for it, Tony,' she continued, looking at her husband. 'And thank God you're not old enough, Martin, and won't be, please the good Lord, until this desperate old war'll be over. Sure, poor Mac'd be no good to them anyway,' she went on. 'Can you imagine him with a rifle in his hand? He wouldn't know which end it went off at, God bless him. But I wonder what is he doing in Ireland at all?'

'I told you before, he's on tour, he's playing leads in some touring company that goes round the country towns,' Maimie explained. She was blushing a little, which was not like her, and her mother's romantic heart went without hesitation on the scent.

'A letter you had from him, did you?' she said, 'Isn't that grand now? Tell me, do you often write to each other?'

'Ah, he writes now and again,' Maimie replied, 'But I don't always answer. To tell you the truth, I don't altogether approve of him running back to Ireland like that, when so many men – Irish as well as English – are risking their lives to win this war.'

'And what about the men who've risked their lives in the Rising?' Martin cried out suddenly.

'You're perfectly right,' Peg agreed. 'There'll be death sentences for all the leaders if they're beaten, and of course they'll be beaten in the end.'

'As long as it's all over soon, please God, England at war with Germany and thousands of Irishmen fighting on the same side with England, and now a few thousand fighting against England and getting help from the Germans. Ah, 'tis all too bad and mad for us to do anything about it except to pray to Heaven to put an end to it.'

'It'll be over in less than a week, I'm sure of that,' was

Father's opinion. 'This tragic business in Dublin, I mean.'

'And then the executions will begin,' Tina muttered. 'You wait and see. The English will show no mercy, you can be sure of that.'

'Ah indeed, they've a great talent for making martyrs out of people. If they were to round this up and give the leaders a couple of months in jail, they'd be the laughing stock of the country before the summer was here.'

'Which country, Mother?' Maimie asked.

'Ireland, of course, where else?'

So the Weldons were sharply divided, one member against another, which neatly and disastrously followed the pattern of the nation from which they had sprung, though their family affection remained untroubled from the first moments of the Easter Week Rising to the last. And it was perhaps because of this that Martin, young as he was, discovered for the first time a theory that clung to him all through his life, and this was that one of the few Irish virtues that was real and not imaginary lay in the fact that most of the people were capable of abstract emotion, and that while they could resent the ruling spirit of a nation, resist it and rise in arms against it, they felt no hatred of the people of that nation, for these were often among their most beloved friends.

The redoubtable Katherine Leigh-Craig however, or Kitty as she preferred to be called by her intimates, was not of this easy-going breed, nor did she attempt to disguise her violent resentment at the turn things had taken. She was 'jolly well disgusted', as she wrote in a brief letter to Maimie, who for over a year had been her son's governess, 'at this stab in the back your dear little country has seen fit to give us, and quite frankly (it is always best to be frank) I don't think that any of us would feel comfy together again. I'm so sorry. Yours sincerely, Kitty Leigh-Craig.'

So that was that and, although she had not officially dismissed Maimie, it amounted, as Maimie's mother observed, 'to the same thing, God forgive her,' and she added with as much pity as she could muster, 'Aren't people very hard?'

The letter arrived a week or two after the capitulation of the rebel leaders, and Maimie, when she had read it to her mother, shed a few tears and fled into the sitting room where she was confronted by the sight of Peg and Martin huddled in each other's arms on a sofa, weeping bitterly.

'Ah, what are you two crying about? she demanded. 'Did you hear my news? No, you couldn't have done, Oh, Pegeen! Oh Martin! I'm sacked!'

'And Countess Markievicz is sentenced to death!' Peggy cried. 'Isn't it desperate, isn't it awful? Ah, try to cheer up, Martin, cheer up darling. Maybe they'll release her. Yes, they're sure to release her.'

'They won't, they won't!'

'Ah cheer up, my darling. Try not to cry any more.'

'Oh my God, how terrible.' Maimie was saying. 'How terrible . . . and it makes this seem sillier and pettier than ever.'

But Martin and Peg were all sympathy for Maimie, and Peg, when she had read the letter, cried indignantly, 'What an old devil!' For she was not yet twenty-two and thought of a woman of forty-three as she would have thought of the Hag of Beare.

It was Maimie who brought the talk back to Easter Week.

'They won't shoot her,' she said softly. 'The most they'll do is to change the sentence to imprisonment for life.'

Martin missed the Richmond weekends very much at first, though he fully realized that, even had they continued, they would not have been, as Kitty had said, very 'comfy' for Irish guests who felt as he did. He recalled with sadness a recent visit, when he had shared a bedroom with an actor called Kenneth Rowe Davison, an Englishman of the quiet, cultivated type and a fervent convert to the Catholic Church. Kenneth had disapproved of Martin's neo-pagan leanings to the ancient gods, but was full of sympathy for many of the

147

interests of the young Irish boy who, he had decided, would doubtless in the end come back wholeheartedly to what he called 'the feet of Our Lady'.

Because of his religion, Kenneth had been commissioned into an Irish regiment, the Munster Fusiliers, and his enthusiasm for Ireland (where he had never in his life set foot) and for all things Irish, knew no bounds, from the friends he had made among his fellow officers and their men to the acting of Sara Allgood, Máire O'Neill and the rest of the Abbey Theatre players, whom he had seen on their early visits to London. It was largely the reason for his attraction to Maimie, though he regretted that she had got 'so anglicized', and to Martin who was, he declared, less anglicized than his sister, and with whom he had so many interests in common. Yeats's poetry and prose, for example, and the drawings of Aubrey Beardsley, and *The Playboy of The Western World*. There were a hundred different subjects they discussed together on that weekend visit with Captain Kenneth, as his hostess Kitty proudly called him (though she wasn't keen about the Munster Fusiliers), his one free leave visit from France for a long time to come.

'Simply everybody is sharing this weekend, Captain Kenneth,' she apologized, 'I'm really ashamed. I've had to put you in with young Martin Weldon. Hardly a companion for a man of your age, but I know you know each other and get on well, and he's quite an intelligent boy. But Captain Kenneth, do me a great favour: don't encourage the boy to smoke, will you? I know he's sixteen, but he seems such a child except when he gets onto the theatre, and even my husband, who is very sensible in most ways, keeps on offering him cigarettes and the boy's not playing any parts at the moment, and I know his people are as poor as church mice.'

Martin supposed it was because the Captain seldom smoked himself that he never offered him a cigarette until the third and last night of the visit. And then, when he had packed up his bags, undressed, and said unusually long prayers, even

148

for him, at the side of his bed, he got in between the sheets, pulled out a packet of Players and, leaning over towards Martin, offered him one.

'I hardly smoke at all nowadays,' he said. 'Gave it up almost completely because my lungs are supposed to be weak like poor Beardsley's. What's more, I sort of promised Kitty not to encourage you to smoke because Teddy and Fuz and even Geoffrey keep offering you them. Well, this is a special night in a way, so we'll both be absolute devils and smoke. Because you see, Martin, I'll never see you again. Not on this earth anyway. No, don't look startled, my dear young friend, I'll never see you again. I go back to France in the morning and in five days' time I'll be dead. I know that as sure as I know there's a God in Heaven. Now don't be sad, Martin. I wouldn't say anything about it, but you're such a wonderful chap and somehow – I don't quite know why – I had to tell you. So good night, my dear very good and very dear friend, and goodbye. Funny way to celebrate a farewell, isn't it? Smoking, which neither our hostess nor my doctor think we ought to do. Goodbye, Martin.'

Martin, instead of saying goodnight, sat up in bed, still smoking, and cried all in one breath: 'Oh Kenneth if that happens God forbid it should but if it does will you come and tell me, will you?'

His companion, looking straight into his eyes through a haze of golden lamplight and the last blue cloud of his cigarette smoke said: 'Yes, Martin, if God allows it I will. I'll come back to you and tell you.'

Then they both stubbed out their cigarettes and Kenneth turned out the lamps.

Next morning when Martin woke the room was empty. Kenneth was gone. So too were his suitcases and all his belongings. There was nothing to remind Martin of his companion but a faint, familiar scent of brilliantine in the air. But a week later the official news came from France that Captain Rowe Davison had been killed in action at Mons.

There had been no ghostly visitation in dream or waking: no moment of foreboding, nothing at all. It was not until twenty years later that the promise was kept.

The execution of the leaders of the Easter Rising had blurred the memory of Captain Kenneth, and the trial and execution of Roger Casement helped further to dim Martin's remembrance of that last night with his English friend. As spring passed into summer, Martin and Maeve became increasingly obsessed with their plans to live in Ireland in the future. Deborah lent a sympathetic ear, and surprised them both by suggesting she should accompany them as Tudor was with the British army in Italy and she was all alone.

'I think Dublin might be a gorgeous place to live in,' she decided, and wrote to Tudor for his approval. But this was not met with any success at all. 'No, my dearest wife, a thousand times no!' Tudor wrote, and underlined the second 'no' three times: 'Dublin has become a city of riots and disorder and I could never be happy at the thought of your living there. Again I say NO!'

'Ah, how I wish I were not so old-fashioned,' said Deborah, 'But I am, you see. Just a dreary old-fashioned obedient wife.'

Mrs Weldon was not enthusiastic either, but for different reasons:

'You want to go back to Ireland?' she asked in astonishment. 'Ah, for Heaven's sake Martin, why? When you've done so well in London and you've so many friends and admirers? And Teddy Swete offering you a part in the new show at the Haymarket he's going to produce there after Christmas is over, and there's a big vogue now for good-looking lads in their teens, weren't you telling me yourself how he said he could get parts for you at any time in the West End? And he and Geoffrey Leigh-Craig are both helping with your fees at the Slade. And what'll you do anyway? No proper theatres - oh yes, the Abbey, I know, sure all they do there is old plays about tinkers and things, not your style at all I'd say. And oh yes, poor Arthur Ellsworthy too, so devoted to you, and getting that drawing of yours into *Punch* and all. Ah Martin, child, think about it before you go lepping over to Dublin. Sure this old war'll be over next year, long before you're old enough for the British to call you up, God forgive them if they bring in conscription at all. I know you wouldn't want to fight for them, why would you? But anyway there's two years yet before you'd be old enough. Now don't go doing anything rash you'd regret, and don't go fighting for those hotheads in Ireland, whatever you do. What do *you* think about it, Tony?'

'The boy,' her husband answered loftily, 'will do whatever he wants to do. He always has and always will, and 'tisn't you or I could stop him.'

Peg was wholeheartedly on the side of the Dublin plan, and so, in an absent-minded fashion, was Tina whenever she made an appearance in the family circle, which was seldom, for most of her time was spent these days with new friends involved in conscientious objecting and at meetings to protest against conscription, where she delivered speeches of a ferocious and warlike character. Most annoyed she became when her father pointed out her inconsistency in the matter.

'And who wants to be consistent?' she demanded. 'Who is consistent in this period of hysteria and murder? What I and my friends demand is freedom for the individual, freedom to be at peace, to live our own lives and not be driven to and fro like a lot of consistent obedient sheep. As for Martin, if he wants to live in Dublin and devote his life and his talents to Ireland, let him do it, of course. Where is the sense, where is the intelligence in making laws that force the individual to slavery even when it's done in the name of consistency? No, you go off to Dublin, Martin, there's more clearsightedness there, I'm certain, than in this well-regulated hell-hole of a country. "Come on young men of London Town" indeed! Mad muddle-headed bloody-minded bastards, the whole lot of them.'

'There's no need for foul language, Tina,' Maimie reproved her, 'Although I agree with you about Martin. He's learned to love his own country through the greatest poet alive, and if he wants to serve her in his own way he must do it. But be advised by Mother, Martin dear,' she went on. 'Don't get too involved with the extremists over there. They're as bloody-minded as any of the Imperialists in this country, and extremists are always a nuisance in the end. But if you keep your head and work hard at your drawings, and those designs you're doing, you should do well for yourself in Dublin. At least I think so. And what a chance for Dublin to get you!'

'Hear, hear!' Peg shouted suddenly. 'All the young men of talent came swarming over to London – all of them from Farquhar and Congreve to Wilde and Shaw until Yeats came along. You'll be helping to make Dublin a real capital again, Martin, and good luck to you!'

And so the year wore itself away with a mingling of hesitation and encouragement, and the surprise that outshone all others was Maeve's mother, Aunt Craven as she was now invariably called, for she, after a series of bronchial colds and lengthy discussions with her doctor, said one day to her daughter: 'Maeve dear, Dr Hargreaves seems to think London is bad for me. My poor chest, you know, and all this clay soil and these winter fogs. Oh dear, well, he says that sea air should do me ever such a lot of good, and what a pity we couldn't find some nice place near the sea. Might make a new woman of me, he says. So what about your plan? I thought it crazy at first I admit, still you never know – I mean about going off to live over there with your clever young cousin Martin, and I could take good care of you both as his mother can't be there. Is he still determined to go?'

'Too good to be true,' Maeve had said, her languid London voice swelling to an unusual enthusiasm. 'So we'll settle everything and go off in the spring. Shall we? Shall we? Perhaps we could get there by St Patrick's Day. Oh Martin, just think.'

But they didn't do that. St Patrick's Day was spent as it had been spent for the last three years, in the rhapsodic excitement of the annual Gaelic League concert at the Albert Hall, and now in 1917, with the memory of last year's Easter Week in every Irish head, the rhapsody and the excitement reached fever pitch.

More than last year, more, oh much, much , oh, infinitely more than the year before that, for that was only 1915 for God's sake, and nobody but the most informed and powerful of the Irish Republican Brotherhood had a notion of what was mounting to a flame in the hearts of Pearse and Connolly and the rest of those fiery spirits who were to strike the blow for Ireland once again and blow the smouldering embers of ancient hope to flame. And now they had done it, and they had died for it, and Ireland's ring of mountain tops was blazing with holy fire like a crown on the heads of the Daughters of Houlihan, and there were the singers and the reciters of old songs and stories, and never a microphone within sight or hearing to blur or blast the lovely voices. There was Máire nic Shiuílaigh like a chaste image of ivory with a light in her face and a voice of pure silver, and she was calling on the words of Fanny Parnell and asking, 'Shall mine eyes behold thy glory, oh my country?' And all the Weldon children rose in a frenzy and added their voices to the rest.

No thought in their heads about the disillusion that ten, twenty, forty or fifty more years would bring. There was no time in 1917 to think of the cruel slow disillusion lying ahead, so many hopes and dreams fulfilled, so many dreams and hopes turned into lost regretful shadows.

No, it was a wonderful year, a great and glorious year of starfire and golden flames, and when Martin was bidding his mother farewell – no, not farewell but *Slán go fóill*! the Irish version of *au revoir*, for which there is no English equivalent, she whispered to him: 'I still don't know are you doing the right thing or not, my darling and my only son, but God knows if I had my way I'd come with you. But you know I

153

must stay with Father, and he must stay where his work is. God bless my dear boy now and forever, and I'll be over to you for a few months in the summer with Peg or Maimie or the two of them if we can manage it, we'll be together again, please God. Goodbye, goodbye – no: *Slán go fóill*!'

She didn't come with him to Euston Station, for she knew she'd only make a holy show of herself if she did, and she wouldn't want to upset him. So Father and Tina accompanied Martin to Euston where they were joined by Maeve and Aunt Craven, and Tina sat for a while in the train between her brother and Maeve, holding tightly to their hands. She said no word as she and Father kissed them goodbye, but her dark eyes glistened, and Father's voice as he whispered 'Hasta la vista, hasta luego! Slán go fóill!' had a vibration and a depth that Martin had never heard before.

That was the night of the 26th March, 1917.

CHAPTER SIX

The Hill of Howth

'We arrive on the 27th,' Maeve said thoughtfully as, the long journey over, they followed the two porters and their luggage from the quayside to the street. 'And I was born on the 27th December, 1897, and ever since then all things, good and bad alike, have happened to me in sevens.'

'Now that's only superstition, dearie,' her mother gently rebuked her. 'Oh, what lovely air. So soft and wild and playful. Do you feel it, Martin? Oh look, and the sun's coming out so brilliantly and just after we arrived I was afraid it was going to rain . . . well, it has a name for it, hasn't it? "Erin the tear and the smile," you know. It was always tumbling down on us during our honeymoon. Well, never mind that, it's getting lovely now. Lovely! I think we're going to be very happy here.'

But they only stayed for two weeks in Dun Laoghaire, still in those days known as Kingstown in honour of some British royal visit, and not to return to its original name for many years. But whatever you called it Dun Laoghaire was, apart from its twice-daily excitement of the arrival and departure of the mail boat, a dull, remorselessly suburban place, with its row after row of consequential shops, its orgy of trams, its high, forbidding walls.

For two weeks they lodged at a red house with a bay-window sitting room whose air of comfortable Protestant security had a curiously unstable quality, as if at any moment something rather upsetting might happen: an echo perhaps of last year's Easter Week events, and of the faint but constant presence of the European war, so far away yet so imminent. Then they moved for a while to Sandymount, to comfortable furnished rooms in a house by the sea. And across the bay on the northern horizon there rose the beautiful shape of the Hill of Howth.

Four years before, a *Peter Pan* tour had included Dublin, and Martin and Maimie had explored the hill and decided that they would live there one day. Now the magic of that rocky headland – azure, deep purple, translucent grey, faint rose as the sun and clouds chased each other over it – seemed to Martin and Maeve to deepen in wonder and mystery through their knowledge of its stories, learned from Yeats's poetry, and the legends gathered by Lady Gregory of the cave where Grainne, the daughter of the high king, had fled with Diarmuid from her marriage to Fionn mac Cumhail, and had at last compelled him to be her lover. That was in a cavern under the cliffs of Beann Eadair of Leinster, before the invading Danes had named the place Hovad, and the English in later days renamed it Howth.

'But its real name is Beann Adair,' said Maeve firmly. 'And it's there we'll be living next year. I'll get Craven to look for a cottage for us.'

But Sandymount was their home for the rest of the year, a happy one in spite of Martin's being struck down with typhoid fever in August. Craven, with all her Weymouth Street *fin-de-siècle* experience at her back, nursed him at home for two fever-stricken weeks until Dr Molloy decided that things would be better for everyone concerned if the boy went into hospital. So Martin was carried into Cork St Fever Hospital where he lay for several days of delirium and several nights of agonizing hunger, meditating firmly not on the life to come but on that succulent chapter entitled 'Food' in Mrs Alfred Sidgwick's *Home Life in Germany*, a book he loved almost as dearly as Yeats's *Wind Among the Reeds*, though in a different fashion. He made a rapid recovery and returned to Sandymount in glowing September weather, looking and feeling well, yet strikingly skinny and interestingly light on his feet. To make things even better there were frequent visitors from Martin's family too: Maimie and her mother were the first to arrive; then Peg and her new English husband, Bill Higginbottom, whose name caused a certain consternation among the more delicate of the Weldons, though Tina decided it had 'all the surprise of frankness, and so much more exquisitely fearless in statement than the ignoble Higginbotham.' And Peg pointed out that Bottom was also a good old Yorkshire word for 'glen, or valley' and that she had no intention of disguising it, still less of cutting it out, as poor prudish little Maimie had suggested. 'A good old Yorkshire name,' Peg repeated, 'and poor old Bill is proud of it, sure it's not his fault that he's English is it? And you know how touchy the English are. No, I'll not breathe a suggestion about it. Higginbottom it was, it is, and ever shall be.'

At the Gaelic League meetings in London Martin had become friends with Miss Una O'Connor, late of the Abbey Theatre in Dublin, and shortly to join the illustrious and wealthy hordes of filmic players in Hollywood. When she heard he was returning to live in Ireland and meant to make his home in Dublin, she had given him two letters of introduction: one to the Reddin family and one to a Mr Joseph Holloway, the architect of the original Abbey Theatre, a passionate lover of the arts of painting and of the stage, and a rival in his diary-keeping enthusiasm to Samuel Pepys himself.

'Come with me and meet them,' Martin had suggested, but Maeve refused.

'I dislike more than I can tell you,' she said, 'meeting people by introduction, especially when the introduction is really for somebody else. Joseph Holloway and the Reddin family expect to to meet you, not some unknown unspecified female attachment. No, my dear, you go along to them alone and leave me with Craven for the evening and my own thoughts. I wasn't made for circles of friends and admirers. You were. I'm like Emily Brontë – without the genius of course – and my own company as a general rule entrances me.'

So Martin took a bus to Haddington Road with (at his host's request) a portfolio of drawings under his arm. In a spacious bare house whose walls were smothered with pictures revealing a widely catholic and not always certain taste, he was warmly welcomed by a stooping, elderly man full of a flowing, croaking educated Dublin cataract of conversation, picked out every now and then by unexpected questions. He seemed to Martin to be very old – he was probably in his early or perhaps mid-sixties – and also to be composed entirely of lengthy curving lines. For everything was in a curve: his white hair, his white moustache, his drooping, heavy-lidded eyes, his shoulders, his back, his stomach, his knees. But he moved with astounding agility, and his face whose chin, and sometimes even the tip of the nose, rested at rare moments of relaxation on his shirt front, shot up whenever some phrase he wished to impress upon his audience flashed into his mind, and his eyes lighted up with humour and, at times, with a melancholy scrutinizing regret.

'There's a lovely head now of W. B. as I remember him nearly seventeen years ago,' he was saying. 'I forget the fellow's name who did it, God forgive me. And he never signed his name either, God forgive him too. For he had great talent. Drank himself to death, poor fellow. Oh yes, I hope you'll never do that now, though I can offer you a sherry this minute if you'd care for one. No? Ah, good lad, good lad. Have you anything to show me now in that portfolio? Yes, yes, of course I'd like to . . . oh now *that's* a very interesting bit of work now for such a young chap. There's true originality. Oh yes. Yes . . . And this! My God, this is a beauty. You'd never think, I suppose – ah well, bit early in the day now to talk of that yet. And look at this one now: oh, this one's a stunner. Wait now, wait, you've a real talent, my boy. Real talent. Oh yes. I wouldn't care for this now. Getting in line you are now with these modern lads you think you are here, I suppose, Derain and Modigliani or whatever he calls himself. Pablo Picasso and all that bunch. And here's a bit of an early Jack Yeats influence. But you're better on your own, boy, and that's from the shoulder. We'll have to show this one here – a lovely thing – have to show it to AE. Tell me now' – and with a curious deftness he selected three from a group and held them up together – 'tell me, would y'ever think of parting with these three?'

'Parting with them, Mr Holloway?'

'That's what I said. I'd like to have them. I'd like to buy them. I'll tell you what – and if it isn't enough you can bargain with me: you tell me you were born in Cork so you should be equal to that, God knows, and I fully realize it isn't much of a price I'm offering, but you're very young after all and not known yet, except our friend Miss O'Connor tells me as a boy actor in London – well, what do you say to two guineas each?'

There was no bargaining.

To receive a cheque for six guineas in exchange for three line-and-wash drawings of (1) bare black boughs enlaced with grotesque aerial dancers and lit by a full yellow moon, (2) dark-robed mourners with bowed heads under a sky thronged with passing half-human clouds, and (3) the kneeling figure of a solitary naked man on a mountain top in evocation of a rising sun, seemed to Martin a stroke of princely fortune: much more than he had earned for being murdered during eight performances a week by Mr Edmund Goulding and his fellow hirelings in *Macbeth* in the heart of the West End: even a little more than he had had for two performances daily as Michael and John respectively in *Peter Pan*. So he said, 'Oh, that'd be wonderful, thank you very much, Mr Holloway.'

Then they shook hands and Mr Holloway propelled himself down in a series of curves on to a chair by a writing desk, and wrote a cheque which he handed to Martin, saying: 'Well now, isn't that grand that we're both pleased with the bargain, for I may as well tell you, young Martin, I consider that it was I got the best of it.' And he rose in another series of convolutions and patted the boy on the back. 'And now when would you be free to pay a call on the Abbey? You're an actor yourself, I'm told, and wouldn't you be glad to meet a few of your fellow creatures? Now let me see what's this today is? Wednesday is it? Would you be free on Saturday? Good man, meet me there on Saturday at half nine, in the foyer, and I'll bring you round and I'll show off my new discovery. Saturday's a good night I may tell you, for the next day Sunday they have free all day: just an old dress rehearsal at half six in the evening, and the previous day, Friday, is pay day, so they'll all be in a good temper.'

Three nights later Martin, accompanied sturdily, yet in a series of slow ambling curves, by his new friend and patron, was ushered into the green room of the Abbey Theatre. It was good to be among actors and actresses again, though with one or two exceptions they were the strangest actors he had ever encountered. First of all it may be because they were all Irish, while the sons and daughters of the theatre Martin had known until that night were almost all of them English. But there was something else, as well as the mere difference of race: here he might as well have been among the members of his own family: Miss Irene Kelly, for example, bore a striking resemblance to Peg at home, though she was a year or two older and still wore her stage make-up (for the play had only arrived at the second act). And Miss Eileen Crowe was Deborah in another mood: almost as handsome in a darker and more severe fashion. But none of them, women or men, were in their presence of their manner like the players Martin had known, with the eager, assertive voices, their restless gestures, their smart clothes, their peals of laughter or operatic groans of disapproval or admiration.

Martin was introduced all round, and a brief and not altogether correct version of his life story given, and the leading lady of the evening – and indeed of most evenings at the Abbey – darted heavily forward and kissed him on both cheeks.

'But of course, me lovely little fella!' she cried in tones as richly deep as the notes of an organ, 'I've seen you play.

160

Twice! Once in *Peter Pan*, wasn't it? – the memory's gone to hell lately – and once as Oliver Twist. When's this it was? Two . . . three years ago. But weren't you Anthony Weldon? Surely it wasn't Martin?'

'No: Anthony. That was my father's name and I think he always wished he'd been an actor. But my real name is Martin.'

'And you've gone back to it. Very sensible. But what are you doing over here in this benighted old city?'

'He's painting,' Joseph Holloway proudly explained in his good-humoured way, turning his head from side to side in a series of arabesques to look round at them all. 'And here are some of his pictures I've brought to show you.'

'Act Three Beginners, ladies and gentlemen, Act Three Beginners on the stage please!' the call boy was shouting from the door of the green room to all the dressing room doors upstairs.

'Ah, bad luck to this old play,' Maureen Delaney cried. She was the leading character comedy actress of the Abbey at that period, and her popularity with the public was as broad and wide as the affection bestowed on her by every member of the company. They never called her Maureen but invariably Delaney, and their spirits rose like some effervescent liquid at the very sight of her imposing, irrepressible face, the light of her swiftly darting eyes, the lilt of her comfortable Western accent, her impatient, good-natured criticism of anything or anybody who did not immediately appeal to her ever-changing fancy. 'Ah sure God help the poor creature,' she would intone after some blighting denigration of some momentary victim. 'Wisha, I suppose the good God made him that way, so 'tisn't himself is to blame at all, but the Man Above. Or let us say nature, dear, yes nature, sure you can blame nature for anything at all and even the Legion of Mary'd never blame you for blasphemy.'

'Darling Delaney,' Sara Allgood murmured after she had gone, and joylessly regarded her reflection in a looking-glass on the wall. 'If one half of her curses worked, there'd be more than a half the population in hell and the rest of them in jail.'

Soon Mr Holloway and Martin were alone in the green room, with only the portraits of Yeats and Lady Gregory for company, and three long, wire-netting-shrouded bookcases crowded with play scripts. But at the end of the play, which Martin was invited by a friendly stage manager to watch from the side of the stage, almost all the players came back, some bottles of drink were produced, and Martin was pressed to drink a glass of whiskey by Arthur Shields, who was addressed by everyone as 'Boss' for some unsolved reason, for anyone less like a boss of anything at all was hard to think of. He was twenty-one, just a bit older than Martin, tall and slim with a hesitant manner and straight brown hair, but very friendly. He kept returning in his inspection of Martin's designs to one fairly large study, in flame colour and black, called *Arabesque*, a female dancer with a strong resemblance to the gipsies of Seville, although the surrounding décor suggested no known place under the moon.

'Forgive me, would you ever think of parting with this one?' he said in muffled tones through a cloud of cigarette smoke. 'I mean . . . I mean I'd like to buy it from you if you'd let me.'

The young artist (Martin was already thinking of himself as that) frankly confessed that he was not averse to the proposition.

'Then how much – I mean . . . could you tell me, I mean – would you want for it?'

While Martin, torn between shyness and greed, hesitated for a moment, Mr Holloway bent above them both in a series of undulations and said, 'Well now, Boss, congratulations! That's one of his best and a fine big one too. Worth at least seven or eight guineas . . .' and then, as young Shields gave a slight start of terror, he went on, 'But I daresay he'd let you have it for five, what do you say now to five, Martin?'

'Oh, I'd be delighted.'

'Delighted? God, aren't you very easily pleased? Well, you're the lucky young man, Boss Shields. Isn't that grand now?'

Boss Shields had fought in the Easter Week Rising in Dublin, and had been incarcerated with the other rebels in the military prison of Frongoch in Wales. He had been released after serving his ten months there but, unlike so many others of the same experience who had returned as hardened fanatics in the the cause of the Republic of Ireland, he had suffered a strange reaction to his national enthusiasm. By the time of his meeting with Martin Weldon he was indifferent, indeed almost averse, to all political movements, to all military shibboleths, to all firing of guns and shedding of blood, and was devoted to the arts, especially to the varied arts of the theatre.

Boss became Martin's closest Dublin friend, and they and Charles Millington, the manager and secretary of the Abbey, were constantly in each other's company. Millington was a few years older than the other two, and added a certain sobriety to their meetings. He knew quite as much about the history of theatre as they did, and Boss and Martin listened respectfully to his opinions on drama, only occasionally exchanging an 'upstage wink' when his theories about acting went (in their opinion) beyond his experience.

The trio was from time to time joined by a fourth, a young Jewish intellectual called Leventhal whom they knew as Con or sometimes Conti, his first name Constantine being considered too elaborate for their fiery discussions. Leventhal was a passionate Zionist, an ardent advocate of the *avant garde* in all the arts, a Dadaist, and admirer of Jean Cocteau and James Joyce, an almost perfect speaker of French and German (he was now studying Hebrew at white heat). Martin fancied that he detected in him certain mediumistic traits, and this theory, so fascinating in its possibilities, induced them all to return, one stormy night long after closing hour at the Abbey Theatre (Boss Shields had somehow got hold of a key), in order to hold a seance in the green room there, lit only by the flames of the gas fire.

'What do we do?' Millington asked of Martin, the ringleader.

'Oh, we sit in a circle and join hands, and concentrate on nothing, and wait. That's all.'

'Complicated. And what do we invoke? Anything? I mean, do we invite spirits or something?'

'Oh no,' Martin replied. 'I told you: we concentrate on nothing. That means we leave it to whatever may come through. Through Con, *I* think it'll be. We may see the people of Faery, the ancient gods, maybe the spirits of the dead . . .'

'That'll be cosy,' Millington murmured.

So then they sat in a circle and joined hands, and after some ten minutes of silence, with brief bouts of rather forced conversation, Leventhal obligingly went into what seemed a genuine trance marked by deep and painful breathing; and later, by a gradual uncanny *disappearance* of his features. Perhaps, as the other three said afterwards, it was just a trick of the dim red light of the gas fire, aided by their own strung-up fancy, but certainly they all observed the dark lines of brows and lashes, the prominent nose and well-defined lips, vanishing steadily until nothing was left, nothing, as Yeats had described of some spirit in *The Countess Cathleen*:

> No eyes, no mouth,
> his face a wall of flesh:
> I saw him clearly by the light of the moon.

Only here it was not the moon, only the red hissing glow of a gas fire.

Three of the four spiritists broke up the seance with a small sense of panic. Charles Millington switched on a light and they watched the gradual return of his features to the face of Con Leventhal who, unlike themselves (who stood about the room staring at him), remained prostrate in a big armchair. Presently he opened his eyes, yawned, and asked what was happening. Martin gleefully told him he had been in a trance, but none of them mentioned the temporary banishment of his features, and the party broke up with a great many cigarettes and with plans for a supper party next week.

'I don't like this sort of this all the same,' Millington said after Leventhal had departed in an outside car, for it was too late for trams or buses, and he was 'too exhausted', he explained, to dream of walking home.

'Exhausted, you see,' Millington went on. 'Sure of course he's exhausted. We're not meant to tinker about with the unknown. Especially you, Martin,' he went on. 'You've a morbid passion for all that sort of thing I know, but you're far too young and far too talented to play dangerous games. Well, goodnight, boys.'

Maeve Kelleher, when she was told next morning of the night's adventures and of Con Leventhal's vanishing features, said, 'I agree with Charles Millington. I think any attempt at the organization of the psychic powers is probably futile in the long run – at best it's a groping in the dark for something whose nature you know nothing about, and it might be dangerous for anyone as young and impressionable as you. But you're strange, Martin. I've heard that old story about once a person has smelt grease-paint it never stops haunting him. Or her. But you don't seem to hanker any more after the stage, yet I have the feeling somehow that if you ever had any great blow, any tragic loss in your life, you'd go back to it sooner or later. I can see you somehow, smothered in grease-paint and velvet and jewels, and with lights blazing down on you. Like Ainley. Like Mac. Where *is* Mac by the way? Still on tour in the bacon-and-cabbages? But never mind that. I've wonderful news for you, Martin. Craven has found a cottage in Howth, and we can go there in the early spring. Ah, I knew you'd be delighted! And now you've begun to sell your pictures so well – isn't it marvellous? – I know you'll be able to help Craven a bit more regularly without writing to London to poor Sophia.'

Martin's mother was now called Sophia (or more often Sophie) by her children because of an almost totally imaginary likeness between her and the mother in *The Severins* by Mrs Alfred Sidgwick, a novel much loved by the Weldons. There was really very little similarity between the two ladies except that both were essentially good-natured, amazingly tolerant, and slow to see evil anywhere. But the name stuck, and now she had become Sophia to all the children. Just then, however, it wasn't his mother that Martin was thinking of.

'A cottage in Howth?' he exclaimed. 'Oh, Maeve, how wonderful. Will it be like the one in AE's poem: A cottage on the mountainside/Hid in a grassy nook . . .?'

'Oh my poor Martin! No. It's just at the top of the village, but the very top of it, you know, with a *bóithrín* – there, did I pronounce it rightly? Isn't it the Irish for a country lane? – leading up to the hills, looking over the sea.'

They arrived there in sunny, showery March weather, and some of the happiest years of their lives began. Howth was only eight miles from the city, though most of it was as unspoiled and as wild and beautiful as the County Clare, and they spent long hours wandering over the hills. On the first few cold evenings they sat round the fire with Craven, making plans for the future, and, when Craven wasn't present, brooding over the ancient gods.

Martin acquired a season ticket on the train that ran from Howth station to Amiens Street in the heart of the city, so he continued to see a great deal of his friends at the Abbey, to sell his pictures, and to learn a lot about Dublin life with its festive and furtive political gatherings, its endless social gossip, and its deadly malicious comments about anyone who did not happen to be present. Not for nothing had the author of *The School for Scandal* been born in this town, thought Martin.

Maeve would accompany him sometimes to the Abbey to see a play, or to a cinema to watch some silent film featuring

Nazimova or Pauline Frederick or Chaplin. Greta Garbo in those days was unknown outside the Scandinavian countries, and the rest of the world had to get on somehow without her. But Maeve expressed no desire to go backstage at the Abbey or to meet any of Martin's friends. She and Dolly Lynd, the Abbey actress from the north of Ireland, had met one afternoon at a matinée and had liked each other from that day, but apart from her and her sister Lucy, Maeve, the strange creature, showed no wish for any companions and she seldom went into town. She seemed perfectly happy to wander over the hills alone, or to sit at home with her mother.

'I'm not a naturally gregarious type, Martin,' she said. 'Craven is really wonderful company when I feel I want any, except of course when she sits wrapped in dreams about her girlhood in Hertfordshire. I was trying to explain one of Tchehov's stories that bewildered her last night, and I wistfully though she was listening, when she suddenly broke into titters of laughter and burst out, "Oh Maeve dearie, I saw two such sweet little girls in the village today while I was doing my shopping: dancing along the road together they were, and both of them dressed alike, and it reminded me *so* much of my sister Edith and me when we were innocent laughing children together at Kitwells. It all came back to me oh so vividly! and I could almost see dearest Mamma sitting at the piano in her pretty blue organdie with a frilled bustle playing Mendelssohn . . . sorry dearie, what were you talking about? Oh that *horrid* Russian writer, so *depressing* dear. Well? Haven't you anything more to say to me?" '

Maeve had an unexpected talent for mimicry, especially of Craven's voice and manner, and Martin wondered for the hundredth time why her nature was so enamoured of solitude, and why she seemed to have so little need for companionship, apart from his own.

1918 sped by through these pleasant and, for Martin, highly contrasted days and nights. Sophia and Maimie came to Howth during the summers, and later in the year they were joined by Peg and her husband Bill of the 'good old Yorkshire name'. During their stay the end of the Great War came, and was celebrated in England with a triumphant and noisy Armistice Night. Far away across the Irish Sea, Bill Higginbottom rejoiced with a little too much imperialistic satisfaction to please his wife and brother-in-law, and there was a renewal of all the age-long Anglo-Irish arguments, while Bill said a great deal about Hunnish tricks and about the Stab in the Back given by Ireland in 1916.

Then, one day, all their talk was rendered futile and senseless when the news came of Sophia's sudden and tragic death in England. It was a letter from Maimie that told them, and all other interests, all other passions seemed to fade into thin air.

Sophia was dead. Their mother was gone, and life would go on and would never be quite the same. Never. The day after the news came through, Peg persuaded her husband to take her back to England for the funeral. There wasn't enough money to bring Sophia's body home to be buried in Irish ground.

The letters of sympathy began to pour in. The most cherished of these for Martin was one from Tina in which she said, 'If any mother in the world was loved by her children it was our mother, our own darling Sophia. And now, beloved little Martin, be sure of this: our mother is having what God knows she earned: a long deep, peaceful rest.'

And as he stood in the little backyard that night and watched the star-laden sky over the stone walls, and the dark hills beyond them, the wind gently touching his face seemed to him for a moment to be his mother's hand.

This melancholy period came during an eventful and, for Martin, a profitable time in his affairs for, as well as the sale of drawings among the Abbey actors and many others, he was introduced to the art director of a celebrated Dublin publishing company, a Mr George Coogan, who immediately commissioned him to illustrate some of the latest publications. Daniel Corkery's *Munster Twilight* was among them, as well as a number of volumes of short stories by various writers. He made drawings in both black and white and in colour, and these illustrations were enthusiastically received by the newspapers, sometimes more enthusiastically than the stories themselves, which naturally irritated the authors.

So the year 1919 was very full and varied for Martin, who had his first small and successful exhibition of drawings and designs which, following the advice of his friend Paul Henry, himself a well-known painter of Irish landscape, he called 'Fantasies in Colour'. He was generously praised by AE in the *Irish Statesman*, nearly all the pictures were sold, and he did his best to forget that most of the purchasers were personal friends or the friends of personal friends.

He and Maeve continued their long walks, lighting fires on the hill tops round about Howth in all the four festivals in honour of the people of Faery who were really, as the two celebrants did not forget, the ancient gods of Ireland, and although Martin remembered his beloved mother every day, and fervently prayed for her every night of his life, the intense pain caused by her death was gradually soothed by time. His friendship with Boss Shields continued happily enough, and there were frequent visits all through the spring from Mac, who bore down on the Weldon-Kelleher ménage and entertained them all in his outrageous Baroque fashion with stories of his touring adventures in the 'bacon-and-cabbage towns'.

'Tired to death of it all, darlings,' Mac cried, floating up and down the room, or striding right and left through the garden like a tall and extremely handsome lion. '*Terrible* melodramas like *No Mother to Guide Her* and *Waifs and Strays of Erin's Isle* dear, *terrible* digs, all Sacred Heart pictures and fleas in the beds, *terrible* actors: so bad some of them that even the *audiences* are beginning to notice. As for our leading lady – Kitty Vere de Vere as she *calls* herself – sixty-five if she's a day dear – and she wears sort of 1903 ball dresses and tennis shoes, such a flaming bitch too dear, and hates me like poison. Well, I have to stay with them till the end of May, because like a fool I signed me name to a letter of agreement – well how did *I* know the war was going to be over? But I'm going to London then, oh I wish you'd come with me, Martin, and you too of course Maeve: oh, I know you don't like living in England, neither do *I* in me heart. A lot of pogs [a compromise of Mac's for expressing a detestable mixture of pig and dog] most of them, but not ALL dear, not ALL; and London *is* a centre of things.'

Martin and Maeve had joined a Sinn Féin club in Harcourt Street, and together they attended its meetings every Monday night, where there were ardent speeches and ferocious arguments and constant confident plans for Ireland's future.

Martin, 'half amused, half enthused, wholly bemused', as Maeve put it, volunteered to go round Dublin canvassing for Mulcahy in some forthcoming election. At the house of the well-known artist, wit and hostess, Sarah Purser, he met with his one failure, being contemptuously turned away by the lady herself, who cried, 'So like the Sinn Féin party to send a boy round town to do its dirty work: no, my poor child, you'll get no vote from me.' He never reminded her in later years, when they became good friends and she a generous purchaser of his pictures, of this incident, but at the moment of its happening took his revenge by going round to the back entrance, where he secured the votes for Mulcahy from all her servants.

But the Monday nights at the Harcourt Street Club, while they amused and stimulated Maeve, began after a few weeks to have a strange, uncanny effect on Martin. These ardent young men and women, these heated speeches, these ferocious revolutionary enthusiasms, had he not experienced them all in the past? Surely they were familiar and brought with them some nameless nostalgic pain, some half-forgotten drama he had lived and died for in days and nights long, God knew how long, ago? Suddenly the thought of Giovanni came into his mind, and the long bridge over the river they had crossed together on so many moonlit nights. And then he understood, and with something like terror in his heart he knew, and it was there in Italy it had happened before and it would all end in that little room with Daddy with the Hard Hat, and he would wake screaming . . .

That was how Martin Weldon grew gradually further and further away from any violent desire for political and revolutionary activity, though his passion for serving Ireland as an artist suffered no change.

But it was too late for this as far as the total security and peace of an ivory tower for the artist was concerned, for he and Maeve were now official members of Sinn Féin, and during the following year (1920) when the British Auxiliaries, known from their uniform as the Black and Tans, came swarming over to keep Ireland safely within the Empire, the two young friends found themselves inextricably involved. The Black and Tans were, in the main, very ferocious gentlemen who drove large armoured lorries about the streets of all the Irish cities, often with a young man, a prisoner, bound to a post high up in front of the armoured cages that sheltered themselves from any missiles of stone or shot from an irritated populace. One day a daring old lady in a Dublin street shouted after them, in uncontrollable irony, 'Well there yous go, bad luck to yous! It took the Boers to put yous into khaki, and the Germans to put yous into tanks, but be Jasus it took the Irish to put yous into hen-runs!'

One of the Tans fired at her but missed, and she danced triumphantly homewards, singing rebel songs out of tune.

Maimie was staying at the cottage in Howth – she had a bedroom next door – when the Tan Terror spread into the lives of the Weldons and the Kellehers. One day, after a series of crashing blows on the door, the house seemed to fill with large and violent-looking characters in the known and dreaded uniform – there were in fact only five of them – and the inmates were informed that it was a Search. They did not call it a raid: no, it was a search, and every corner of every room was ransacked while unpleasing comments were made

171

about the number and the nature of the books and almost everything else. Nothing more incriminating was found than Martin's Gaelic League card of membership, which was described as 'something suspicious in that bleedin' lingo', and his and Maeve's Sinn Féin club cards, which were thrown contemptuously aside with the comment, 'Got those already, ta ever so.'

And no arrests were made. But the raid had a strange effect on each different member of the household: Maeve silently resentful, Craven agog with terrified excitement, and Maimie giving a somewhat overdone performance of a half-witted simpleton which, she explained when the Tans had disappeared, was 'an awfully subtle ruse, as even those horrible creatures couldn't imagine anything important could be, as you might say, afoot with a village idiot in the house. But *you* were really alarmed, my poor Martin,' she went on, 'you were as white as a sheet.'

He had been and, catching sight of his blanched features for a moment in the glass he had suddenly realized the truth of Maeve's words to him, long ago, that the actor was still alive in the depths of his soul, for he had thought of himself: 'Yes, I think it would suit me to be really pale . . . like Hamlet,' and then the second thought came: 'Maeve was right as usual. Only a born mummer would react like that.'

His second reaction was a prayer of gratitude, for the first time since her death, that Sophie his mother was no longer on this earth. The news of the raid would have been torture to her.

The general election at the end of the previous year had proved an overwhelming victory for Sinn Féin: but a curfew was arranged and came into force at varying hours of day and night, which was confusing because sometimes Martin and other residents of Howth or Killiney could go freely if dangerously about the city until ten o'clock p.m.; on other days the streets were emptied by two in the afternoon, and no sign of life but the silent lorries with their cages of steel and their occasional tragic hostages driving through the abandoned streets under the bright summer sunshine.

It was during that long, storm-riven winter that Maeve developed influenza, and when it was over an obstinate and exhausting cough. After Christmas her cough grew worse and she became alarmingly thin. The presence of the Black and Tans had been a constant brooding menace, and after the raid on the cottage at Howth everything in life took on a more sombre tone than she or Martin had ever experienced. Craven was the busiest and the most cheerful in the ménage, though she too found the food rationing from Britain and the accompanying coal shortage tiresome. With searing memories of the Black and Tans still fresh in her mind she took refuge, like so many impressionable English residents in Ireland, in becoming more Irish than the Irish themselves. So many bitter arguments raged in the kitchen between herself and her spinster sister Hilda, who had come over for a long stay and remained staunchly British in the intervals between lessons on piano and violin, which she gave to young ladies of the village to augment her small income.

Aunt Hilda, known to Martin and Maeve as 'Bruja', the Spanish for 'Hag', was a tall lady of high principles and determined utterance, as well as being an unwavering supporter of the British policy in her sister's adopted country.

'Well really Florence,' she would cry in her clear and powerful voice, 'I don't know what's come over you. There *has* to be law and order especially in these times of disturbance, and if the Irish won't behave themselves properly we shall just have to teach them how. That's *all*. And if they continue to be disloyal and if they try and rise up against us any more, we shall just *tread* on them. Oh dear me, there goes a cup. Broken. I knew it would be if you *will* upset me with your renegade remarks. Oh well, I'm sorry I'm sure, but it wasn't *my* fault. *And* if I choose to wear my little Union Jack in my jacket I shall continue to do so with or without your permission. *And* my poppy on Armistic Day.'

'Oh very well, Hilda,' came in the softer, wearier tones of

173

poor Craven, 'I'm just as English as *you* are, dear, but the way our country is behaving to poor old Ireland, after all their talk about small nations' rights and brave little Belgium, makes me absolutely sick. Really sometimes I feel as if I'd have been quite glad to have seen the old Kaiser goose-stepping all the way down Piccadilly, it might have taught us a lesson on how it feels to be occupied against your will.'

'Florence!' The voice rose on the air like a steam whistle. 'How can you – oh, how *can* you? Oh there goes a plate! Never, never, never did I think that a sister of mine could be so wicked. Glad to see that Hun, that *German Kaiser* . . . oh, Florence, I never thought you could be so . . . so . . . why, do you *realize*, Florence, if the Huns had succeeded in invading Britain, you might have seen your sister – yes, your sister Hilda: me! – slowly gyratin' on the end of a *German bayonet*. Or on the end of something worse!'

One day Craven, in her famous pleading voice, said: 'Really Hilda, I *do* think it unwise to go about all over the village simply plastered with Union Jacks and Armistice Day poppies. I mean the whole of Ireland is up in arms about these horrid Black and Tans, and I shouldn't be a bit surprised if it made you most unpopular in Howth and everywhere else if you will go about all decorated like that with what everybody resents so bitterly! You might be insulted at any moment. You might be attacked.'

Aunt Hilda's voice dropped to a most ominous and sardonic contralto, almost to a baritone. 'I should like to see them *dare*, Florence.'

'Well, don't blame *me* if something disagreeable happens.'

But on this one point Craven did underrate her present heroes, the poor persecuted Irish people, one of whose rare virtues was that the strenuous resentment, even hatred, felt towards an abstraction – to the armed and alien presence of an unwanted power that had ruled them for God knew how many centuries of continuous protest and rebellion – contained no shadow of personal grudge against individuals. So that Hilda-

174

Bruja was right in her way to insist on her partisan patriotism and to express it in wearing her flags and her poppies, for nobody in Howth or anywhere else seemed to blame her in the least. Indeed, on the occasion of an illness of King George V, when she paraded the village with bowed head and stricken mien, she was frequently asked in tones of apparent sympathy: 'How was her poor royal patient? Sure, God help the poor man, I'm sure you must be worried about him, Miss Chattock, but cheer up now, sure God's good!'

Meanwhile Maeve's cough grew worse and worse, and one cold windswept March day in the following year, as she and Martin were mounting the steep hill of Ball Glas that separated the top of the village from the wilder hill beyond, she faltered a little and stopped, her face pallid and sharp as a knife, her breath coming in broken gasps, and said: 'I don't think I can do it, Martin. I'm sorry. I'd better go home again.'

Of course Martin went with her, and for a long while sat at her side as she lay on the sofa by the window and Craven brought them toast and tea and started to talk of a doctor.

'That nice Dr Molloy who was so good to Martin when he had typhoid two years ago, you remember, dearie?'

'All right, I'll go to him,' Maeve answered, and somehow she produced a smile, 'But don't worry about me, darling,' and she started to cough again.

Miss Bruja had returned to her native land and was enjoying a brief holiday in Hampshire with Brother Percy and his wife, 'Horrid little Emily' as she was described on a picture postcard that depicted pleasant green meadows and clusters of elm trees. 'Hampshire is a wonderful spot,' she added in her wobbling yet determined hand, 'Scenery every bit as lovely as anything you can describe, and it's England, *Mother England*!'

The last two words were underlined three times, and the card was signed, very large, 'Love H.'

Somehow it cheered them all and gave them a little laughter.

* * *

175

The appointment with Dr Molloy at his address in Merrion Square was on April 1st – 'a significant date, we hope,' Maeve said between two bouts of coughing. Martin accompanied them into town, but not to the doctor's house, and waited for mother and daughter at the appointed meeting place on Stephen's Green for what seemed an eternity, wandering up and down by the lake between duck-haunted lawns and trees that were misty with buds of green, wondering what was going to happen.

At last they appeared. To Martin's eyes there was something new and faintly ominous in the aura that hung almost visibly above their heads and about their bodies as they came slowly towards him: Maeve with a determinedly valiant smile, Craven with undisguised despair.

'Well?' Martin asked as they drew nearer.

'It'll be all right.' Maeve murmured.

'What does Dr Molloy say?'

'We've got to go home at once: this instant!' Craven said. 'She's very ill. The doctor says she's very *very* ill. Cod-liver oil and six eggs a day beaten up in milk. Six a day! And oh Martin, he even suggested a sanatorium might be the best thing. I don't know, I don't know what to think.'

'Well don't think about a sanatorium, darling,' Maeve said as they walked slowly towards a tram that would take them to the station for Howth. 'Because I wouldn't go. I'd be dead in six weeks.'

'Oh Maevy dear, we must do what is best for you. Careful dear, how you get up that frightful step. Remember what Dr Molloy said. No more climbing, whenever we can avoid it.'

'But what's wrong with her?' the boy asked as they sat down in the tram.

'Phthisis!' said Craven, in a strangled voice.

'But what's that?'

'Oh my dear Martin, the girl's in consumption. Left lung almost on the verge of collapse, he says, and the right lung badly affected too. Oh Martin, isn't it dreadful?'

176

Martin tried to say something that would relieve the nightmare hanging over them like a pall, but he found it impossible to speak. Maeve herself broke the silence.

'Oh, I suppose what was good enough for Chopin and Keats and Aubrey Beardsley ought to be good enough for me,' she observed after a bout of coughing into her handkerchief. She scrutinized the handkerchief. 'Oh well, no blood,' she continued with forced cheerfulness. 'That's already something, as the French say.'

'Cod-liver oil three times a day and temperature three times too, morning and evening at six, and last thing at night. And six eggs daily . . . I'll get everything in the village . . . you take Maeve straight back home from the hill-car.'

'Of course.'

'You're a great comfort to me Martin,' Craven whispered as they climbed into the hill-car at Howth Station. 'Such a comfort. I knew you wouldn't desert us in this awful trouble.'

So for more than two months the cottage at Howth reeked of cod-liver oil and various medicines, and Martin developed and almost professional skill in making what they all called egg flips, and he and Maeve took gentle twenty-minute walks in the mornings along a level road close to the cottage that they called in later years 'the Naples road' because of their talks about spending the autumn and winter in Naples. They both had the old-fashioned idea that salt air was good for consumption, and though Maeve questioned Martin about Spain the idea was dismissed because of the absence of the sea at Seville, the only Spanish place he knew. No, Naples. Yes, Naples!

So it was not until Maimie came to stay with them that they learned about mountain air being the latest, the most advanced and successful setting for afflicted lungs, and then, inevitably Switzerland took her place in their talk and Naples seemed to fade into the air.

'Davos Platz, Grisons, Switzerland: that is the most famous cure-resort for your complaint in Europe,' said the learned Maimie. 'Ah yes, my dear Maeve, Davos is the place for you. I know Naples sounds fascinating, but it's not for people with consumption. Poor darling Maeve! But truly,' Maimie went on, warming to her subject, 'truly, Maeve my dear, Davos is the place for you. Six or seven thousand feet above sea level, with taller mountains all about, sunshine all year round, Alpine flowers in summer, snow and winter sports all through the dreary months. Ah, of course you know, Davos is Thomas Mann's Magic Mountain . . . Do persuade her, Martin, and persuade Craven too. And I'll help Craven compose a letter to your father, Maeve, to increase your incomes. I'm sure he'll do it if we can word it tactfully.'

He did. Maimie was really wonderful the way she went about things, and everything worked out as she had said. She even persuaded her friend, Susan Perrin, with whom she had just been touring France, Italy, Egypt and Palestine, to rent a small and pleasant house in Bayswater where they could break their long, adventurous journey for a few weeks. Susan was the soul of kindness. A fascinating creature, described by Maimie as having 'the eyes of a gipsy and the mind of William Blake', she had lost her young husband in 1919 when he was killed in an Air Force exhibition flight to celebrate Armistice Day, leaving her with his unborn child in her womb.

In addition to her very practical kindness, Susan had an ethereal side to her nature. A little while after her husband's death she had developed a form of mediumship, which was expressed in an amazing series of automatic paintings and drawings. These came to her mind and hand, she said, from 'places beyond the stars'. She had also begun to sing, and many of her favourite songs, which were enjoying a vogue in the London of the early Twenties, seemed to be accompanied, as it sounded to Martin and Maeve as well as to many others who had heard her, by an invisible chorus, a host of male and female voices. This effect gave her listeners an uncanny pleasure, and several begged her to give a public recital. But she always refused.

'I must never commercialize what has been given to me from so far away,' she would say, half-closing her eyes as she spoke – a habit which, Martin discovered in later years, was common among many mediums, whether professional or, as in Susan's case, determinedly private.

It was during those weeks in London that Peg and Tina once more entered the lives of Martin and Maeve, who by this time was regarded by the Weldon girls as a welcome addition to the family circle, and they were all passionately sympathetic about her illness. Peg, accompanied by her devoted Bill of the proud old Yorkshire name, was the same as ever: time did very little to change her golden blonde charm or her alternate fits of wild laughter and moments of solemn earnestness.

But Tina was different. She too was married – 'thanks be to God!' as her mother would have said. To look at she was unchanged: the same great dark eyes, the same Sphinx-like 'hairdo' – 'that atrocious new expression for a chevelure', as she described it – and the same wide, unsmiling, scarlet mouth, but there was also an undeniable husband, a distinguished English painter and stained-glass window designer whose name was Mervyn Treacy, complete with an Irish grandfather – Cork Protestants, as Tina announced in sepulchral tones as though she were a priestess at the head of some dubious dark mass. But there was no more of the black mass in her mood. Her present role seemed to be that of a devoted wife and mother of two children, a boy named Nicholas and a baby girl called Sally.

Now she sat in a beautifully cut tailor-made gown of the latest style, passionately clasping her Sally, who resembled nothing so much as a gaily smiling Chinese doll, to her breast, while Sally's father hovered suitably near. She was the picture of domestic delight, and the only detail to suggest that the eternal Tina had not succumbed forever to a decent sense of British decorum was that her slim ankles were bare but for the golden bangle on each one, and that her feet were clad in gold sandals which had nothing to do with the rest of her conventional toilette.

'There's a great deal to be said for stodgy respectability,' she intoned. 'There's nothing more lovely than a plain gold wedding ring and all that it means. My God, when I think of those disgusting Bolsheviks in Russia – just imagine, they wanted to do away with marriage. Did you know that? *Did* you, my angel?' she murmured, blowing cigarette smoke into Sally's face and making the Chinese doll splutter and screw up up her eyes so that she looked more Chinese than ever.

'Oh do mind the darling baby, Tina dear,' Craven cried in dismay.

'So good for her,' was the answer. 'Helps her to conquer fear. My baies will be afraid of nothing: not even of those foul Bolsheviks, bad luck to them all.'

'But I thought you adored them, Tina,' Martin, not invariably the soul of tact, remarked. 'Don't you remember the dog you called Trotsky?'

'Did I? Well if I did it was to show what I thought of Trotsky. A dog. Just a low dirty dog. That's why I called him after Trotsky. It obviously was that!'

And good husband Mervyn, 'always so loyal, so understanding,' as Tina had rightly said, stroked her hair affectionately and murmured something about going home to Nicholas and not wearing out the invalid.

'Of course, of course, silly and inconsiderate of me,' she murmured. 'Goodbye, my dear Maeve: have a glorious journey and get strong and well again. And make my darling brother take care of you. As you will without being asked, dear Aunt Craven.'

She kissed them all with great affection and made the Chinese doll wave her hand. 'Isn't she divine? Oh, the joy of my babies! So wonderful. And how I envy you all going up to that marvellous place in the Alps: what's it called? Ah yes, of course: Davos! Davos Platz, Grisons, Switzerland! My love to it – and to you!'

CHAPTER SEVEN
The Long Sickness

They arrived at Davos on a day of summer sunshine that spread like honey over a high mountain valley. The valley was divided by a small town of white and russet brown houses with an imposing grey Kurhaus among them, and the town in its turn was divided by a main street, the Promenadestrasse. High up on either side still loftier mountains rose to the sky, their lower slopes swathed in the branchy dusk of pine woods and speckled with more chalets and villas, with bulky sanatoria here and there seemingly composed of balconies with windows half-hidden in their inner recesses, and here and there one could see recumbent men and women, a man or a woman to each balcony, taking 'the cure' on the chaises longues, referred to locally as *Liegestühle*.

'Patients,' Maeve murmured to Martin as she gazed about her from the public balcony of their own Pension Thalmann, where Craven had decided to stay for a week or two while she and Martin searched for a suitable flat. 'Patients taking the cure, and now I suppose I'm a patient too, so I'd better start away.' And she stretched lazily out on her *Liegestuhl* in the cool shadow of the balcony, and a little Swiss maid with flaxen plaits twisted in coils over her ears brought them afternoon coffee and cakes on a big square tray.

Craven found a pleasant flat in a white and brown house called Villa Verna. It was in Davos Dorf, which was quieter and more residential than the adjoining Platz, so bustling and lively with its horse-bus (no petrol was allowed for the sake of the patients), its Kurhaus and its Kornzertsaal, its Rathaus and all the rest of it. And the windows of the sitting room in this pleasant flat all faced south and had a roomy balcony with two *Liegestühle,* and there were two bedrooms, a big one with two beds for Craven and

Maeve, and a smaller one with a double bed for Martin.

Villa Berna was owned and managed by a Herr Otto Leisinger, his plump and smiling wife and their two sons, a grown-up young man called Hammi and a fifteen-year-old boy familiarly known as Fritzli, following the Swiss passion for replacing the German diminutive of *chen* by *li*, which gave a touchingly childlike quality to the astonishing dialect they all spoke, regardless of education or rank, and called Schwitzer Duitch.

At Davos Martin had an exhibition of his designs and pictures at the Bibliothèque and Objets d'Art shop of Heintz und Roussel on the Promenadestrasse, and through it made, as well as an encouraging sale, one of the greatest and most permanent friends of his life.

Five of his pictures, he learned from Herr Roussel, who spoke excellent French with a strong Swiss accent, had been bought by a young man who, like himself, was an *Irlandais*. And this unknown Irishman had been madly enthusiastic and had expressed a desire to meet the artist. His name, Herr Roussel added, was 'Jacques quelque chose,' and he had been very insistent and *agréable*.

A few days later the unknown purchaser introduced himself to Martin at the Kurhaus Café, where Martin was drinking coffee with two Russian friends, Anton Nikolaieff and Serge Belski. He was a tall, athletic-looking man in his early thirties, with fair hair and complexion, and his name, he told Martin, was Jack – Jack Dowling: a Kildare man, a lawyer, an enthusiastic Wagnerian, and an earnest student of Freud. They all walked together to the door of the Russian sanatorium, where they left Belski and Nikolaieff, and then Martin and Jack strolled back to the Villa Verna. By this time they seemed to know all about each other, and still wished to know more. Jack said he wanted to meet Maeve, so Martin invited him up to the flat, and that first meeting was an immediate success.

'At last,' Maeve remarked when Dowling had gone away after arranging to walk with Martin the next day to the forest on

Schatzalp, 'at last you've found a friend who's really worth your while. And don't, my darling,' she continued, 'go falling in love with him if you can help it. Because I somehow think he won't respond, I don't feel he's the type who would. And I don't want you to be hurt.'

She was perfectly right. Jack and Martin saw each other every day, and Jack came to the flat almost every evening, but though he seemed, and indeed was, completely devoted to Martin, no shadow of romance was to be seen anywhere beyond the most cursory embrace from each other when the evening's long talks with Maeve were done.

And Martin of course was hurt, and the hurt lasted for nearly three years before coming to an end in the oddest way.

Jack Dowling was the most important of their friends in Davos, but there were many others, so many indeed and so varied that they formed a constantly shifting spectacle in the lives of Martin and Maeve. There were, for example, the two Russians, Anton Nikolaieff and Belski, whose first name was Serge though he always remained Belski to Martin. An art critic of experience and taste, Belski hailed from Odessa and was the most lively-minded and impatient patient at the Russian sanatorium. He was also a brilliant linguist (though he had no English), and tried hard to teach the elements of Russian to the young Irishman. Martin soon mastered the Cyrillic alphabet and a few words and easy phrases, but no further progress was made because he was only able to learn a language through conversation, and since both he and Belski were almost wholly at their ease in superbly fluent and imperfect French, it was tedious and pointless to limit themselves to a few stuttering commonplaces when they had so much to say to each other. So poor Martin gave up the original ambition which had first prompted him to this difficult task, which was to read Pushkin and the great nineteenth-century masters in the original, and continued with Maeve to enjoy Tchehov and Dostoievsky and Turgenev and the rest in translation. At the Russian sanatorium, too, was Mademoiselle

Maryla d'Orlitt (nobody seemed to know her real name), a surprisingly young lady of enormous vivacity and enterprise who gave frequent exhibitions of dancing at the Kurhaus and other centres, told endless tales of her misfortunes in Russian, German, English and French to anyone she could persuade to listen, and, as Anton Nikolaieff said, 'cherchait profiter de tout le monde'.

In the flat next door lived Francisco Gomez with his wife Rosa and their enchanting seven-year-old daughter, Isabelita. Francisco rapidly made friends with 'Martinito', on hearing of his Spanish connections, and begged to be known as 'Paco'. He, like Jack Dowling, had had what was known in Davos as 'the rib operation' and, unlike Jack, had claimed the extracted ribs as his own special property. Whenever he was in melancholy mood, which was often, he would call out, 'Rosa, mis costillas, por favor,' and Rosa would obligingly bring the ribs to the balcony where he could admire them with pride and show them off to Martinito. On very melancholy days Paco would retire to his room, his ribs laid out on a stool close by his bed. Then he would ask Rosa to draw the curtains, and with true Iberian passion for the intensification of a mood he would ask her to play records of funeral marches and slow, sad pavanes on their horned gramophone.

Above their flat were two middle-aged spinsters of great charm and intelligence: Bláthnaid (Irish for Florence), and Una (Irish for Agnes). Bláthnaid had contracted tuberculosis of the spine while studying the Irish language on the Island of Aran, and her devoted English friend, Una, had insisted on staying with her as companion and nurse. They had been living in Davos for many years when the Weldon-Kelleher ménage arrived, and they all became good friends.

Above Bláthnaid and Una, in the highest flat of the Villa Berna, lived Daisy Carroll, a handsome and hilarious blonde lady, a Londoner by birth, and in her middle forties. Her husband George, who had for many years practised as a dentist at Frankfurt am Main, was interned during the war as an enemy alien and contracted tuberculosis of the spine, 'like poor old Bláthnaid, or whatever she calls herself', as Daisy would remark. Here he was in Davos, a bedridden invalid with little to cheer him but his wife and their two daughters, Lillie and Baby, whose respective ages at this time were ten and six years, and who spoke English with a strong German accent and were, like their mother, almost equally at home in English, German and French. Daisy was the life and joy (if not the soul in its more lofty aspects) of the household, and it was she who kept things going in that top floor flat by teaching languages to various Davos residents and patients.

Her English, when she spoke it, was the slangy, allusive, English of the London of the late Nineties when, as she said, she was 'a ravishing young thing that all the Johnnies were nuts about,' but she seldom kept even to her own native tongue for very long, continually breaking into French or German phrases as spicy as *Zucker Kuchen*.

There were countless others: a young lady from Ireland, a Miss Patricia Mac Curtain, who father had been Lord Mayor of Cork and who would say: 'After all there aren't many girls whose Daddy had King Street renamed in his honour and called Mac Curtain Street instead!' And a scintillating and dubious Parisienne whose name, so she said, was Alice Champagne; and Biddy Healy, another star in the Irish firmament, and Jean Zervos, a handsome, dissolute *Makak* (the Swiss name for any Greek they did not much care about). Jean pursued with amorous fervour anyone at all of the most modest claim to attraction, regardless of age, rank or sex, and met with scanty success in spite of his good looks. He was too eager, too indiscriminate in his quest for prey.

'*So ein frecher Kerl!*' Daisy Carroll would cry. '*Hat mich so öffentlich fixiert* in the Kurhaus last night and finally chased me out. But I was up to his little game, cheek of him! Catching me by the hatrack when I was pulling on my snowboots to come home, and leering right into my face. I said, "*Genügt, genügt, Du impertinenter schamlosser Schwein,*" and gave him such a clout! Right across his dirty chops. I don't think I'll have any more trouble with *him* . . . Jim – Jam, that's the girl I am, free and easy! For I like to play the Umpty-umpti Ay! In High Society!'

And with a saucy wink and a high kick worthy of Lottie Collins, Daisy made her exit.

Then there was Kurt Schupp, Kurti as he soon became known to Maeve and Martin, though any close friendship with Maeve was circumvented by the fact that she had only a few hesitant words of German and he no English at all.

The Family Schupp lived in a chalet a few yards away from Villa Berna, and consisted of the Swiss Mamma Schupp, a widow of two bereavements; her daughter by her first marriage, Margarethe, known as *die Deda*; her older son, also by the first marriage and so, like myself and *die Deda*, of purest Swiss origin, and known as *der Hammi*, a solid, serious schoolmaster; and finally, her youngest child by her second union with a gentleman from Stuttgart, now also dead, and this, Mamma's youngest born, was none other than *der Kurt*.

Kurt had first seen the light in Stuttgart. He was passionately German and called Mamma *Mutti*, which annoyed her. Unlike his worthy and hard-working brother, Hammi, Kurt had no job of any kind, but his days and nights were busy enough in their exotic way. At night he would sleep in his narrow bed in a simple nightshirt fashioned by Mutti and adorned with a monogram, but when the sun shone out in glory, as it did almost every morning over that Alpine valley, Kurti would rise, shave and make a carefree toilette, exchange the homemade nightshirt for a dazzling pyjama suit of scarlet and gold, or blue and silver, with trousers wired at the sides to give the appearance of wide-spread riding breeches, and clad thus in what he called his *Frühstück Pyjama* he would sit brilliantly in view on the balcony to enjoy his coffee and rolls, hoping, a little wistfully perhaps, that some passer-by would enquire who was the lovely young man on the balcony of the Chalet Sonnenfried.

For the rest of the day he would saunter or flutter up and down the Promenadestrasse clad in a series of tasteful polo-necked jumpers and variously tinted riding breeches, also wired at the sides to give them a more daring line, and he would greet and be greeted by his many friends.

Kurti made great but unavailing efforts to attract the attention and favours of Martin. To gain this end he tried a number of approaches, including the assumption of a manly stride and a domineering manner, and even the cultivation of a neat moustache. But this too, alas, met with no success, so in the end he settled for straightforward companionship, so they had many long talks together, combined with a surprisingly practical system of teaching conversational German, as well as a little coffee-drinking in the Kurhaus, and a little beer-drinking in Buols Kurgarten, where they indulged in the playing over of many records, generally of the lighter schools of music by such composers as Lehar and Weber, and Kurti would explain the Berlin musical comedies and revues from which they came, and would warble bits of the songs with explanatory gestures and shouts of enjoyment. Then there were walks in the mountains and through the pine woods about Davoser See, the search for mushrooms in the autumn and for wild strawberries in the spring. And on winter days, thanks to Kurti's inspiration of replacing the wheels of Maeve's bath-chair with small toboggan slides, she would be propelled with ease up hill and down dale through the dazzling sunshine over the snowy roads, with Kurti and his Irish friend pushing together, clad for these brilliant but icy days in the heaviest of jackets and breeches with thick woollen stockings and short snowboots of black felt.

Martin still carried Maeve upstairs to the flat on the first floor of Villa Berna, and was still in charge of her bath-chair, with or without Kurti, when any expedition of more than half a mile was in question. But there was no doubt about it, she had made amazing improvements since her visits to Dr Spengler had begun. Martin had been in Sicily for three months during the spring, and when he returned at last to Davos he found a radiant Maeve who told him of Dr Spengler's treatment, and said she would like to walk with her truant cousin as far as the post office which was on the borderline of Dorf and Platz.

'But can you walk as far as that, my darling?' Martin cried, and she, as if remembering Peer Gynt, had answered heroically, 'Ay! And farther still!'

So that year was in the whole a joyful one, especially as it included a lengthy visit from his beloved sister Maimie, and when Martin painted a study of the two young ladies, so beautifully clad in the Greek-looking gowns that Maimie had bought in Paris from their creator Raymond Duncan, the brother of the celebrated Isadora, they were all in the highest spirits, proudly confessing to the early (or was it late?) Grecian inspiration of the Raymond Duncan designs and of Martin's handling of these in his picture, but justifiably denying any influence from the fell compositions of Alma-Tadema.

However, the arrival on the scene of Jack Dowling, and the close friendship between himself and Martin, was not a cause of delight to Kurti.

'Since that der Schacki is arrived,' he complained, 'art thou not at all the same Mischli. Not at all the same. Ach! of course I can see that he all of handsome, of manly bearing, not? and perhaps as thou sayest of quite gross intelligentz, but if that is so why so much of tennis play, of card gamble, how calls it? Bridge or so what, so tedious and longtimeish? Why? Answer canst thou not because thou quite blind art. Quite blind, my poor Mischli!'

And with all its brilliance, its anguish and hope, with Maeve under Dr Spengler's eye growing slowly stronger, and with Jack Dowling established in their lives as a friend of rock-like permanence – for did he not return to his own Kildare each summer and to Davos each winter, and was not Kildare a few miles only from Dublin? – the Magic Mountain Valley with the dazzling snow and sun of its days, the Arctic cold of its nights, faded out of their lives as winter melted into spring and Maeve, with full Spenglerian approval, decided to leave the highlands for the comparative lowlands among the hills above Vevey. At last, on a golden day in May, the Kelleher and Weldon ménage found itself in a little pension surrounded by fields of wild narcissus sloping down to Lac Leman, with the coast of France in a haze of dragonfly blue on the opposite coast, with Vevey below them and Montreux away to the left, and beyond Montreux past the Château de Chillon to the end of the lake, guarded by the peaks of the Dents du Midi, or was it Mont Blanc? – Martin was never certain – crowned even through the summer days, like Andersen's Snow Queen, in eternal, dazzling white.

The pension, run with truly Swiss efficiency by Monsieur and Madame Bonjour, was clean and comfortable, with good food and an atmosphere of deadly peacefulness. It was largely inhabited by old ladies well into their eighties, so Maeve and Martin spent a lot of time wandering among the gentle hills a-blow with wild narcissus, and when they weren't doing that they would watch together from the balcony outside Maeve's bedroom for the twice-daily excitement of the arrival of the hill-car in order to see, as Maeve put it, if anyone under the age of 195 would ever arrive.

One day they were rewarded. From the hill-car stepped down a solidly built young man with closely cropped golden hair, who turned with brisk gallantry to assist the descent of a young lady very much like a feminine – as extremely feminine as he was masculine – edition of himself. Both husband and wife – for surely she was his wife? – had the same gold and pale tan colouring, both seemed about the same age, and both were, so Maeve and Martin decided, in their middle or late twenties. What was their nationality? Maeve thought perhaps Danish or Dutch, and Martin thought German or Swiss. At dinner that evening the couple came together to their table, and with concerted bows and hearty smiles they introduced themselves, or rather the husband introduced, first himself and then his 'dear vife'.

'Good evening ladies and young schentlemahn,' he said with three swift bows for each of them in turn. 'I name myself Tiede Klaasen, and this,' he added, holding his wife's hand in his, 'this is my dear vife, Mevrouw Margarethe Klaasen-Pinkster. I name her always Guus [pronounced Hooss]. And for me she always names me, not Tiede but Tim, isn't it?' Then they all shook hands and laughed, not from embarrassment but from a feeling of sheer pleasure.

Tim's English was superior to Martin's German, so English was the medium that both adopted for the friendship that grew and developed with breathtaking rapidity between them. Breathtaking in every sense it was, for it entailed long vigorous walks together over the hills and through forests set about with dykes and ditches, entangled with the twisted roots of the trees. Tim rightly considered himself Martin's superior in physical strength and agility, as well as being four years older, and while he was strenuously ready to help his Irish friend over seemingly impassable places on their way, he objected always to any offer of assistance for himself. Even when he once fell into a wet ditch overgrown with brambles and twigs, and Martin offered him a hand, he said indignantly, 'Many t'anks, dear chappie, I can hallup mysalluf!'

His accent in English, like his deep hearty voice, was incurably Dutch (though Martin did persuade him to abandon the term 'dear chappie') but his knowledge of the language was sound and adaptable, and they discussed a thousand subjects together from religion and sex to revolutionary politics and national characteristics, from personal memories, passions and prejudices to the Russian Ballet and the art of the Theatre.

'So you have seen the great Nijinsky?' Tim said one day. 'Ach! How vunderfoll. I envy you so very much, dear cha—I mean dear Martin! How young you must have been! But you yourself were already at vork as a boy actor! And now a painter. But how quiet and dull for you must seem this life here! Ach of course, I foresee, isn't it? I foresee already: you vill return. Ach ja! I am so certain of this. You are very vunderfoll, dear Martin

190

Never once before in mine whole life have I met someone like you. Give me ein kiss, Martin. Ein brötherlik kiss.'

So Martin, nothing loath, put up his face for Tim to deal with it as he chose. But never, surely, thought Martin, did two brothers kiss quite like that.

It was soon after that that Guus, true to her Nordic femininity, frankly informed Martin that she considered him the cat's whiskers, or some Dutch-sounding equivalent, and proposed that he should make löve to her, isn't it? Martin, not feeling up to this, replied with true Irish hypocrisy that he could not possibly betray his good friend Tim by making Tim's wife his mistress. 'Ach w'y not?' cried the indomitable Guus. 'Tim shall not, I tenk, mind at all, isn't it? He had already himself in Eindhoven had en mistress, and I have not so much mindet. You shall see, dear Martin, yes, I tank already you shall see.'

But nothing came out of it except on the moonlit nights when the five of them, Craven and Maeve and Guus and Martin and Tim, sat in a row on the balcony outside Maeve's bedroom, and Guus would hold one of Martin's hands and Tim the other, and an occasional sigh would escape from them, one in Dutch baritone, the other in Dutch mezzo-soprano, and Maeve would refer to these occasions, when she and Martin were alone together, as 'the moonlit hours of the groaning Dutch'.

And then, at a telegram of urgent request from Alexander McMullen, the marvellous mad Mac, Martin left the pension and the 'white ghost' of the Dents du Midi, and Maeve and Craven, and Tim and Guus, and travelled by train to Naples to meet the *Indomitable*, the ship that was carrying Mac back from his triumphant three years in Australia as leading man to Oscar Asche in a repertoire of Shakespearean plays in Sydney, Melbourne and other centres of culture, in that faraway continent.

The meeting finally took place, after endless complications that included the hiring of a rowing-boat to take him to the side

191

of the *Indomitable*, whence he was shouted at in affectionate abuse by a golden-haired Mac in an elaborate silk dressing-gown to 'go round to the other side, you silly God knows what!' The boatman declared this to be impossible: there were too many cables and other obstacles in the way. 'Then go back to the shore and wait for me in Napoli: Napoli dear and all that "O sole mio"!' screamed Mac when Martin had translated the message. 'And don't go wandering about the town; stay where I can see you. You're so unreliable, Marty, but your hair's looking lovely.'

It was long past two o'clock when they found each other, and Mac was accompanied by a Jewish-looking lady of perhaps forty whom Mac introduced as 'Donna, me new friend, Donna Raphael. Donna darling, this is Marty. (Husband the famous pianist, she's a *dear* too but we'll have to get rid of her. But how, dear? How?) Donna darling, now we *have* found each other let's all go and have *nourishment* somewhere. Lunch dear, lunchuary!'

So they did, and later on they dined together at Sorrento and 'looked in', as Mac put it, at San Carlo, and heard the last act of *Il Barbiere de Siviglia*, and on the following day Donna had disappeared. 'Where, dear, God knows, but she's *gone*,' said Mac triumphantly, throwing four extravagant-looking gold cigarette cases onto his own bed in the room they shared together. 'A few more 'undreds of those in me luggage, dear. Oh yes, the Australians are very generous. I'll say that for them.'

Then, flinging the windows open, he stepped onto the balcony and addressed the almost empty piazza. 'My popolo!' he roared, 'Back at last from the Hantipodes, I send you greetings!'

Next day he and Martin left for Capri. Mac was seasick all the way and demanded raw lemons. 'Not a day's illness on that endless trip, Marty, and now this tiny little journey and I'm so ill I thought I'd be dead. So this is Capri! Looks marvellous, I must admit. Wouldn't it be Heaven if we met Compton

Mackenzie or Norman – what's his name? – Douglas, yes, that's it. But I don't imagine we will. They've *left* you see . . . Oh Marty, look at that sea! Look back at Naples! Vesuvius! You don't think it might go off while we're here, do you?'

It didn't, though Martin, after drinking a lot of the wrong water, became ill and kept to his bed for five days, but soon recovered and began to work again.

One of Martin's studies, a figure in gouache against a background of blue rippling water and apricot-coloured rocks, so delighted Mac that he insisted on buying it for himself.

'Or perhaps for darling little Maimie,' he said. 'Now what sort of frame would you suggest, Martin?'

'Oh, the colouring is so vivid, I think my usual dreary neutrals, Mac, don't you? Grey mount, black frame.'

'Grey and black do you think?' said Mac. 'Oh well, maybe you're right. Grey . . . and black, dear.'

But a fortnight later, when they were not only in Rome but on a tour of inspection of the Catacombs, Mac interrupted himself in the middle of an impassioned sentence about 'the poor Early Christians, dear, poor darlings, having to celebrate Mass down here!' to shout joyfully in Martin's ear, 'Or perhaps Green, dear? Yes Green – peacock or – olive green, what do you say?'

'Mac, what *are* you talking about?'

'What do you *think* I'm talking about, you poor slow-witted thing? The *frame*, of course.'

' . . . what frame?'

'Oh dear God! And I always thought you were so bright! Why *the* frame of course, for the beautiful nude I bought from you – brown nude, blue sea, canary-coloured rocks. Do you think – let me put it in simple juvenile dialogue, dear – do you think Gr-r-een? Gr-e-en frame, Martin. Gr-r-reen. *Now* do you understand?'

'But Mac, dear Mac, that was weeks ago in Capri.'

'And what, pray, has *that* got to do with it? *Gr-r-reen frame*,

193

you poor half-wit.'

'Oh, green then, if you want green.'

'No dear, I meant puce, that's why I said green. Grrreeen dear!'

Thus ended the visit to the Catacombs.

The next day they were in Florence, where Mac, who knew little about painting, was disappointed to find there was no discoverable portrait in any of the great galleries of Sarah Bernhardt: 'In Rome at least they had the Terrazza di Tosca, dear!' (which was all that really thrilled him about Hadrian's Villa), and expressed astonishment that Martin had arranged no ticket for his (Mac's) return to London, or his (Martin's) return to Switzerland.

'But I do realize it's my own fault really!' he cried in mellow tones. 'I mean, to expect you to be businesslike and managerial. You're too artistic, Marty, you're too like me, you see. It's like two prima donnas travelling together.'

And two days later they parted with deep mutual regret. But before the final farewell, the final *au revoirs*, Mac said suddenly, 'Poor little Maimie, Martin! I'm always worrying about her. How does she live? I ask her and she says, "Oh, I sell my books and things." But you can't live on selling books and things *forever*, dear. Nobody could . . . I'm going into a new show thanks to Oscar Asche's influence, a modern show (expect I'll be no good in it) with Gladys Cooper in the West End. And I'm going to take a flat in London – I know you hate London, Marty, but it *is* the centre of things at the moment – and I've a good mind to ask Maimie to come and live with me. I'll take care of her financially, and she can take care of the flat, and I know she won't expect any nonsense about lovemaking and all that. Do you think she'll come and take care of me?'

'I hope she will,' Martin said solemnly.

And she did. And Martin went back to Maeve and Craven. The Klaasen-Pinksters had returned to Holland, and all that was left of Tim was a stout book-like package of letters written daily by him as a sort of diary, and ending with messages in

Irish – and in the old Gaelic characters (which he had insisted on learning from Martin) – begging his friend 'to be a good boy, and never to forget his devoted Tim'.

A few weeks later Craven, Maeve and Martin went back to Ireland, to beloved and familiar Howth, where they took a furnished – a rather dimly furnished – house in the village for a couple of weeks. It stood near the church and opposite a row of shops, and they badly missed their own old house standing on its corner further up the road, where they had had all their own furniture and their many books, now all stored away in packing cases. That house, with all its poignant memories, was now occupied by others. So Craven, during their two weeks in the dim recesses of St Kevin's and its view of grocers' and chemists' shops, lost no time in discovering a charming little house high up near the summit, facing the lonely, legend-haunted Loughoreen mountains, where they were to spend the summer.

Meanwhile Maeve, calling in to Doyle's provision shop, was heartily welcomed by Mrs Doyle, who looked up from the basin of flour she was dealing with and cried, 'God bless us and save us, Miss Kelleher! Oh welcome back home again, isn't it fresh and well you're looking, and I har'ly reckonized you at first because me arms was up to the elbows in flour! I'm making a cake for poor little Michael's eighth birthday you see. Welcome again a thousand times, and would you like a cup of tea?'

The offer was politely refused with many thanks, but Maeve felt all the happier for it, and said that that sort of thing was what made ramshackle furniture and chests of drawers whose handles always fell off when you opened or shut them worth while enduring.

A little later that month Martin received a letter from Craven's elderly and very wealthy cousin, Walter A. Dixey (known as Wad to his family and friends), asking him to meet him with his wife Fanny in Paris where, as they frankly admitted, 'they could show him Paris and he could help them out with the language'.

He had a delightful two weeks with them and was taken to
the Opéra, to the Théatre Sarah Bernhardt, to the Casino and
all the rest of it, and was housed with them in great splendour in
one of the grandest hotels at the corner of the Avenue de
l'Opéra. Then they extended the invitation, suggesting that he
break his journey back to Ireland and spend a week at their
home in Holland Park Avenue. 'We can make you quite
comfortable,' said Wad, 'and you'll be able to see Mac, and
your dear little Maimie too.'

On the evening of their arrival Martin found a postcard for
him from Maimie, which stated: 'Do hope you'll come and see
us darling, very happy here, mind now that you come before
going home to Ireland, by the way Mac and I were married this
morning, isn't the weather gorgous, tons of love Maimie.'

'They're married!' cried Martin, showing the card to Fanny.
'Now what for in Heaven's name?'

'Oh I think that's wonderful,' cried Fanny, 'I often thought
they would in the end, you know, and Maimie *does* need
someone to take care of her.'

'If I know my sister Maimie,' Martin observed. 'it's she
who'll be taking care of Mac.'

So he called at their flat that evening and the door was flung
open by Mac, radiant and resplendent in evening trousers and
a smart white shirt that he wore under an extremely decorative
dressing jacket in puce and gold, with a purple tasselled belt.
'Welcome, welcome, dear Marty!' he cried. 'Come upstairs
and meet everybody. And I may Hadd,' he went on, 'we are
'usband and wife' – an enormous flourish – 'in NAME only.'

'I wonder,' thought Martin, bearing in mind the unstable
and easily stirred temperament of his new brother-in-law. And
his doubts were fully justified when, some eighteen months
later, Maimie gave birth to a baby boy, baptized John
Christopher, and, another year and a half later, to a tiny and
very beautiful daughter, whom they called Mary Rose.

It was a wonderful wedding party, with Ivor Novello and

Bobby Andrews and Constance Collier, and the lady known as Donna when they had met in Naples. ('She *would* come dear, bloody nuisance, but she's very clever and kind and sweet, and after all what could I say?')

'What a cow,' Ivor Novello whispered when, for a moment, she had glided from the room. 'But what a *Dear*,' as she made a sudden reappearance, a bottle of champagne in either hand, and they all drank the health of the happy couple.

'Registry Office, dear!' Mac explained, 'and Maimie didn't like it, but we can alway go to a proper Catholic church later on. Have some more champagne, Martin!'

'And something to eat,' Constance Collier cried, and she put a plate of pâté sandwiches in his hand. 'Mac tells me you and I played together in *Oliver Twist* with Herbert Tree a thousand years ago,' she murmured, 'and isn't it terrible of me, I can't remember it! Can't remember you either, and can't think why not,' she continued. 'Oh, it's age of course: not your age, dear Martin. Can't remember. Such a vivid face too. You were a little boy then – Anthony, wasn't it? Oh I'm getting so old, can't remember a thing any more, isn't age *hell*?'

Mac put the *Scheherezade* record on the gramophone, and Ivor whispered, 'Remember Nijinsky in that, Marty?' and everyone became silent and sad for a little while, remembering the god of the dance and his tragic fate, and Martin went back at last to Holland Park Avenue with Rimsky-Korsakov's music ringing in his ears.

That summer Mac and Maimie were frequent visitors to Howth. There were picnics and walks on the hills, and it was after one of the picnics that Craven, watching the newly married couple walking down the hillside together said to Martin:

'Poor little Maimie. Look at her, walking beside that great brute she's married to,' and Martin, without passing any comment on the strangeness of the misnomer when applied to such a person as Mac, inquired, 'Why poor little Maimie?'

'Well dear,' said Craven, 'she's so tiny and he's such a great tall tree of a man: things must be terribly painful for her, dear.'

And Martin, guessing immediately what was meant, said: 'But you can't always judge by a man's height, dear, or indeed his lack of it. I mean, some short men have enormous noses, just as some tall men have perfectly reasonable ones. Mac's nose is a very reasonable one: so are all his proportions. I've bathed with him very often and I know.'

'Oh I see what you mean, dear,' Craven replied. She was not to be led astray from her purpose by this mention of noses. 'But a nose, dear,' she continued, without a trace of Victorian embarrassment, but looking him straight in the eyes, 'a nose – and I'm very glad to hear you mention it because it shows how innocent you are, dear, so I suppose you don't realize – a nose, you see,' she repeated relentlessly, 'is stationary.'

This astonishing revelation left Martin for once with no reply ready so he meekly said, 'Yes I see. Of course, dear.'

'So let's change this horrid subject,' said Craven, 'and see what we can do this evening. There's a Pauline Frederick picture on at the Carlton . . . We might go to that.'

So they went and were once more entertained by the brave beauty of the silent screen.

Friends had told Martin and Maeve that Roquebrune in the Alpes Maritimes was a wonderful place to go for the winter months. So they went, and were perfectly happy from the first moment. The train from Marseilles, where they had spent a night, stopped for a few minutes at Monte Carlo before continuing its journey to Roquebrune and Menton, and at Monte Carlo they gazed up at what seemed a vast wedding cake in a setting of green forest and savage rocks, backed by grey and golden mountains under a sky as blue as the skies of Spain.

And after wandering about together down the sunbaked roads by the sea they found what they were looking for: the Pension Mirasole, set between the hills and the sea in a garden of cypress and pomegranate trees, a cheerful white-walled house. They were shown two pleasant, plainly furnished single bedrooms, a pleasant small salon, and a cool, spacious dining room with a marble floor and about twenty tables.

'The terms?' Martin asked in French, terror in his heart.

'Trente-cinq francs per jour, Monsieur.'

'Et la nourriture?'

'La – ? Ah! Les repas? Inclusifs, Monsieur. Trente-cinq, ça veut dire trente-cinq francs par jour, c'est la pension.'

'Just under five bob a day,' thought Martin to himself. 'Nous acceptons avec plaisir, Madame,' he said.

So that was where they spent the winter of 1925/26, and their one regret was that Craven was not with them. For the sake of economy she had stayed behind in a portion of the little house at Loughoreen in Howth.

'And she would have loved it so much,' Maeve said mournfully. 'What a curse money is: or the lack of it!'

'Never mind,' Martin reassured her. 'Next year we'll come back and bring her with us whatever happens.'

'Yes. Whatever happens,' Maeve answered and they both looked out over the sea and thought of Craven alone in a half of the house at home in Howth.

'The Ballet opens next Monday,' Maeve went on after a pause. 'I wish you'd go into Monte Carlo some evening and find out what programmes they're doing and what sort of prices we'll have to pay. Go in without me, Martin; it'll do you good not to have to drag me along with you at quarter your normal pace.'

So Martin went alone and found out at the booking office that on Monday next the season would open with *Les Sylphides*, then *Les Matelots*, and then *Barabau*, a new ballet with a décor by Utrillo, and that the prices were high but not unreasonable and well within their reach, thanks to the remarkable Pension Mirasole.

Then he went to the Café de Paris for a cup of coffee, and saw at a table close to his own a pleasant-looking elderly Englishman in difficulties with a waiter who knew no English while he, the Englishman, had no French. So Martin came to the rescue and the Englishman said, 'Oh mercy, mercy beaucô!'

So Martin said, 'Oh, we needn't speak French together, you know!'

'Oh then you're English, what a relief!'

'No. I'm Irish.'

'Irish are you, bejove! I say, what fun! My old great-grandfather was Irish. Same name as mine, Jeffreys. He was an army man you know. Know any Jeffreys in Ireland?'

'Oh yes, one or two. Cromwellian settlers like one of my ancestors. My name's Weldon.'

'Ah, I wondered how long you'd be before you mentioned Cromwell. Well, how do you do, Mr Weldon?'

'How do you do, Colonel Jeffreys?'

'Oh I'm not a colonel. Not army at all. I'm a doctor. Just call me Jeff. What's your Christian name – you don't mind my asking?'

'Not a bit. My name's Martin.'

'Martin. I like that. Well, you call me Jeff and I'll call you Martin. How's that for a start? Look here Martin, may I offer you a drink?

'Thanks so much but it's a bit early for me.'

'Good boy. Very sensible at your age. And remember, I speak as a medical man. A coffee then?'

'Thanks. I'd like another coffee.'

'I say, would you be free to have a bit of dinner with me tonight, Martin?'

'I'd love to, but I'm afraid I can't tonight. I have to get back to my cousin. She's at Roquebrune.'

'A cousin at Roquebrune? That's a charming little spot. And do you both live in that hotel: top of the cliff, just outside the village?'

'Oh no, you see Maeve – my cousin – she could never climb up there. She's an invalid – T.B., God help her.'

'T.B.? Oh poor girl. And poor old you too, Martin my boy. Not much fun being tied to a T.B. patient.'

'Ah well, we're used to it now, both of us. She's been ill now for nearly five years.'

'And you're devoted to her, of course. Must be, you young rascal.'

'Oh, not that you know . . .' Martin began and then he stopped. How impossible, he thought, how abysmally idiotic it would be to explain Maeve's temperament, or his own either, to this bluff, kindly Englishman. But almost at once he was informed by Jeff that he wanted to meet Martin's cousin. Jeff himself, he told his new young friend, was a widower who had lost his wife and their two children on the *Titanic* nearly fifteen years ago.

This pleasant friendship, consisting chiefly of lunches *à trois* followed by a matinée at the Ballet, or dinner *à trois* followed in its turn by an evening performance, lasted all through that winter, and sometimes there were exchanges of entertainment when Jeff, as he speedily became known to Maeve as to Martin, would come over to Roquebrune to spend an afternoon or two bathing with them.

One day Maeve said to Martin, 'What a superb visual artist Mother Nature, the daughter of the Almighty, is as a rule, and how she takes after Him in so many ways – except in this one: I consider the divine visual arts are all supreme, and they don't always work very well, in nature, do they? The body of a man or a woman, children, flowers, trees – they don't function: they're not well organized. Teeth fall out, arthritis creeps in, animals devour each other, the strong prey on the frightened weak . . . Now we three are the contradiction. You have a very beautiful body, Martin, and I'd have one too, but tuberculosis has made it piteous, and neither of us can swim, I because of T.B., and you because you were too lazy to learn. And look at old Jeff out there swimming away like mad and with that poor old body, those sad wrinkled legs. No, life is very unfair!'

'Water's simply wonderful today, children,' the doctor spluttered as he waded ashore, shaking liquid diamonds about him. 'I do wish you'd let me teach you to swim, Martin, you'd be a champion after a couple of lessons. Well, that *was* a jolly morning. You don't know what you're missing, my boy!'

It was during an interval at the Théatre du Casino that Martin found himself reading the news of the latest triumph of Suzanne Lenglen which, in those days of the mid-1920s was silently announced to the public by means of a long broad sheet of paper passing slowly and steadily downwards and announcing the latest events, artistic, political and sporting, mainly of French interest, to the public.

Martin was standing alone until a tall, strongly built man with dark eyes and hair and a small moustache of the same hue said to him:

'Evidemment, elle va encore triompher, la merveilleuse!'

'Qui ça, la marveilleuse?'

'Mais la belle Lenglen, ça va sans dire, n'est-ce-pas?'

'Ah oui, elle gagne toujours, la petite Suzanne.'

'Pas si petite, non plus!'

Then Martin was invited to a drink: the two strangers shook hands and inclined their heads in the French way, and murmured their own names barely audibly. Over their drinks the tall dark stranger, whose accent was unnoticeable – he could have passed as a Frenchman anywhere – said, as they discussed the next item on the programme, that he was not madly keen, much as he admired Utrillo, on 'la décor' which that artist had designed for *Barabau*.

That was what caused Martin to say, rather rudely as he often reflected later, 'Vous n'êtes pas français?'

The stranger reddened a little.

'Vous ne l'avez pas remarqué jusqu'à cela? Je suis flatté! Non, je ne suis pas français, et je vous en prie de me corriger toujours quand je fais des erreurs: je sais bien que j'ai quantités de défauts.'

'Cher Monsieur, c'est pas moi qui pourrais vous corriger. Moi non plus je ne suis français.'

'Vous n'êtes pas français? Vraiment? Alors de quelle nationalité êtes-vous?'

'Je suis irlandais.'

'Hollandais? C'est incroyable.'

202

'Non, pas hollandais: Irlandais.'

'Irlandais? Irish! And I'm an American. You're Irish and I'm American. So what the heck are we making friends for in French?'

And so they laughed together, enjoying the moment and remembering it together as long as their friendship lasted, and it lasted, not forever, but for many years.

Since that night in the Calle San Fernando, when the bold brazen Juan Fuentes had forcibly made love to his 'cousin', Martin had been perfectly aware of his own prematurely awakened but undeniably inborn sexual nature. So it was no surprise to him to observe the unmistakable look in the American's eyes, the unmistakable deepening in his voice, when he added to his last words about making friends in French: 'Because I mean that's what we were doing, isn't it? I mean, making friends. Real *friends*, I mean in any goddam language. You get what I mean, don't you? Say, do you realize? I don't even know your name! What is it? Mine's Robert. Robert Hamnet. So, just plain Robert please! tell me yours.'

'Martin. Martin Weldon.'

'Well I won't *forget* the Weldon, but I certainly am not going to call you by it. Say, you don't mind, do you, Martin?'

'No, of course I don't.'

'I'm glad. Say, how old are you, Martin?'

'I'm twenty-five. Same age as the year.'

'As much as that, are you? I figured you were about twenty or maybe twenty-one. But I'm glad all the same. That means there's only four years between us. I'm twenty-eight: but I'll be twenty-nine next April. Say, why don't we spend the great occasion together, you and I? What do you say to that, Martin? April the First: April Fool's Day. That's me. Now will you dine with me tonight? Gosh, I do kind of rush things don't I? But looking at you I can't help it. I just can't help it, Martin. Tell me you'll dine with me tonight.'

So then Martin had to refuse and explain about Maeve. His new American friend listened with attention and with respect, and with a sudden remorse that was of course redundant and made things for the moment absurdly complicated.

'And you love her as much as that, do you Martin? Why then, I've done something unforgivably wrong. I've made a perfect April Fool of myself . . . please Martin, please try to forgive me. Because what I wanted was for you and me to be – yes, Goddammit, I will say it, why, I've already said it – to be more than just friends, because I thought you were as free as I was. Five years ago, when I was about twenty-four, I guess, I was in love, deeply – painfully, as it turned out. It was with a girl from my own part of the States. We'd been engaged to be married for quite a while, just over two years. And then one day she told me it was all off. "Why?" I said. I couldn't understand what was wrong. And then she told me, oh so calmly, you can't imagine, she said, "Well, Robert, the truth is I'm in love, see? Yes, I mean in love, the real thing, not this playing around that you and I've been up to all this time. *You*?" she said, and her voice was like a knife, "You're not a fool," she said, "you *must* know yourself, it's been nothing but a kind of acting around with passion – just sex and nothing more, and even there we never really got down to anything real. You never touched me except to kiss me every little while, till I got sick of the whole show. And then three months ago I met Peter and we've been living together ever since, and I'm going to have a baby and Peter's going to marry me next week, see, and I'm sorry Robert and all that, but you're just going to have to make the best of things and forget all about me. Maybe you'll understand one day, maybe you'll realize it's all been for the best." '

Robert stopped talking for a few moments, and then he said, 'And since that day, Martin, I've never looked at a woman – in that way, I mean. Couldn't, somehow. Oh I don't mean I became a woman-hater: it was just that I knew I could never trust myself – or any of them – in love. Even the physical urge for them faded away. I turned – not with any real ease, because I'm not a true born homo – but I turned towards my own sex. But – and you can believe this or not, because it's true – until today I've never met a

204

single person I felt I could love. Oh, the occasional rather sordid sort of slap-happy affair with some reasonably attractive young effeminate: I'm no saint and I'm not setting myself up as one: but no one, not one solitary soul did I feel I must love and be with. Then I saw you, Martin: I saw you and you know the rest. And it seems I was meaning to play the same hateful trick on you that that girl played on me. But with me it was not intentional – please, please believe that – and now that I know about you and your Maeve, isn't that her name? now I guess I'll have to face up to it and come to terms – what's the expression?—'

He broke off again and sat for a few moments in silent misery. So then there had to be another lengthy explanation from Martin about the essence of his devotion to Maeve.

Once again Robert listened with attention, with respect, and then with a slow dawning of relief in his eyes. 'Well then,' he said at last, 'maybe it's going to be OK . . . Mind you, Martin, it *is* kind of hard for an ordinary guy like me to really understand a friendship like that between a man and a girl. I figure it's only a true hundred percenter like yourself on the one hand and the most remarkable type of young woman on the other that could make a friendship as deep and devoted and yet as passionless as that possible. Oh, but you don't know, you just couldn't understand what happiness it means to me.'

'To us both perhaps,' Martin, feeling astonished by his own words, heard himself say, and they shook hands together quite formally, as though they had just been introduced for the first time.

So all things worked out happily for them both, and for the next five or six years they spent a lot of their time together.

Yet a curious trick was played on them by fate: on Martin perhaps more than on his American friend. It was almost, he felt at times, as though an echo from past years was resounding in almost exact reverse from the old days in Davos when his unhappiness about Jack Dowling was at its height. This was neither complete nor exact as far as the romantic side of the relationship was concerned. That was perfectly and agreeably in order: there was no inexplicable holding back by one man, or any bitter answering heartbreak felt by the other. But there was no doubt, and this became clearer and clearer as time passed by, that Robert was the obsessed and obsessive adorer, and that this persistence of his adoration, although invariably accepted by the other, was not returned in full measure. There were trips to Italy together, to Venice and Florence and Rome, as well as to various centres in France like Vence, which was where Robert spent most of his time, where indeed he was stationed in a sanatorium by the American university that had financed him, the head professor of Romance languages, for a period of four years for the treatment of incipient tuberculosis of the lungs. There were frequent short visits to Paris, where every night they would see a play together at the Comédie or the Odéon, or visit the Opéra where Diaghilev's Ballet was performing. There were three wonderful days and nights in the remote grandeur of the Gorge du Loup . . . and it was during this visit that Martin realized with a dull sense of regret and ingratitude that the never-ceasing protestations of love in his ears and pressed on his lips were growing tedious.

Besides, he had begun, just before the first meeting with Robert in Monte Carlo, to write a play in Irish on an ancient Gaelic mythological theme, and these endless amorous journeyings to and fro, all of them financed with unquestioning generosity by Robert, were interrupting his work. And the ultimate reality of his work and his life was bound up, not with dear generous Robert, but with Maeve. With Maeve, above everyone else, but also with Craven and now with a strange and, for Martin, a completely new sort of friend, a slender, smiling golden-haired young man called Hubert Dunstan, the son of a distinguished English father and of a handsome American mother.

From the first moment of their meeting, Hubert and Maeve and Martin were friends. The two young men first met in the little village post office in Roquebrune, where Hubert was having a sharp dispute in impeccable French with an irascible elderly man on the other side of the counter about a registered letter that had, it seemed, gone astray:

'Mais je vous assure que vous avez tort . . . Cette lettre est perdue, voilà tout!'

'Eh bien,' Hubert snapped back, 'Eh bien, c'est moi qui vous assure que c'est vous – oui vous! – qui a tort. C'est moi-même qui envoyait cette lettre il y a plus qu'une semaine, et elle était raccommandée par moi-même. Donc, si elle est perdue, tant pis pour vous, vous m'entendez? Tant pis pour vous.'

'Assez d'histoires!' spluttered the official. 'Si c'est vous qui l'a vraiment envoyée, raccommandée ou non, c'est pas avec moi que vous l'avez affaire. Non! Alors, finissez, Monsieur, et plus d'histoires.'

'Ah vos eternels pas d'histoires. Vous allez voir, je vous assure.' And he stood aside for a moment for Martin who was buying some stamps.

'Oh, sans blague il a un toupet, ce jeune homme!' the elderly man hissed under his breath to Martin. 'Alors ça sera douze francs cinquante s'il vous plait, Monsieur, alors bonjour, Monsieur, et merci.'

Martin slipped swiftly past the still infuriated Hubert, who stood at the door looking like Nemesis.

'Pardon, Monsieur,' Martin murmured as he jostled past Nemesis and regained the sunshine of the street.

He was swiftly joined by Nemesis.

'Horrible little brute!' Hubert said. 'Do excuse my talking to you, and in English too – but you *are* Irish aren't you? And I've simply got to tell somebody sensible that there are moments when I feel I simply *loathe* the French. Just imagine, a most important letter to a friend in America, with quite a lot of money inside it too, and he has the nerve to deny all responsibility. Oh well, let's forget all about it, such a marvellous day, isn't it? And life's so short and all that, and I've longed for the last three days to talk to you and that tall interesting-looking girl who's always with you. Is she your sister? Why, here she comes! Do introduce me, will you? My name is Hubert, Hubert Dunstan.'

And so the meeting came about and the feeling of ease and friendship was established from the first moment. It grew and developed as well, and when the time came at last to say their regretful au revoirs at the end of the Roquebrune period, they felt they had known each other for years.

Perhaps it was with Maeve that Hubert found a greater kinship even than that which was so swiftly established with Martin. For Maeve was definitely and distinctly a woman, and Martin, in whom a feminine streak undeniably existed where his reactions to certain men were concerned, had little if anything of the woman in his character. Hubert, on the other hand, was fundamentally and predominantly feminine, from end to end of his being: his delicate build, the silky gold of his hair, the nervous timidity of his smile, his glance, his easily stirred irascibility, the nervous excitement of his wit and humour, all these things proclaimed him as what he was: a slight and touching misplacement in a world that could never understand him. Of course it was to Maeve he turned for his truest companionship and understanding. Was she not a woman? And was she not singularly and inexplicably a woman who saw him clearly, who sympathized with him deeply, who made no demands of any kind on his manhood, and who never seemed to find the crepuscular quality of this either mysterious or amusing?

But they were all happy together, the three of them. Even when, as inevitably happened when a personality like Hubert formed a third of a group of friends, a slight tiff would blow up over nothing at all, the tiff would end in comedy though it had begun in strife.

At the end of April 1926 Martin and Maeve went back to Howth, to the great joy of Craven, back to their Loughoreen cottage among the haunted hills, and during the summer there were visits from Hubert and a long visit too from Robert who was enchanted by Howth and found it infinitely more beautiful than Killarney, which disappointed him. ('Perhaps,' thought Martin with unusual irony for him, 'because there were so many Americans about.') And Martin finished two acts of his

Gaelic mythological play but got stuck in the third.

And then, as they had planned with Hubert, at the coming of late autumn days they decided to take an apartment in Menton with Craven to arrange things for them. There in their new flat in the Avenue de la Victoire things started happily enough until one day, about two weeks before Christmas, Robert told Martin that his doctor was far from pleased with his health and insisted on his spending the rest of the winter in Davos. Robert, in his turn, insisted on Martin accompanying him there – he to pay for everything as always, poor generous Robert.

Davos again! It was a nostalgic time for Martin to find himself back in the old Alpine valley that had been home to him for so many years. But now there was no Daisy and no Kurti, for Daisy was still in Locarno with George and the children, and Kurt Schupp had returned to Stuttgart. True, Bláthnaid and her devoted Una were still in the Villa Berna, and so was their dreary curly-haired dog Nello, but Davos was a dull place without its leading comedy characters and without the old Russian friends. Still worse, there was no Craven or Maeve there any more, and no Jack Dowling, and Martin was secretly glad when the week was at an end and he returned to Menton. But, true to his temperament, Martin had forgotten to write or wire the date of his homecoming, taking for granted that Maeve and Craven would be in. However, after carrying himself and his two suitcases up the stairs, he found the door of the flat locked. So, cursing softly to himself in his usual mixture of English, Irish and Spanish, he left the suitcases in front of the door and decided to take a walk and get a drink – a coffee or a vermouth or anything at all – and as he crossed the street to the Café des Fleurs, who should he walk into but Charlie Bordley.

Charley Bordley was an American like Robert, though he bore no likeness at all to his compatriot. For Robert, apart from the occasion of his sudden swooping down on Martin in Monte Carlo nearly two years ago, was a studious, sober, well-conducted sort of fellow. Charlie hailed from Los Angeles; he had a pronounced, not unattractive, Californian accent, a roving eye, an uncontrollable temper, and a still more uncontrollable passion for strong liquor.

This evening he was plainly under the influence of all these aspects of his nature for, on seeing Martin, he bore down on him with loud Bacchic cries of delight.

'Well if it isn't the great artist from the land of saints and bollux,' he shouted. 'How are you tonight, you hard-hearted son of a starchy old Irish gun? Come along with Charlie and he'll give you the most beautiful goddam liquor, and if you don't want to, you'd better change your mind quick, see, because Charlie isn't the man to take a refusal from any goddam son of a bitch, no sir!'

He pulled Martin by the arm into the Café des Fleurs and up to the bar, where he bashed into a group of three tough-looking Italian youths who seemed to take a poor view of the experience, and a still poorer one of Charlie.

'Questo maladetto Americano ancora – ubriaco come sempre!' one of them shouted. 'Ah! Fa attenzione tu, sporco mio, fa attenzione Carlino: fa attenzione, sporco pazzo obuttarò un bichiere d'acqua in faccia tua!'

Charlie then landed his fist into the eye of his opponent, who straightaway retaliated, and a hideous fight began, to be interrupted by the barman throwing both of them through the door into the street. The two remaining Italians gathered about Martin, who knew too little of their language to respond either in a friendly way or with cold aloof dignity, so he smiled, shrugged his shoulders, explained his lack of Italian, and ordered a coffee for himself. Suddenly, as he was beginning to drink it, the door was flung open and through it staggered Charlie, swiftly followed by his adversary, whose left eye was badly bruised. He was not, however, in as wretched a condition as poor Charlie, whose brow and eyes were streaming with blood, and who lurched desperately towards Martin and leaned over his shoulder muttering, 'Filthy Guinea, he's killed me, Martin, he's wearing knuckledusters on his lousy fingers. Jesus I'll kill him – no, Martin, let me free, I'm going to kill the bastard . . .'

This time Martin got between them and, in spite of his hatred of brawling, found himself shouting whatever he could summon of abuse in his limited Italian at the young man who, luckily for Martin, had fallen to the floor in a faint. Finally Martin succeeded in dragging his unlucky American friend back to the house. The suitcases had disappeared and the door of the flat was open, and there stood Maeve and Craven with horror-stricken faces. Martin, dragging Charlie, who was still streaming with blood, over the threshold, explained as well as he could what had happened. He hauled Charlie into his own bedroom and left him lying on the floor with a pillow, prudently covered with a bath towel, under his head, and then went into the sitting room where poor Craven, panic-stricken by the situation, gave voice to the chaos:

'Oh Martin, what a tragedy! If only you'd let us know, dear, what day and what time you were arriving back we would never have gone out to the pictures, would we, Maeve? But you see, I thought it would do her good to have a little distraction, and me too, so we went to La Muette and saw such a lovely picture with Mary Pickford in it, and if we'd known you were coming we never would have gone – well naturally, I mean – and you would never have met that horrid Charlie whatever his name is, poor fellow, I'm very sorry for him, I would be for anyone in such a condition, but what are we going to do, oh what *are* we going to do with him? I suppose he'll have to sleep here and where I should like to know, there's no room for him, could you ever put up with him in your room, in your bed too, lying beside you with all that blood, poor Martin, but I don't see what else can be done for tonight anyway, oh what a tragedy, how awful everything is, why don't you say anything, Maeve dearie, you might tell Martin how sorry you are for him, don't you think dear?'

'Martin knows me. He knows I'm sorry for him. Craven darling, do let's stop all this blather and give Martin something to eat and let him get to bed with "the bleeding sergeant". What would you like, Martin?'

But Martin was too unnerved to take anything but a pear and a few grapes and a glass of wine, so he said goodnight to Maeve and her mother, made some elaborate, futile apologies about bringing this trouble on them, and went back to his room. Having undressed, he with difficulty removed the supine and still sleeping Charles Bordley into bed, and crept gingerly in beside him. The wounded man lay quite still except for an occasional stirring of his head and a few mutterings in incomprehensible Californian. Martin tried to cheer himself up by recalling what Wilde had to say in *Intentions* about the peasants 'taking refuge in dialect'. But what was really in his mind was the memory of an old superstition – or had he made it up himself? – that to bring a bleeding man or woman over the threshold was to invite inevitable disaster . . .

That thought, and the presence of Charlie Bordley's bruised and battered body and his still bleeding head, kept all sleep away from him until dawn, and this was swiftly followed by the grim task of getting the wounded man out of bed and into a bath tub, and finally into what was left of his clothes. All this was accompanied, between groans and curses, by profuse apologies and protestations of gratitude, and still more humiliated apologies and still more passionate gratitude to dear Maeve and that cute old mother of hers who had both been just too wonderful to talk about, though he did a great deal of talking and promised to send them flowers as soon as he got back to his apartment, and Jesus what a fool he'd been, oh no, he certainly could never forgive himself. Never. No sir!

At last he was gone, wearing on his wounded head what looked like a turban – Martin's talent for bandages was not a strong feature – and a sort of grisly peace descended for a while on the flat in the Avenue des Victoires. Martin resorted to his habit, learnt from his sister Maimie many years ago, of tying a silk scarf round his eyes in order to induce sleep and to keep any light of sun or lamp far away. But sleep would not come, and in its place were hordes of almost visible forebodings, battalions of dim, dreaded images he could not explain or understand.

A little later Hubert came in with coffee on a tray, and they began to drink it. There were fresh rolls and butter too, but neither of the young men had any appetite for food.

'I've seen Craven and Maeve,' Hubert said, 'and I'm worried about them. Especially Maeve. She's lying there silent as the grave but for occasional fits of the most terrible coughs . . . Martin, I don't want to be a scaremonger but I do feel we ought to get hold of a doctor. She's not strong, as God knows we know, and her life is much too precious to risk. What do you think?'

So a doctor was sent for and he arrived that evening: Dr Didier, a kindly middle-aged man who took a serious view of the situation. He diagnosed influenza in Craven, and expressed his fear that Maeve was suffering from a violent chill which might develop into pneumonia.

'I understand that Mademoiselle has suffered during five years from tuberculosis of the lungs,' he said. 'Pneumonia following that condition would not be easy to treat. We must take the greatest care.'

He kept his word, and for three days he was a constant visitor.

Two nurses arrived: a large, cheerful, competent Englishwoman, and a gentle, equally competent little French nun. Up to Christmas Eve and beyond it the flat took on the air of a hospital, for Craven seemed to grow worse, and Maeve did develop pneumonia. But by New Year's Eve Maeve had passed the crisis 'inseparable from pneumonia' (these were the days before penicillin), and a faint rejoicing temporarily took the place of the terror and foreboding that had gone before. 'She's far better, a wonderful improvement,' cried Dr Didier, and prescribed champagne. Two bottles arrived and they all drank together with thankful hearts to the New Year.

But three days later, when Maeve, half sitting up in bed, was telling Hubert about her first meeting with Martin, and relating the events of that magical thunderstorm when Martin and she had looked out through the pealing thunder and lightning, and the hissing rain that overflowed the London gutters, and how they both knew that they were old friends – friends of a million years, as she said – and the dark storm became slowly illuminated with the golden light of a half-forgotten valley . . . she fell back on her pillow with a cry.

A relapse had swept over her like a dark cloud, dilating her eyes and causing her breath to come in rapid, painful gasps. 'T.B. was heaven compared to this,' she murmured, half smiling.

Six days and nights went by hideously, and one morning just before midday she died. It was the morning of the 7th of January, 1927. The others in that room of death were Martin, Hubert, Dr Didier, the French and English nurses, and poor Craven, who had come in from her own sickroom in a dressing-gown, and lay silently halfway across the bed. There was such anguish in her eyes as she watched her child slowly and terribly dying, for Maeve could not lose consciousness until the last moment, and it was clear from her eyes that she heard the death-rattle in her own throat.

CHAPTER EIGHT
Return to the Theatre

They never really recovered from Maeve's death, those three odd people who constituted her 'family'.

She had expressed a wish that her body should be cremated and the ashes scattered on the summit of Shiel Martin, the highest of the hills of Howth and, although Hubert with his usual kindness and affection had offered to have her coffin sent to Marseilles and to 'take care of everything', Martin insisted on doing it himself. Before the coffin was closed he crossed Maeve's hands on her breast, and left a copy of Yeats's collected poems between them. Then he drove in a taxi to the station in Menton for the Marseilles train and, when it arrived, had the coffin, duly addressed to the crematorium, put in the luggage van, and walked listlessly homeward. They had a sad enough evening, he and Craven and the devoted Hubert, and the next day they had lunch together on the *terrasse* of a good little restaurant *tout au beurre*, and they drank two bottles of red wine between them and felt a little better because, as Craven said, 'Maeve would hate to see us all being mawkish old miseries just because she's gone away for a little.'

'For a little'. Did that mean, could it mean, that Craven was beginning to share perhaps only half-consciously in her daughter's and Martin's belief in reincarnation? That after death, what was in store for the soul was no immediate and static heaven or hell but a cycle of repeated rebirth, of new adventures and discoveries, a form of continually repeated purgatory in different bodies and in different places before the ultimate union with God could be achieved?

Maeve had been right again in her prophecy about Martin, that if some great grief, some seemingly incurable tragedy were to overcome him, he would go back to the stage.

He went, after writing a letter to Mac and Maimie explaining that he was filled with an urgent desire to act again, and would welcome the discipline of the theatre which demanded regular action, whether one was in the mood or not. He also admitted that after ten years away from the stage he had forgotten how to act.

The Macs, as Mac and Maimie and their company were known to their friends, accepted Martin with joy and gentle sympathy. 'It's you I'm so sorry for, Marty,' wrote Mac. 'One need never be sorry for those lucky enough to die, especially to die young and get out of this bloody awful world, dear. It's the people who loved them and are left behind who stir my pity, and I absolutely understand your devotion to her, Martin. What a strange girl she was. So cool and aloof and yet somehow so close to you and so full of understanding. Oh yes, you must miss her horribly, so come along as soon as you can and we'll work you to death. I'll only give you small parts at first like Rosencrantz or Guildenstern, and I think Count Paris in *Romeo*. Poor little Maimie is up to her eyes directing the men to set the show for tonight – *Macbeth*, dear, and Paula quite good as Lady Mac if a *trifle* overplayed – so I'm writing it out – still – all love to you dear Martin. As ever, Mac.'

That spring the McMullen company was touring England, not in the great cities but in towns for the most part of charm and distinction, and it was at Canterbury that Martin joined them. There it was that Mac began to teach him his more than half-forgotten craft of acting. There and in other English towns ranging from Oxford to Woking Mac, as reliable in all theatre affairs as he was outrageous outside them steered Martin through the labyrinths of the difficult art. And so he taught Martin how to enact the presence and the personality, not of a child, but of a young man in his twenties.

'You're *not* little Anthony Weldon any longer, Marty,' he would say again and again, 'so don't look up at everything and everybody with that trusting winsome expression. The other players are mainly of an equal height with you, and if you gaze up at them you're looking over their heads. And if you look up at the audience they'll only think you're looking for the gallery, which in most of these terrible town halls and things we're playing in, these *terrible* towns, is non-existent anyway. And stand firmly on your two feet dear; you're a big boy now and you have to shave every morning. Your old boyish charm is still with you, but it's the boyish charm of a young man, and Don't Forget It! Now let's try that Cassio scene again where Iago makes you drunk: you're still inclined to make us think it's your first glass of port at a children's Christmas party. See what I mean dear? Let's try it once more with Iago – David, David, where are you?'

David Vivian-Hill was playing Iago, a tall pleasant-looking actor and son of the well-known Vivian-Hill with whom Martin had often played in the old days with Tree at His Majesty's Theatre. His wife Olive was a pretty dark-haired creature who played Nerissa in *The Merchant of Venice*, and was permanently convinced that everybody, both male and female, was in love with David and wished to steal him from her. She need not have been so worried. David Hill was not at all an amorous man. Acting was his first passion and drink his only other one. But he and Martin got on quite well together, and the Iago-Cassio scene made excellent progress.

So the season passed pleasantly enough. At the beginning of May came the regular weekly play outside the Shakespeare repertory, and Martin thanked God he was not playing in it, a contemporary comedy, of the type described as whimsy, entitled *Smilin' Thru*.

'We have to do it in this country,' Mac explained with a tragic expression, 'because the English don't really like Shakespeare. Outside London anyway. Well, would you expect them to, Marty?'

They were walking at that moment through the main street of Woking and everywhere middle-aged ladies, carrying shopping bags, passed up and down with nice expressionless faces.

'*Look* at them, Marty,' Mac hissed as a very determined specimen passed him by. 'Look at *this* one!' He went closer, brandishing Mephistophelian fingers at her. 'Would you expect anyone with a face like *that* to appreciate Shakespeare, dear? WOULD you?'

'Goodness gracious,' the determined lady said, and popped imperturbably into Boots Cash Chemists.

'God how I long to be back in Ireland! But of course, you went over last Thursday, didn't you? On your free night. Maimie was terrified you wouldn't get back in time, but you *did*, dear. Of course, I knew you would. How I envy you: just *one* night and I'd feel better. How was Howth looking?'

Howth had looked very well on that translucent evening when Martin had carried the casket containing the ashes of beloved Maeve to the summit of Shiel Martin. That was where she had wanted her ashes to lie, and this was the 30th of April, May Day Eve. And as Martin laboriously climbed the rocky mountainside, he felt that she was very close to him in spirit.

But when he set about the task of opening the casket from Marseilles, he found it impossible. Almost an hour he spent wrestling with it, but the aids of a key, and old penknife and his own strenuous efforts were all in vain, and in despair he hid the casket, still unconquered, in the shadow of a furze bush by the side of a great stone.

The law-abiding conductor of the hill tram-car, which had left Martin at the foot of the mountain of Shiel Martin, was suspicious of the young man's purpose and later that evening informed the Garda Siochana, the Civic Guards, of what he had seen. A month later Martin received a courteously worded letter from the Superintendent, informing him that the Guards had removed the casket, had opened it, and were keeping it in safety at the Howth Barracks.

'May I add,' the Superintendent wrote, 'that the casket is waiting for you here, and that we fully appreciate the sacredness of your mission. Yours very sincerely . . .

And a year later, on the anniversary of that date, when May

218

Day Eve came, Martin once more carried the now open casket up the mountainside, and at last fulfilled his promise to Maeve Kelleher.

But on the night of that first climb, after he had failed to complete his task for her, he was just in time to catch the night mail-boat from Dun Laoghaire and arrived in an exhausted condition at Woking between the hours of six and seven next evening. He was just in time for the show, which was *Hamlet*, and he had been promoted from Guildenstern (not even Rosencrantz, he had sometimes bitterly reflected) to Laertes, which gave him great joy.

But his sleeping hours troubled him, for the old familiar terror of the Italian nightmare returned at this period, and once again he found himself crossing the long bridge over the Tiber with Giovanni. Once again they were in a box at the Opera together to hear the newly imported Gounod version of *Faust* . . . Once again he stood tense and alarmed behind the sheltering curtain for fear of recognition by government authorities who might be among the audience. More vividly still, he was saying goodnight to Giovanni at the entrance of the house on the corner facing the river, letting himself in to the hateful room where, on the following morning, he would be arrested and marched away to face death. The last moments of all were forgotten, but terror ended the episode and now there was no dear Mother to walk him up and down the room at home in Ireland, or Father to soothe him to sleep with his husky laughing voice as he sang the old song.

And where were all the others of that half forgotten life in the past?

And where was Giovanni?

At the London station where the Mac Company assembled on that warm June morning to take the southern route boat from Fishguard to Rosslare (they were to open in Enniscorthy in the County Wexford in a week's time) panic reigned. For there was no sign of Mac or Maimie, and no sign of David or his wife Olive.

219

'They'll miss the train!' someone said.

But no! For here came Mac in a light and very striking overcoat, and Maimie close beside him and—

'My dears!' Mac cried in tones calculated to reach the back of any gallery in the world's largest theatre. 'My dears, David and Olive aren't coming! Oh no, they're not coming with us: that bloody bitch has decided to *let us down*, dears. Yes, we've been let down, and Maimie and I will have to stay in London for a few days to find a genius of unbelievable memory and concentration as well as talent, because he'll have to play Iago, King in *Hamlet*, Macduff in *Macbeth*, Tranio in *The Shrew*, and Taffy in *Trilby* on Saturday nights when Mother Church puts on the Rival Show dears, which is the Retreat for Men. Oh, *and* Gratiano in *The Merchant*. Oh, and Lysander in *The Dream. I* don't know where we shall find such a man: you'll all have to help him, darlings. All hands to the pumpuaries. See you in a few days' time in Enniscorthy, we hope, and God help us all! Of course we'll have to postpone the opening!'

It was about ten days later, during a desultory morning rehearsal at Enniscorthy, when Mac's voice interrupted them all. Headed by Martin, Paula Savila, the slightly overacting Lady Macbeth, and Doreen Sheridan, a fair and gracious Portia, they rushed to the top of the steps from where the voice rang out triumphantly: 'Found him, darlings! A *real* actor at last and a baritone singer as well: Old Vic for four years, bloody expensive but what does it matter, he's a Real Live Actor.' And Martin, standing in front of the group, saw what seemed to be Giovanni. Giovanni! It was impossible, but the impression lasted for a few dazzled minutes and slowly faded away. For the young man who was following Mac up the stairs bore no physical resemblance to Martin's recollection of his old Roman friend, yet the image – for those few moments – was the same. He was of medium height and of sturdy build, and looked about thirty, though in fact he was only in his early middle twenties.

'Mr Linden Evans,' Mac cried, and pushed him in front of

himself and the beaming Maimie at his side. 'And he's going to transform all David's parts so you'll hardly recognize them. So we won't miss *dear* David in the least, my dears! Linden, this is me brother-in-law, Martin Weldon: Martin, this is Linden Evans.'

Their friendship developed rapidly, in spite of Mac's gloomy prophecies that, apart from admiring his work and his incredible swiftness in learning seven major roles within the space of as many days and nights, Martin would not get on at all with the newcomer.

'He's so English dear,' Mac cried, 'and although his large nose and his sheer brilliance would make you think he was a Jew, it seems he's not one. Not that I'd object to him if he *was* one, dear, but I don't think he is. No, he's just a John Bull with the lid off, Britannia's son, and I'd be very surprised if I found you could tolerate him for five minutes.'

So it seemed that Mac was doomed to surprise, for Martin and the English newcomer were friends from the beginning and soon became inseparable. There were long mornings together when Martin heard Linden through his lines for Iago, for the King in *Hamlet*, for Tranio in *The Shrew*, for Demetrius in *The Dream*, in which Martin was to play Lysander, and for all the rest of the range of parts the amazing Linden was to interpret night after night. Then, when the task had been achieved, including matinées at the various convents that were almost as plentiful in Eniscorthy as were the inhabitants of the town, there would be long walks together through the countryside. On Midsummer Eve there was a memorable climb to the summit of Vinegar Hill where, in honour of St John, the mountain top was crested with flame and with boys and girls of the town who danced round and round and filled the curling smoke with loud songs and laughing cries. Linden's summer overcoat was soon stained with paraffin oil and with scorched patches from the fire but, far from objecting to this, he kept the coat for years, scorches and stains and all, as a memory of that mad magical interlude, and always regarded it as a memento of this true initiation into the secrets of Ireland.

They stayed with the McMullen Company all through that summer and then Linden, like John Ernest Worthing in *The Importance of Being Earnest*, caught a severe chill at Cobh in the County Cork, and Martin spent all his spare time in helping to nurse him back to health. By the time the summer season was over Martin and Linden (or Linden and Martin, as they were to be known henceforth), set out on an adventurous journey to Cork and Dublin. Martin had small unimportant exhibitions of his pictures at various art centres in both cities, and Linden gave small but remunerative singing engagements at various musical centres, and then, with the stealthy approach of autumn days and nights, they returned to the McMullen Company tours and stayed with them a year.

When that was over they discovered in Dublin a small theatre, a branch of the Abbey Theatre, where, on a minute stage on which as Linden correctly stated 'you could hardly swing a cat, so we might as well throw discretion to the winds and be bold and daring for once,' they opened one night with *Peer Gynt*.

Linden, who had a better head for essentials than Martin, had organized a body of shareholders – Craven was among them – and enough money was soon available to make things practicable. Realizing that the Abbey's programme put a national theatre for Ireland on solid foundations, they decided that their work should be to provide Dublin with an international theatre. A little later, in the January of the new year, they had discovered a somewhat larger theatre on the north side of the city and here, in February 1930, they opened with Goethe's *Faust*, with Martin in the title part and Linden inevitably as Mephistopheles.

The present chronicler of this trivial record is tempted to say, in the manner of Charlotte Brontë, 'Reader, had you forgotten Tina? I had not.'

It happened that, after the end of this story, the hideous warnings of Aleister Crowley concerning monkeys were fulfilled. Tina was on holiday in South Africa when, in a grove of palm trees near Durban, a monkey dropped down onto her back and bit her shoulder in the very spot that the magician had indicated. The bite developed rapidly into meningitis, and of this she died in the year 1934, filled with a terror that Crowley was sitting at the foot of her bed, watching her. Of course there was no one there, but the devoted friend who was nursing her sent for a Catholic priest who calmed and reassured her. She died in peace, but the Catholic cemetery where she was buried had to be guarded at the gate by the police, who successfully prevented the magician's followers from removing the body from the grave for the purpose of magical experiment. She will rest in peace, free from all evil, for powers like that of the Great Beast cannot triumph over the love of God, and in her heart she had been aware of this all through her strange life.

Had you also, Reader, forgotten Anthony Weldon, the father of the Weldon family? Martin had not, and after his death, which occurred in the same year as Tina's, he seemed much closer in spirit to his only son. For when they had been on earth together Martin had been ill at ease with him, as he had never been with Sophie, their mother, who was always a familiar and beloved figure in the lives of her children. Sophie had always been the darling of the family. They had worshipped her, Martin perhaps most of all, while Father had been to him a kindly but remote figure with his adoration of fine, pompous phrases, and his alternate passionate love for, and violent rage on behalf of, all his children.

After his death, he became increasingly close in spirit and in thought to Martin, who every night remembered him in prayer and in fond images of his generosity, his singing of old Irish songs learned from his own father, his presents of goldfish and goldfish ponds, and of subtly carved wooden ornaments for the fireplace, of little delicate stools and tables, his brilliant line drawings – for his colour-blindness prevented any possibility of his being a painter – his plays and his comic poems; as well as the effortless, eloquent stories of Beppo the Brigand, which he told extempore to Martin every night in the darkness of the bedroom they shared for so many years.

Successes and failures followed one another in dazzling succession, and the results on the whole were so encouraging that by the Forties of our century the couple were established figures in the city and beyond it. They toured in Egypt, in Malta, South Africa, Canada and America – the United States as well as Latin America – and even in Australia and New Zealand, and by the Sixties and Seventies were fairly well known and widely recognized. So that one day, when Martin was invited by a famous publishing house in London to write his autobiography, he was of course pleased but puzzled.

'An autobiography,' he thought. 'That must start at the very beginning, with the first thing one can remember, and what is that? Where does my memory begin?'

And he took up a copy book and began to think, 'Of course! It was that frightening Italian dream of Giovanni and me, and Daddy with the Hard Hat, and then waking up with Mother carrying me over to Father's side of the bed, and Father taking me in his arms and singing:

I'se a going to bite you, I'se a going to bite you. I'se a going to bite you; All down here.

Michéal mac Liammóir.